SUSAN DWYER

Strangers
Saints
and
Sinners

Carolyn,
Best wishes !
Susan Dwyer

Dedicated to
My son Ryan Young
daughter Courtnay Smith
and my Aunt Rita, also known as Sister Thomas Ann Reynolds-STAR

CONTENTS

CHAPTER 1

TOILET PAPER SNOWBALLS

1964

Trouble began that school day near the end of recess. Kaylee Reagan studied the high ceiling of the girls' washroom of St. Patrick's Grammar School, wondering if her skinny arms would be up to the challenge. Her best friend, Louella McDermott, turned up the volume of her transistor radio. The Beatles' hit "I Want to Hold Your Hand" crackled on.

Her fifth-grade classmates who packed the washroom sighed with relief that Kaylee wasn't singing along. Even the nuns who taught at the Catholic school in the Hudson Valley had ordered her to mouth the words to songs during choir practice.

Louella turned to Kaylee and screeched above the music. "So give it your best Mickey Mantle. Fling it high and sure like a fastball. So make it stick!"

Estimating the ceiling to be two stories high, Kaylee took aim, wound up, and hurled the wet toilet paper snowball. Miserably, it plopped down onto the octagon-shaped black-and-white tile floor and grazed her scruffy saddle shoes. Except for Kaylee's, most of the wadded toilet paper balls stuck, and the ceiling grew into mushy mounds of white toilet paper moons.

"So try an underhand throw. Don't make it too wet, or it won't stick. So watch me." Louella whirled her head and whipped her long brown braid around to her back. She eyed her toilet paper ball, squeezed a little water into the rust-stained porcelain sink, wound up, and flung it high. Louella grinned. Lo and behold, it stuck. A few sloppy ones hung on for a bit and then plopped down because of an incorrect formula of too much water, making the snowball too heavy to stick.

The first bell rang. Brenda Mullarkey lingered until the other girls scurried out, with Kaylee trailing the pack. With no witnesses, Brenda shoved Kaylee. Her head snapped back, and Kaylee slammed through the doorway and into the wall, elbows first.

Bratty Brenda smirked and pointed at the ceiling. "Hey, dummy, the ceiling is that way. Your half brain makes you a dimwit. Besides, your stupid snowball will never reach the ceiling."

Kaylee froze. Her fingers curled into her palms. Nails dug into flesh. She wiggled her shoulders, shaking off the impulse to throw a punch. Instead, she pinched her nose and yelled, "You stink."

At that, Brenda slithered away without another soul around to witness what had happened.

With greater determination, Kaylee spun on her heels and flew back into the washroom. The second bell rang, the one that meant everyone must be seated at their desks. But Kaylee remained behind.

I can do this. I'll prove it. So what if my grades rot? It can't get any worse. I already sit in the dumb row. For once in my life, I'll show them. I will plant a glob of mushy toilet paper on the ceiling.

Kaylee tilted her face upward. With more resolve than ever, she intended to land her first toilet paper snowball and christen the ceiling with a wicked pitch.

As Louella suggested, Kaylee wound her arm backward for a tremendous underhand whirl. She lobbed it up, landed it high. The wad hung on for a moment, but the formula was too wet. Gravity called, and down it plopped. After taking a deep breath, Kaylee tried again. That time, it stuck. Satisfied, she turned to the mirror, flexed her biceps, and beamed. Just then, Sister Killian stormed in. Kaylee braced herself.

Sister Killian's big black habit flowed from the top of her head down to her toes and swayed side to side like a pendulum marking time. Her scowling, pale face appeared stark against the blackness of her outfit. Clenched fists peeked out from beneath her voluminous dark cloth. Sister stood ramrod straight, eyes sharp. She placed her hands on her hips and glared. Kaylee's snowball loomed above her.

Glancing upward to the heavens, Kaylee prayed the wad would stick or that Sister would move—just in case. Kaylee's jaw fell. It was as though the snowball had a mind of its own. Down, down it came, plopping smack on Sister's head. An involuntary squeal escaped Kaylee's lips.

Drips rolled off Sister's clamshell-shaped bonnet, missed her face, and landed on her chest. Her breath came hard, like bellows fanning a fire. Her bosom rose and fell. Kaylee cupped a hand over her mouth, but it was too late to muffle a laugh. Sister looked like a sorry clown. Kaylee's hands turned clammy. Sister's cheeks twitched in nervous confusion. Trouble.

A guttural sound Kaylee had never heard before emerged from deep inside the gigantic black mass that enveloped Sister. It rumbled and shook, sounding like the old woody station wagon Mother drove. Her face pinched tight, Sister Killian turned toward the mirror. She slid the wet mush from her head, bared her teeth, and pointed at the door. Kaylee followed in the finger's direction to the classroom as Sister's breath crept up her spine like a locomotive pumping steam.

Kaylee took her seat in the classroom, but Sister bellowed, "Stand in the back corner until school ends."

Bratty Brenda let out a well-practiced pig's snort. A ripple of giggles erupted. Kaylee stood and looked out the window as squirrels whisked by in a game of tag. She closed her eyes. She soared with eagles.

Sister gave the desk bell a wag. "Kaylee Reagan." Sister waited. "Miss Kaylee Reagan!"

Louella slid her foot and nudged Kaylee's.

Kaylee turned to see Brenda Mullarkey smirking at her while the rest of the girls in the class just plain stared. There were no boys because the school separated the boys and the girls once they reached the fifth grade.

"Face the wall!" Sister barked.

Not again. Kaylee would hold back the tears until she was home and alone in her bedroom.

Sister Killian swiftly rang the bell on her desk with a snap of her wrist. "Girls! Mark my words. If... in... three years, you want to be part of the eighth-grade graduating class of 1967, you must work hard. If you expect promotion to the sixth grade will be automatic, think anew. You must take school earnestly and complete the assigned homework!"

Sister performed her routine scrutiny of homework notebooks, which the girls had stacked on her desk first thing in the morning. She studied each one for a parent's signature, proving the student had completed the homework.

"Forgery!" she barked. "Forgery!"

The word pounded against Kaylee's eardrums. Knowing the outburst was aimed at her, Kaylee once again turned her gaze heaven-ward and sighed.

Sister strode up and down the aisles, returning homework note-books. Kaylee's notebook met her desk with a slam, commanding complete silence in the classroom.

After school, Sister ordered Kaylee, without the other classmates, to go across the street to the convent for detention. Kaylee suspected Sister did not want to trouble herself with detaining a dozen girls, so like it or lump it, Kaylee remained her victim.

Kaylee speculated about why this time Sister Killian was sending her to the convent for after-school detention. She would rather go to the principal's office during the school day and miss arithmetic or gram-mar. Even so, Kaylee had wondered what it was like inside the convent, where nuns lived. Now she was about to have a peek.

Kaylee had signed her mother's name to her homework, but she didn't understand what the big deal was. Mother wouldn't notice if Kaylee had finished her homework anyway, even if she had signed it. And Sister Killian hadn't given Kaylee detention for sticking her chewing gum to the underside of her desk or for ticking Sister off during the spelling bee. Sister Killian had directed Kaylee to spell the word ship. Kaylee repeated the word, pushed her proud shoulders back, and spelled out s-h-i-t. It had sent the class into hysterics and sent Kaylee, without knowing what had gone wrong, to the principal's office.

Kaylee had not been sent to detention in the convent the time she aimed her peashooter at Brenda but hit Sister instead. Sister had fumed. She hadn't seemed to care that she hadn't been the intended target.

But this time Kaylee realized she was the only one who had signed her mother's name to homework—or at least the only one who got caught. That provided the teacher with enough reason to single her out and confirmed Kaylee's suspicion that her teacher was out to get her.

Kaylee followed Sister to the convent office. Sister found it occupied, so Kaylee followed her to the dining room and was given instructions to wait there. The fifth-grader set down her bulging, worn leather book bag. It held a three-ring binder and a composition-style homework notebook. The books, covered with protective brown paper crafted from discarded grocery bags, peeked out the top.

Straining to listen, Kaylee put her ear to the door. Sister telephoned her mother, and the barren, hollow hallway echoed her words. "Mrs. Reagan, please come and pick up your daughter at the convent, where she's in detention." After a pause, Sister said, "She committed forgery by signing your name on her homework notebook."

Kaylee supposed her teacher had enough on her without mentioning the snowball, the one that seemed to have a mind of its own. If Sister grumbled about the snowball incident, she would have to include most of the other girls in after-school jail. It was unfair since they had also thrown snowballs that stuck to the ceiling, but they hadn't gotten detention. Sister knew it, too, but she was out to get

Kaylee and Kaylee alone. It had to be why she stuck to the forgery grievance.

The door of the dining room swung open, and Sister stepped in.

"You're mean, soooo mean!" Kaylee whined. "Why do I have to sit in your stupid convent? I want to wait for my mother in the classroom!"

Sister pulled her mouth tight. "The school building is closed while the custodian polishes the floors, and there's a meeting in the convent's office, but it's none of your business. Stay put on the chair until your parent reports here."

"But it could take forever and—"

"Zip your mouth shut. Make not a sound, or the back of your head will meet my knuckles."

Kaylee continued, "There are eight of us kids, and she's busy! Who knows how long it'll take for her to get here? You're making my poor mother pay too. You're punishing Mother by making her drive to school and pick me up, and she's a crummy driver. What if she gets killed in a car accident?" Kaylee looked away. Maybe Sister hoped her mother would pay more attention to Kaylee's homework in the future, but with eight children, seven of them girls, that was a long shot.

"I have to go to the bathroom," Kaylee said, crossing one foot over the other.

"Don't even try it, you sneaky little thing. You're full of brass. You're disrespectful, disruptive, disorganized. Belong in fifth grade, you do not. You will repeat this entire grade next year."

Kaylee closed her eyes at the unbearable thought of another year with Sister Killian. Even worse, her brother, Joey, younger than Kaylee by one year, would catch up to her in grade and taunt her every day for the rest of her life. But in another year, he would be upstairs in the boys' department and taught by the Brothers, who also covered themselves in voluminous black and had eyes everywhere.

Kaylee turned her thoughts to the proud feeling that swelled through her when she wore her Girl Scout uniform to school. The only time classmates could wear something other than the school uniform was when the scouts met after school, but things had gone south during that last boastful day.

It had been one of those rare days when Kaylee stood with her shoulders back and her head high. She showed off her Girl Scout sash, adorned with hard-earned badges. It made it easier to brush off the sting of being the dummy in the dumb row. But after the daily reciting of the Pledge of Allegiance, as each girl held hand over heart, Sister told Kaylee to remain standing. Kaylee stood as if she were a peacock spreading its dazzling feathers.

She will let everyone see me for the goodness that I am. Show me off like a good example. Maybe I should pirouette or stand up front so there is no mistake or confusion about what I can do.

Sister pointed. "Remove that sash of badges! There is *no* way you could have possibly earned them."

Kaylee ran her fingers over the colorful embroidered medallions. She knew the feel of each one. The sewing badge for the dress she'd made. The dancing badge. The Red Cross badge. And even a badge for storytelling. She had stitched them onto her sash beneath an emblem of golden wings and stars. Kaylee kept a stiff upper lip. Chin up. She slipped the sash over her head, fighting off the impulse to hold it high. Arranged it in her book bag. With ruffled feathers, she sat.

Kaylee stood in the convent's dining room, folded her arms, and met Sister's eyes, the eyes of the Wicked Witch of the West.

I'm not scared of you. If I had a bucket of water, I would throw it and melt you.

Sister glared. "Sit!"

Kaylee sat. Sister slammed the heavy door, rattling the crucifix on the wall, and left Kaylee alone. Kaylee stood and stuck her tongue out.

"Sit down, and put your tongue back in your mouth," Sister said from behind the door.

Not only does she have eyes in the back of her head, but she can see through doors too. I'll escape this dungeon.

"Where there's a will, there's a way," Kaylee murmured, remembering what Grandma advised when you're in a pinch. *I'll get even.* Kaylee didn't know how, but somehow she knew she would.

In punishment, Kaylee sat next to the head of the table and shivered on the ladder-back chair. Elbows on knees, arms crisscrossed, each hand holding on to the opposite elbow, she curled into her cocoon.

Kaylee raised her chin and looked around the dining room. Neat rows of straight-back chairs flanked each side of a long wooden table. A monstrous armchair marked the head of the table. Nothing sat at the other end, not even an empty chair. Kaylee squinted at a familiar painting of the Last Supper, which hung near the dreadful chair. Then she turned her gaze toward the wall behind her. An image of a bloody, beheaded man stared right at her. Kaylee's jaw dropped. She rose with a start, scrambled backward against a hutch, causing the china to rattle. Then she bumped into the Last Supper, making it rotate sideways on its hook. She crouched in horror. Petrified, she couldn't look away from the bloody head.

The door swung open. "Caravaggio," said a woman whose apron covered a housedress and whose arms held a basket of fresh linens.

"What? Who?"

"Caravaggio," repeated the stout woman with smooth bronze skin and matching amber eyes. Her long black hair spun into two long braids.

"Do you speak English?" Kaylee's voice shook.

"The artist," replied the housekeeper, smiling. "Caravaggio," she said, enunciating each syllable, "is the artist. And the head belonged to St. John the Baptist."

"Mortal sin? Did he get detention?"

"Excuse me?"

"How did he lose his head? Where's his body? Where's the rest of him? Did he kill someone?"

The housekeeper set the laundry basket down and put away the table linens. Then she straightened the picture of the Last Supper. "It's not like that. St. John was misunderstood."

Kaylee, her mind filled with questions, stared in fascination and fright at the housekeeper.

The woman scooped up the remaining linens. "I need to take these bed cloths to Sister Killian's bedroom. *Bendiciones*."

Kaylee held the door open for the housemaid, then her eyes followed the path she took to Sister's bedroom. Kaylee waited. When the housekeeper emerged and shuffled away, Kaylee backed away from the portrait of the beheaded St. John and looked up and down the corridor. She shook her head to clear away the bloody image then tiptoed into Sister's bedroom. Kaylee softly closed the door behind her.

CHAPTER 2

DETENTION

The chill rose from the terra-cotta tile floor, penetrating the worn soles of Kaylee's unpolished saddle shoes. She felt a chill run up her spine. Kaylee pulled up the threadbare knee sock, which had fallen around her skinny ankle. As soon as she moved, the rubber band holding it up snapped, and the sock slumped down.

A brown bedspread draped a twin-size bed in a cold, odorless room. No lumps, no headboard, no footboard. No teddy bears. Not a family photograph. The walls of Sister Killian's bedroom held only a crucifix. A well-thumbed Sunday prayer missal rested on the night table beside the bed. Beneath it sat a large, shiny Bible with paper edged with gold. It looked like it had never been opened. A narrow shaft of light slanted through the center of the window where the bulky curtains did not quite meet.

Kaylee listened hard for the sound of footsteps.

If I get caught in Sister's bedroom, she will send me to jail. I'll never see my family again.

Kaylee stood on her on her tiptoes, roamed Sister Killian's bedroom, and parted the curtains. A statue of the Blessed Virgin Mary stood guard over the convent in the garden below. Oak leaves smothered the ground at her feet while a few dingy brown leaves clung to the branches.

Hoping to escape, Kaylee struggled to open the window. It took the strength of both hands to move the latch. Kaylee hesitated as she listened for the sound of footsteps. Hearing none, she turned back to the unlocked window, but a keyhole in a top drawer distracted her from her impulsive plan. Why a nun would need a lock? What could she be hiding?

Like a curious cat, Kaylee inched over to the dresser, ran her fingers along its top, down to the keyhole, over the knobs, and pulled. Nothing happened. She turned to the nightstand and easily opened its drawer.

Yellowed holy cards lay like a deck of cards. Kaylee flipped through them. Buried within the deck, she found a black-and-white photograph of a family and a picture of a pleasantly dressed couple. The pair looked to be about eighteen years old. The man with light-colored hair gazed in adoration at the smiling young woman. An open vest covered his shirt, which was unbuttoned near the collar. His tie dangled loosely around his neck.

The woman's dress, dusted with roses, fell to midcalf. Kaylee envisioned the light material swaying in a gentle breeze. The young woman's hand hung by her side with her pinky finger set in an easy hook to the man's pinky finger. It was as though the loving pinkies were swearing a future promise. A statue of a man on horseback stood in the background. The horse's strong hooves were ready to charge forward as if in battle. Who could the couple be? Was the photo hidden here for a reason?

Kaylee placed the picture back into the drawer. Something in the face of the woman was familiar, something she couldn't put her finger on. Kaylee felt around the drawer until her hand rested on a skeleton key. Grasping the key, she tiptoed back to the dresser, worked the locked drawer, and wiggled it open.

The drawer held a stack of old letters tied with a tattered pink ribbon. Kaylee was not sure what seized her, but she wanted to read them. The ticktock cadence of footsteps echoed down the long corridor.

Her heart throbbed. It pumped so hard she thought she could hear it. She held her breath—waiting, waiting.

When the footsteps passed, she exhaled and impulsively tucked the stack of letters into the bodice of her uniform. She closed the curtains, locked the drawer, and returned the key to the night table. Heart pounding full speed, fingers shaking, she peeped into the corridor, swiftly padded to the dining room, and squeezed the pack of letters into her book bag.

The heavy door of the dining room flew open to reveal the familiar squinty-eyed, scowling face of her fifth-grade teacher, Sister Killian. Kaylee had experience reading Sister's facial expressions, and much of the time this one was all Sister Killian needed to quiet an entire gaggle of girls' chatter.

Kaylee had long since known there were legs somewhere under the voluminous black habits that covered the nuns from head to toe. At their waists hung a circle of rosary beads. The Sisters wore tight bonnets held on by thin cloths tied in small bows under their chins. The fronts of the bonnets fanned out and framed their faces like giant clamshells, telltale emblems of this order of nuns, the Sisters of Charity. Like a pair of extra eyes, black polished shoes peeked out at the ankles' hemlines.

Kaylee grinned while remembering first grade, when Sister Dominique fell into the snow and exposed her black stockinged legs. That was hilarious—a big black spot in the soft, pure-white snow. "Make a snow angel," Kaylee had said. The girls had giggled. Sister had made no snow angel.

Sister Killian pointed down the hall, and Kaylee flew out of the dining room like Jonah spewed out from the belly of a whale. She marched in the direction of her mother, who appeared small standing at the enormous entrance to the convent. Kaylee clutched her book bag, with its secret stolen treasure, close to her chest. The music of Onward Christian Soldiers played in her mind. She made a conscious effort not to march her feet to the tune for fear of a knuckle whack to the back of her head.

CHAPTER 3

THE LONG RIDE HOME

Slowly, deliberately, Kaylee set one foot in front of the other as she marched down the long black-and-white tile corridor toward her mother. Mother looked stern. Sister looked severe. Kaylee was scared. Her footsteps echoed until she stopped where her mother stood. Mother gave Kaylee the silent treatment, and for added insurance, one of her looks, the one which meant *you wait and see.*

Without a word, Sister opened the convent door, and Mother quietly exited. The only chatter came from the rattle of car keys in Mother's hand. Kaylee followed the sound of the jangling keys to their old woody station wagon and, for the first and maybe the last time, sat in the front passenger seat. She looked over the lonely, quiet wagon that did not carry the rest of the ten-member family. Then she looked at her unspeaking, pretty mother.

It's just me and an angry mother who won't even talk. I wasn't bad. I threw toilet paper snowballs just like most everyone else. Mother didn't have to bother signing her name to my homework. I did it for her. She's too busy.

Old woody's engine sputtered and reluctantly woke to life. A pelt from her brother, Joey, would be better than this silence, this penance.

From the car window, Kaylee watched trees and houses fly by. They crossed railroad tracks and followed newly paved suburban streets lined with neat new homes, two-car driveways, and knee-high swimming pools emptied of their summer fun. Kaylee wondered if more punishment would be doled out at home. They rode past the house with the hand-crafted grotto constructed from an old claw-foot bathtub. The tub stuck halfway out of the ground, and its hollow dome framed a three-foot-high statue of the Blessed Virgin Mary. They were getting close to home.

Kaylee knew women were preparing dinner while fathers, home from work, turned the pages of newspapers.

The sleepy bedroom community hummed with dinner preparations as televisions buzzed with fuzzy, rolling images. Unlocked doors swung open and slammed shut. Neighbors shared lawnmowers and borrowed cups of sugar. All of this seemed unreal compared to city life.

Kaylee gazed at her mother from across the car seat. "You're so pretty. I'm plain—plain ugly," she said.

"Oh, for the love of God, not now. I know what you're trying to do," Mother said.

"What do you think I'm trying to do? You really are pretty. Oh, to look like you. I'm ugly."

Mother had curly, jet-black hair that fell to her shoulders and was only a little frizzy. Her black almond-shaped eyes, set deep over high cheekbones, graced an oval-shape face. The circles under her eyes had taken months to disappear after the youngest baby's christening. Mother walked tall and sat straight like a movie star. She often wore a tea-length dress beneath her apron and walked in sensible shoes.

Kaylee turned away, bit her lip, and closed her eyes.

The cropped cut of my mousy brown hair is ugly and too short to try one of my older sisters' curling rollers. And my younger brother, Joey, likes to wrap his paws around my skinny arm and twist it in opposite directions, leaving a burn. All red and itchy. Even Dad calls me Skinny Bones.

Detention was not over yet. Mother remained quiet. She hadn't scolded Kaylee, which made Kaylee feel even worse. Punishment, detention, penance—all for signing Mother's name in her homework notebook just to prove it was done. Sister punished Mother, too, for not looking after Kaylee's homework assignments and by making her drive to school to pick her up.

Mother never asked Kaylee if she completed her homework. Kaylee figured it was because she had eight children to look after. Fifteen-year-old Courtnay was the oldest and attended Catholic high school. Thirteen-year-old Mary, who was two years older than Kaylee, loved playing the piano. Joey was ten and liked being an altar boy so he could steal wine. At five years old, Liz still sucked her thumb and dragged a blanket around. Next came four-year-old Lucy, three-year-old Orla, and one-year-old Emma.

When Mother was too busy to sign her name, which was most of the time, Kaylee simply forged a decent rendition of her signature—or so she thought. It had worked until today. It would have been a better forgery had Kaylee practiced those Palmer Method penmanship lessons, like everyone else in the class. Kaylee worried about the letters. She worried about penance, penmanship, and punishment. She and her classmates practiced making continuous slanted ovals, trying to stay in the lines. Once she even practiced with her eyes closed, but it made little difference. Even Mary told her to stop holding the pen like a lollipop. Kaylee tried. She tried to hold it correctly and to keep the center of the oval on the dotted line between the upper and lower bold lines. The left hand wanted to take over, but Kaylee was not allowed to use it. Whenever she put the fountain pen in her left hand, her knuckles felt the sharp slap of a wooden ruler. A ruler with a barely visible metal edge.

The metal always landed first. Once, it drew blood that Kaylee wiped on her uniform. Then she scratched an itch on her cheek and, unbeknownst to her, left behind a bloody red zigzag running from her right nostril to her earlobe. Her friend Louella had chuckled with admiration, but Kaylee wondered if she would ever learn to slide and swirl the words across the page and make them look pretty. Why was it so hard? She didn't understand why Sister wouldn't let her print. When she grew up, she planned to buy a typewriter just like the one Uncle Pat owned.

Kaylee should have doodled less and swirled more, yet looking out the window held more appeal than penmanship or the fine art of forgery. The truth was that the number of Kaylee's fake signatures outnumbered Mother's authentic ones, so Kaylee was no longer comfortable asking her mother to sign her name.

Kaylee turned to Mother. "I told Sister she's lucky you can even drive to school at all. She had no idea you flunked the road test five times before you finally passed."

Mother rubbed her belly then tightened her grasp on the steering wheel. "You told Sister Killian that? Dandy. That's just dandy."

Kaylee exhaled with relief. Mother had finally said something.

Few people had a driver's license while living in the Big Apple. Mother had rarely ridden in a car, let alone driven one. She had walked to church with her family and ridden the train to school. Grandma carried groceries home by pulling a wire basket on wheels.

The suburbs of the Hudson Valley, where they had moved, were within commuting distance of the city where Dad worked.

After the move to the Hudson Valley, Dad told Mother she should learn to drive. Mother reluctantly agreed. It took time before Mother became comfortable driving without him sitting beside her. The driver's test presented other problems. Granted, the first failure was not altogether her fault. Dad drove her to the driving test site, but out of habit, when he got out of the car, he took the keys with him.

Kaylee had overheard Mother telling Dad what had happened. Mother had fumbled around and searched for the keys.

"Start the car," the driving examiner said.

"I can't start the thing. I need the key."

The examiner slid his spectacles down to the end of his pointy nose, glaring at Mother with what she said was a look of amazement. Mother jumped out in quick pursuit of Dad, but by the time Mother got back in the car, her hands shook so badly, she put the car in reverse and stepped on the gas. The car shot backward, and the instructor pulled up the emergency brake.

"You get a mulligan," Dad had told Mother, as if she were playing a round of golf and he was granting her a do-over.

He didn't know it then, but it would take four more rounds before Mother passed the road test. Dad never took off with the keys again, but as for the other four times she'd flunked the driving test, no one knew for sure what happened. One failure could have been because of the snake Joey placed in the back seat. He had pretended not to know anything about it, but his sisters had been on to him and gave Mother an A for effort.

Anyway, Kaylee felt safer when old Mr. Melbourne, the bus driver, was behind a steering wheel. Mr. Melbourne always stopped at railroad crossings if the lights flashed and sometimes even if they didn't. Mother never stopped. She rode over bicycles, garbage cans, and once had hit the telephone pole at the end of the driveway. "Oh, someone must have moved the pole," Mother had complained.

Kaylee peered out the passenger window, relieved to see the familiar, fresh neighborhood houses all in a row. They sped past the neat rows of one-story ranch-style homes, occupied, for the most part, by second-generation Irish-American families. Like the Reagans, many had moved from Washington Heights in Manhattan. Others had moved from Inwood of Manhattan or the Bronx. The liberated families exchanged the city's symphony for the suburb's lazy hum. Most of the neat houses matched neat cars parked squarely in driveways, but a few ramshackle station wagons sat in front of some of the new houses.

They were almost home, and Kaylee still did not know what punishment would befall her.

CHAPTER 4

KAYLEE AND HER FAMILY

Mother's tight fists gripped the steering wheel as she aimed the old woody station wagon up the winding hill. The car lurched into the driveway after rolling over a garbage can lid and a baseball bat and nearly hitting the neighbor's cat. Her foot slammed the brake.

Kaylee held her ears, blocking out the high-pitched squeal of the brakes. They halted in time before crashing into the only two-story home on the entire block.

Next door, Mrs. O'Malley parted her curtains, and Kaylee waved.

"Back in the city, her mother did the same thing, sticking her nose everywhere," Mother said.

"Did she inherit her nose from her mother?"

Mother exhaled and wagged a finger at Kaylee. "Never mind. You're grounded! You are lucky. Dad thinks you are getting too old to be spanked. No going out to play. No friends. No leaving your bedroom until you clean it! If it is not clean, you will go without supper. Cleanliness is next to godliness, you know. Now go tell Joey to put out the trash."

Kaylee ran into the house and took one look at her younger brother.

With one hand on her hip, she put on Sister Killian's scowl and pointed to the garbage.

Joey gave Kaylee his best King Kong stance and ran outside. Prancing like a ringleader, he returned with two garbage can lids and hunted for Kaylee. Then he smashed aluminum trash can lids like cymbals in her face.

"Yeow!" Kaylee screamed.

"For heaven's sake. If I told you once, I told you a thousand times. Be quiet, Kaylee, or else." Mother yelled.

Joey fled.

Kaylee didn't wish to test the "or else" part, so she cleaned her room and got closer to God. But she couldn't go outside.

She checked out Joey from the window as he bumped and dragged metal trash cans to the curb, creating enough ruckus to make the neighbor's curtains part again. All he had to do was take out the trash, nothing else. He hardly ever placed the lids on the cans tightly enough to keep stray dogs and other random critters from knocking them over. Sometimes the cans rolled down the street, spewing garbage all over the neighbors' yards. Dad made all the sisters, except for the two youngest, pick up the litter.

When Dad arrived home from his engineering job, he beeped the horn for someone to open the garage door. There was no way he would get out of the car and open it. And no way Joey would budge.

"Someone better run fast before he climbs from the car and opens it himself!" Mother yelled.

Mary, Kaylee's older sister, stopped playing the piano, dashed out, and yanked open the garage door. The girls knew better than to wait for Joey.

Kaylee spied her brother from her bedroom door, sneaked out, and bonked him in the arm. "Just because you're the only boy, you get away with everything," Kaylee yelled and raced off.

Joey tackled her and deliberately let his drool land on her face.

Kaylee, so mad she couldn't see straight, kicked him with all her might until he backed off. Finally, he landed a monkey punch, leaving a knot the size of a chestnut on her arm.

"I'm telling Dad on you. You kicked me in the family jewels," Joey said, knowing the thought of Joey someday carrying on the family name pleased Dad.

Kaylee stuck out her tongue. "Boys don't wear jewelry. You're stupid."

"You're an ass."

"I know you are, but what am I?"

"An ass," Joey said.

"I know you are, but what am I?" This could go on forever, so Kaylee got in the last word before running into her room with her hands over her ears and slamming the door behind her.

The worst punishment Mother could give Kaylee was to forbid her from going outside, but now she couldn't even call her friends.

Her sister Courtnay hogged the phone, rapping with her boyfriend. Courtnay ran the telephone cord under the bathroom door and could gab for hours, thinking no one could hear her. But if Kaylee was careful not to make a sound, she could pick up the receiver on the extension and listen in. It didn't help that Courtnay tied up the children's bathroom. If you had to go, well, it would not be in Courtnay's conference room.

Once, when Courtnay was putting on Mother's makeup, Kaylee snuck up behind her and cut out a lock of her curly blond hair. Courtnay never even knew it.

Piano notes drifted from the living room, drawing Kaylee from her bedroom. She sat on the bench beside her sister Mary and swayed to the captivating notes of Beethoven's "Fur Elise." Kaylee cheered when she played the last note. Mary squeezed her then cracked her knuckles.

"Hey, Kaylee, I want to be a concert pianist," Mary announced.

"Mother said not to crack your knuckles because it's not good for piano fingers. Anyway, you are a pianist. You make the piano sound so pretty. Why can't I get lessons and play like you?"

Mary pointed at Kaylee's feet. "Because you are pigeon-toed."

"But what does that have to do with anything?" Kaylee fiddled with the high keys on the piano.

"Because you get ballet lessons instead so your feet will turn out, not in." Mary chuckled.

"That's not fair." Kaylee played another high note. "If I practice turning them out like a penguin, will I be able to take piano lessons?" Kaylee rose, pointed her toes, and pranced like a ballerina but looked like a duck waddling.

Mary exploded with laughter. "You might be better off with the piano."

By this time, Mother had finished cooking. The ringing of the supper bell beckoned the family to the kitchen table.

Kaylee squirmed in her seat, expecting Mother to tell Dad about her forgery, but she said nothing, and Kaylee wondered if Mother felt guilty for not checking her homework. Dad might not be so pleased if she didn't sign Kaylee's homework notebook regularly, regardless of its completion. This time, Catholic guilt favored Kaylee.

As usual, grace began with the sign of the cross. With hands in prayer pose, the family gave thanks for the blessings the parents, seven sisters, and one brother were about to receive. Before ending with the sign of the cross, Mother added a prayer of her own—a request. "Lord, let at least one of our children join the vocation of the clergy. Amen."

"I want to go to Atlantic City or Coney Island for vocation," Kaylee announced.

"Idiot," Mary said.

"Why? Where do you want to go?"

"A vocation is something you are called to become when you grow up. Like a nun or a priest," Mother said.

Kaylee's detention in solitary confinement in a convent was enough to keep her from a nunnery.

Little did Mother know altar boy Joey was the one closest to heeding the call. He was already practicing the fine art of priestly communion, making his sisters kneel before him so he could administer his stolen hosts. He greedily kept the stolen wine to himself, which may have encouraged his Sunday-night behavior of jumping out of his bedroom window to go rob a train or something else like that.

After dinner, Kaylee worried about what to do with the letters she swiped from Sister Killian's bureau. Finally, she removed them from her book bag and hid them in the back of her closet, next to her piggy bank. She didn't know why the devil had made her take them, but she had and now couldn't imagine what would happen if she got caught.

Back in her bedroom, Kaylee thumbed through the letters. *I'm too frightened to read them. Suppose God strikes me with lightning. Tomorrow, I'll return them. I'm sorry. I'm guilty.*

All night Kaylee schemed how to return the letters with no one knowing. She took the letters from the closet and was about to place them back in her book bag when the edge of a photograph sticking out from an envelope caught her eye. She untied the tattered pink ribbon and stared at an image of the same couple she had seen in the picture inside Sister Killian's night table.

* * *

The next morning at school, Kaylee looked away from the out-of-focus words on the chalkboard, rubbed her eyes, and gazed out the window. Often, she closed her eyes and imagined she was flying with butterflies and bees. Flying far away from school. But sometimes, Kaylee would shift her gaze from the window overlooking the playground and pay attention to her schoolwork. It was no surprise that her favorite times of the day were lunch and recess.

Since there was no cafeteria, each day the girls removed their lunches from brown paper bags and set them on their desktops. The Sisters brought in milk cartons. Bratty Brenda held her nose a little higher than usual. She tossed her head just enough to make her curls jiggle and spring back like tiny Slinkys. She had been jiggling those perfect finger curls since first grade and wore a purple satin ribbon above one ear. Brenda raised her steak sandwich to show the difference between it and Kaylee's peanut butter and jelly, but Kaylee was too busy eating, and she restrained herself from taking aim with her peashooter.

"Not again. Not another overcooked steak." Brenda moaned. "You would think my mother would know how to fix my lunch by now."

Brenda turned to Kaylee. "At least it's not a PB&J on stale bread with crust still on it."

"Try again. Bread has no time to get stale in my house. Besides, the crust is the best part. I got a peanut butter and jelly. Come near me, and you get a punch in the belly," Kaylee said, but she unexpectedly bit into an all-peanut butter Wonder Bread sandwich. She washed it down with milk before spoiled Bratty Brenda noticed.

Every morning when Mother prepared lunch for her school-age children, she lined up twelve pieces of bread. She spread peanut butter on six of them and jelly on the other six then slapped the two opposite pieces of bread together. But sometimes, someone got an all-peanut butter sandwich or an all-jelly sandwich.

What was worse was the time Mother made a bologna sandwich for Dad. Instead of bologna, she accidentally placed the picture from the package in the sandwich. Mother spread the cardboard picture with mustard. Kaylee had wondered if Dad had been hungry enough to eat it —mustard, paper, and all. Mother prided herself on making fresh sandwiches each morning, unlike their neighbor Mrs. O'Malley, who made ten sandwiches for her two children every Sunday night. Mrs. O'Malley saved two for Monday and froze eight for the rest of the week.

Each school-age child in Kaylee's household received three cents for a carton of milk. If anyone at school forgot to bring their milk money, they still got the carton of milk, but Sister kept a record for the future. After lunch on Fridays, schoolmates with extra pennies could go to the seventh-grade classroom and buy penny candy from Sister Theresa. Kaylee felt lucky to spend the money Grandma gave her.

Grandma was an excellent source of coins. Kaylee loved riding the train to Penn Station and transferring to the subway to visit her in the city. Grandma was generous and let the children reach into her Tetley tea tin and grab a handful of coins. The old tin had lost its scent of tea and smelled like rusting metal. Kaylee, well versed in grabbing pennies, could spread her hand as wide as a peacock's tail feathers and scoop up a bazillion.

When Kaylee finished her lunch, she hid a scrap of bread in her hand to feed the birds during recess. Then she scooted past Brenda to throw out the trash, hoping Brenda was too busy eating to open her big mouth.

"Hey, dumbbell, if you cut your hair any shorter, you'd look like a boy," Brenda said with her mouth full.

Kaylee rubbed her head and felt the short crop of her hair. She didn't want to look like a boy, and even though her brother, Joey, said Brenda was cute, she didn't want to look like her either.

Kaylee's older sister Mary had trimmed Kaylee's tangled, sticky hair to remove the bubblegum that had dropped from her mouth and rolled into her hair during sleep. She couldn't do much about her new, choppy look except to make her hair even shorter. So, to improve her appearance, she planned on asking Mary what else she could do besides polishing her shoes. Maybe Brenda would find less to bully her over.

CHAPTER 5

READ THE LETTERS

Kaylee wanted to forget the letters. So she practiced ballet and turned her feet out, attempting a ballerina's first position. She stared at her saddle shoes, realizing they did nothing to improve her plies and releves. Still, Kaylee didn't bother to change into her pink slippers but kept thinking about the photo of the couple in which even she could see their love for each other.

Finally, while sitting on the edge of her bed that night, thoughts about bad things that happened at school whirled through her head. Considering the injustices of spelling bees, the unfairness of rulers with sharp edges that slapped knuckles, and detention, she thought that at least something good had come out of being sent to the office. Principal Sister Agatha gave her licorice. Sister Killian didn't know about the candy, and Kaylee was not about to tell her. Kaylee clenched her fists then opened the first letter.

An hour later, Mary entered the bedroom they shared.

Kaylee didn't hear her until it was too late. She scrambled to hide the letters behind her one-eyed teddy bear.

"Too late," Mary said. "What are you hiding?"

"Nothing," Kaylee said.

Mary yanked the only arm of the shabby teddy bear, and the letters fell to the floor along with some of Teddy's stuffing. She grabbed a couple and waved them. "Where'd you get these? What are they about?"

Kaylee picked up the loose stuffing and pushed it into the bear's shoulder. "Love letters. I don't know who wrote them, and I don't know who got them." Kaylee rolled onto her side and read more.

"Where you found the letters might give a clue."

"Sister Killian's bedroom. They were locked in a chest. I found the key and took them."

Mary's mouth dropped. "You're kidding, right? Thou shall not steal! It's the seventh commandment."

"I'm already on my way to hell. Remember, I sit in the dumb row."

"That's not a sin, but stealing is. Add that to your list of sins. If Sister Killian doesn't kill you, you'll be in the confessional booth for so long they will charge you rent. But you'll get off with less penance if you're lucky enough to have Father Halligan hear your confession instead of Father Cunningham. Otherwise, plan on kneeling with penance for a century. And be ready for sore knees."

Kaylee curled her hands over her head and stuck her index fingers out, making devil's horns.

Mary wagged her finger. "You're a devil! You might get struck by a thunderbolt. And nuns don't write love letters, so they must belong to someone else."

Kaylee pointed at herself. "They belong to me now."

"No, they don't! Do you want to die? You're an idiot."

"I know you are, but what am I?"

"Idiot."

"I know you are, but what am I?" Kaylee chanted over and over until Mary stopped calling her an idiot. "Just don't tell Dad."

Mary cracked her knuckles. "Are you kidding me? I'll tell Mother, and she'll tell Dad. Then expect to die. He'll shoot you."

"Don't, pleeeeease don't," Kaylee begged. "I'll tell on you."

"Tell what? You can't get much on me."

"You crack your knuckles."

"Big deal. They already know that."

"Just don't tell."

"Maybe, but it doesn't make it right." Mary smirked. "If I keep your secret, you'll have to take my turn doing the supper dishes for a month of Sundays. And if I think of anything else, I'll let you know."

"I won't be your slave!" Mary picked up a letter and read it aloud.

To my darling Olivia,

As I lie here at night, thinking of you, I want you to know how I truly feel. I am very much in love with you. I did not know what I was missing before you came into my life. When I close my eyes, it's as if you're here with me. The silk of your voice. The lovely curls of your soft chestnut-brown hair, the sweet dimples when you smile, the sparkle in your green eyes are what I see. I love the fullness of your lips, your style, and how your scent stays with me like a freshly bloomed lilac.

"Did my heart love till now? forswear it, sight! For I ne'er saw true beauty till this night."—Shakespeare.

Remember the first moment we met? If you had not trespassed, I would have never met you. I held you in my arms. We were on the boat, and you were unconscious from a fainting spell. You hadn't yet opened your eyes, and already you moved me. Remember when we made our way from the galley and up onto the deck? I tried to take your hand, and you pulled away. It was forward of me, but it felt right. It feels so right. I've never felt this way. As sure as the wind fills the sail, you fill my heart. You are the face of love, the face of life, the fountain of bliss. Home, you bring to me. My love for you will never end. Sweet dreams of you lull me to sleep.

With your hand in mine, I'm sincerely your man.

Love,
John

Mary's eyes bugged out. "Man, oh man, this is good."

Kaylee flung her arms wide and, in a deep dramatic voice, said,

"Darling, oh, darling." Then she collapsed in a heap on the bed and crawled under the covers. "What will I do when you're not here?"

Mary looked around the room. "Where art thou?"

Peals of laughter rippled through the bedroom. Kaylee threw off the covers, lay on her back like a turtle trying to right itself, and wiggled with glee.

Kaylee reached for another letter and held it up. "Olivia can't be Sister Killian. Could she?"

"Maybe. Why not?"

"Because she doesn't smell like a lilac. She smells like fish sprinkled with chalk dust."

Mary held her nose. "Ew. P U!"

Kaylee opened the letter. "It's my turn to read one."

To my darling Olivia,

The days are so long without you by my side. I miss your touch, the sweet perfume of you, the scent of your hair, your warmth. When I look into your deep-green eyes, I am overcome with joy. Even the guys on the job remarked on the difference in me.

It's incredible to have the opportunity to work on the construction of the Empire State Building. I can't wait for you to see the view from the observation deck. It's thrilling up there. By the time it's completed, there'll be one hundred and two floors. Even though I dropped out of college prep school, it was worth it. I pay the rent. An' I've been luckier than most. Even luckier than my enterprising father, who is out of work.

Sadly, with barely a thread of hope, Mother wrings her hands with worry over the Depression. When all this is over, she wants me to return to Fordham Prep and later become an English literature professor like her brother. But I'm not as sure as I once was. I love the thrill of building skyscrapers. Especially the tallest one in the world!

Mother can't seem to find any joy these days. There are so many neighbors out of work and going hungry. My cousins are here for dinner five times a week, and we're glad to share our food. Hopefully, it won't be long before the country is up and rolling, putting a most-wanted end to the soup lines.

Fill your days with my sincere love. Fill your heart with joy as you have filled mine. You're in my dreams. Until next time.

Loving you,
John

"How did people get so depressed?" asked Kaylee.

"The Depression made them depressed."

"Duh. Why?"

"The dads lost their jobs, then lost their houses, then had nothing to eat."

"I think we should hide food in the attic just in case we get depressed."

Mary grinned. "It'll just go rotten. Besides, the Depression ended over thirty years ago. Grandma will tell you about it, but only if you ask. She says it brings back sad feelings."

Kaylee wet her lips. "Could be why she licks her plate when she thinks no one is looking."

"Yuk!" Mary scratched her head. "Maybe."

Kaylee waved a letter. "One more, one more!"

"It's too late," Mary said. "Save it."

Kaylee pounced and opened the letter. A pressed flower floated to the floor. Kaylee picked up the fragile buttercup and held it to the light. "What secrets do you hold, little flower?"

"Go to sleep." Mary switched off the lights.

* * *

The following day after classes, Kaylee jumped off the school bus and headed straight for the bedroom she shared with Mary. And the letters. Mary wasn't far behind. She dropped her book bag on the bedroom floor. "We're going out to play."

29

But it was too late. Kaylee had already opened the letter addressed to John Sullivan.

"This is wrong," said Mary. But she was not about to miss it.

"Look, Mary. There are a few letters from Olivia to John that were never opened." She pointed to a stamp on the envelope—RETURN TO SENDER. "Why were these letters returned? I'll bet Olivia sealed them with a secret. We should open one," Kaylee said.

Mary rubbed her forehead. "I can't imagine why the postman returned them, but I don't think we should open them."

"Why not? We read so many. We may as well read this one. What's the difference?"

Mary shook her head.

"Okay. How about we read this one? It's already opened." Without waiting for an answer, Kaylee slipped the letter from the envelope and read.

> *Dear Olivia,*
>
> *Soon, I will hold you in my arms again. I loved strolling along the footpaths of Central Park, your hand hooked around my arm. I loved posing with you in front of the great statue of Simon Bolivar. Our picnic by the Conservatory felt like our secret garden, our secret place. Olivia, how I long for you. Our love feels ageless. Endless.*

"Ouuuuueee," Kaylee said and squinted her eyes to read more.

> *There are so many beautiful monuments and statues to see. One of my favorites is Shakespeare. "Come what sorrow can, It cannot countervail the exchange of joy. That one short minute give me in her sight."*
>
> *Sadly, though, it's hard to come down to earth and think about the lot of the unfortunate homeless. Hooverville shanties are sprawled across the Great Lawn of our Central Park. I'm sorry for the hobos who have to live in them. It seems President Hoover has forgotten about these people. Next time, I'll pack extra sandwiches*

for some of them. It may not be much, but it's a godsend for a hungry person. There's talk about removing the sheep from the park's meadow to keep them out of starving hands. It's ironic to see the double towers of San Remo luxury apartments looming high in the background. How they can look out over the shanties and do nothing escapes me. The poor are in my prayers.

There is something important in the park I want to show you. Bethesda Terrace is a beautiful fountain with an angel at the top. It's believed the gospel of St. John inspired the architect Calvert Vaux's design. Jesus, while in Jerusalem, healed a man of great faith at a pool known as Bethesda.

It'll be a very special place for us, so we'll go by horse and buggy. A place to visit year after year with the fondest of memories. The world is our oyster.

"Parting is such sweet sorrow. That I shall say goodnight till it be morrow."—Shakespeare

Sincerely in love,
John

"Wow, this is good! What's that word?" Kaylee asked, pointing.

"Sound it out. It has three syllables."

"Sin-cere-ly. Oh, I see, and now I know how to spell it too. The first syllable is sin. Is John sinfully hers? What sin do you think they committed?"

"You're an idiot," Mary said. "Sincerely means heartfelt."

Mary moved her hand over another word, exposing one syllable at a time. "Now, read this."

Kaylee sounded out the word opportunity and practiced spelling it. Then, impulsively, she slid a bobby pin along the fold of an envelope and tapped it until the paper fell out.

Dear John,

It has been a while since I heard from you. Where are you? I went to your apartment, but no one was home. Your neighbor knew nothing about your family or their whereabouts.

It's not like you to simply disappear. You have always been reliable.

There is something I must speak with you about. I am beside myself with such heartache. I need you. I miss you. Where are you?

I love you,
Olivia

Kaylee fanned herself with the letter. "Wow. What happened? What was it Olivia wanted to tell John? It sounds so serious. I don't understand. I want to know what went on. I want to know where John is. And why did the letters come back?"

"It's none of our business."

"But I'm curious."

Mary wagged her finger. "Grandma says curiosity killed the cat."

"I'm curious, not curiosity." Kaylee giggled.

The two sisters spent several days and nights lying in bed, taking turns reading the letters. They enacted dramatic love scenes. Placing hands over hearts, they moaned with passion. The bed became a stage, the dolls and the one-eyed teddy bear an audience.

Mary put on Mother's pearls and waved a sheer purple scarf as she pirouetted and sang, "Don't Sit Under the Apple Tree."

Kaylee put on their brother's tweed cap and got down on one knee. Then, with a key ring, she proposed to Mary.

"No, I won't marry you."

"Why not?"

"Because you're my brother," Mary teased, and they burst into peals of laughter.

"Hey, let's put on a play about love. I could get another Girl Scout badge. It'll prove I'm not dumb. And best of all, we can save the money to track down John. We'll call the play *Romeo and Juliet*. It's probably one of Dad and Grandma's favorites. They love Shakespeare."

"Maybe," Mary said. "About the play part, I mean."

"Who do you think Olivia is?"

Mary handed Kaylee a piece of paper and a pencil. "Do the math."

"I don't do math. Besides, how is math going to tell me who Olivia is?"

"Grow up, idiot! Who do you know that is old? Like about fifty ancient years old and has big green eyes and dimples?"

"Oh my God. Are you saying Olivia is Sister Killian?"

"Yup. I am now."

"She can't be. Sister doesn't have a heart."

"She did at one time."

"Where do you think her heart went? And why were the last of the letters returned to her?"

"We'll never discover why. Don't need to. Don't want to."

"You know why the Sisters wear those big black clothes?" asked Kaylee.

"Why?"

"It's a habit." Kaylee giggled at her own joke. "A bad habit."

"Ha ha. That's a good one!"

"Come on. Let's find out why the letters came back," Kaylee said.

"How? How can we possibly do that?"

"I have some money, and we'll make more putting on the play. And I'll babysit if Mother lets me," Kaylee said. "Then we could buy tickets and tokens, take the train to the city, get on the subway, and go to the last address posted on the envelope. Besides, I'll probably earn another Girl Scout badge and look smart."

"Don't be an idiot," Mary said. "They don't make Girl Scout badges for being sneaky."

"Maybe they make a detective badge."

"I doubt it. Besides, this happened thirty years ago. Do you think anyone will still be at the same address?"

"Grandma has been at the same address forever, and I'll bet it's close to her apartment. And you know how to get there."

"That gives me an idea." Mary rushed from the bedroom and returned with a phone book. "Instead of going there, you can call him." She fanned the phonebook until it opened to S and ran her fingers down the page, stopping at Sullivan. "There's no John listed. There are many Sullivans but none with the first name of John. Well, it was a good idea to try the telephone book. Anyway, where did you get money?"

"It was in Margaret Riley's blue coat pocket, the coat her mother gave us when Margaret grew out of it. You know, the one you wouldn't wear, so I got it. Ha ha. So there."

"I wouldn't be caught dead wearing a charity coat."

"So what," Kaylee said.

The letters hounded Kaylee and kept the girls reading long into the night and well past their bedtime. They took turns reading, listening, and learning about the sad, trying times of the Great Depression. They learned about the construction of the tallest building in the world and about the beauty of Central Park. The two sisters wanted to know more, but the letters from John had stopped. And it was already late, time to turn out the lights.

As the house took its goodnight breath, Kaylee overheard Mother moaning to Dad about money and too many bills. Kaylee tucked her head under the blankets. *I won't ask for anything.* With that, she gave up the idea of piano lessons for the time being and dreamed of ways to make money. Kaylee had learned that the Girl Scouts sold things besides cookies. Selling greeting cards earned points, but the points were for a select few items in a small brochure, not cash. She could exchange the points for things like a basketball hoop or a jump rope, but not piano lessons or train tickets. Kaylee put the thought aside but remembered the S&H Green Stamps. She planned on helping Mother lick them and stick them in the little books so they could go to the redemption store. Mother could get something for the kitchen. Maybe something that didn't burn food.

CHAPTER 6

SISTER KILLIAN/OLIVIA

1964

Sister Killian folded her hands in prayer at about the same time the Reagan family was saying grace.

"Sister Killian, will you please lead us in grace?" asked Sister Agatha.

The nuns blessed themselves with the sign of the cross, and Sister Killian prayed, "Bless us, O Lord, and these Thy gifts…"

Before "Amen" announced the end of dinner prayers, the principal turned her attention back to Sister Killian. "Would you care to include any special intentions in your prayers?"

Sister Killian nodded. Her closed eyes held the image of the brave warrior St. Joan of Arc, who helped save France from the British during the Hundred Years' War. Nearby knelt St. John, known for his Christian teachings, and St. Anthony, the patron saint of lost things.

Sister Killian bowed her head. "Yes, I pray to St. Joan of Arc to help children find the courage to do the right thing, and I pray to St. John for wisdom and faith." She paused, squeezing her eyes shut more tightly. "I also pray to St. Anthony to help me find what I have lost."

After a quiet moment, Sister Agatha said, "Amen."

Sister Killian kept her eyes closed as the nuns ate. Sister Agatha nudged her arm and gestured to her plate. The two nuns exchanged glances and finished their meal with little said.

After supper, Sister Killian went to her room, suspecting that more than her secret letters might be missing. She rummaged through her meager belongings until she happened upon old photographs hidden away between holy cards. She sat on the edge of her bed, lay back, closed her eyes, and allowed herself some rare moments. Moments where she recalled a time when she was Olivia. The scene played in her head like a movie.

* * *

The blazing sun held promise as its rays spilled across an azure sky. Promise lit the faces of a young couple strolling hand in hand along the footpaths of Central Park. The woman's steps moved with a certain lilt. The smiling couple paused for a photo in front of a statue of Shakespeare. His name was John. Hers was Olivia. Soon they lay upon a blanket spread on the Great Lawn of the park. Olivia gazed up into John's eyes. The blue sky framed his face, making his eyes appear an even deeper blue. Enchanting violin music played in the distance, and as if in a fairy tale, a soft puffy cloud drifted by. Yet for a moment, an uneasiness stirred within Olivia as the cloud cast a shadow over them. The shade drifted with the passing cloud. The glow of the sun returned and graced her face as she melted into John's embrace. With a gentle touch of his hand, he brushed a lock of hair from her cheek.

Later that afternoon, the couple found themselves at a cafe, the look of love in their eyes. Love showed in their touch. It showed in their light, easy laughter. Colors became vibrant and took on a new life of their own. It seemed as though they were destined to always be together.

During the weekdays, when they were apart, they exchanged letters. Olivia watched from her bedroom window for the mailman to climb the steps of the brownstone dwelling. When he neared, she would run downstairs, taking two at a time before her mother could intercept the mail and question her. Each time the postman delivered a letter, Olivia swooned and swirled her hips. After reading each one, she placed it at the bottom of the stack, retied the pink ribbon, and hid them away in her hope chest.

Sister Killian touched her cheek, as though she were back in the past, remembering the gentle feel of John's hand, the musky scent of him, and how he moved his lips to hers. Her eyes remained closed to the memory.

* * *

The sudden toll of the chapel bell, signaling evening prayers, jolted Sister from her reverie. Within moments, she heard the echo of her heavy footsteps as she walked down the corridor that led from her dark room to the convent's sanctuary. She prayed for John. She prayed for her parents, whom she had not seen in years. She prayed for her students and, finally, for herself.

That night she woke in a sweat. She had dreamed about the events that drew her to take vows to become a nun. She had long ago tucked away the memories of past years, the time of her life, the time of another world. She had tucked away her photos, her letters, her feelings. Yet that time came rushing back as if it had been only yesterday. She wanted to forget, but forgetting was not easy.

CHAPTER 7

OLIVIA'S ADVENTURE

1931

Two high school seniors, Olivia Hunter and her friend Millie Hayes, walked around Columbus Circle and headed south on Eighth Avenue.

The sound of a man's flirtatious whistle caused Olivia to quicken her pace.

Millie hesitated, blew a kiss in the stranger's direction then hurried to catch up with Olivia.

When they turned the corner and headed west on Forty-Third Street, the somberness of the times stretched out before them. Men had turned out their empty pockets to symbolize President Hoover's new flags. The two girlfriends crossed the street to avoid the forlorn stares from those on the mournfully long breadline that stretched along the sidewalk. A firetruck sped by, its siren screaming.

Olivia kept her eyes focused ahead. "They are staring at us. Gosh, there must be two hundred men on the breadline. Where are the women and children?"

Millie looked at the breadline. "I don't know, but many of the jobless men abandoned their families. They can't feed them, so they leave. They must feel ashamed and embarrassed, even though it's out of their control. I've seen their makeshift camps in the park."

A pigeon flew by, cawing. Millie glanced up. "Even the birds are asking for spare crumbs."

Olivia's head and shoulders drooped as she clutched the picnic basket tighter. "Hunger has a smell. It's like something damp, and… and… sour and mixed with rotten eggs and fish."

"Won't be long now. They'll be dishing out dog soup by the time they reach the end of the line," Millie said.

Olivia looked into the picnic basket and took out one of the sandwiches. She passed the basket to Millie, crossed the street, and headed for the breadline.

"What in the world are you doing? Wait!" called Millie.

Olivia held the sandwich out and offered it to the last man in line.

"God bless you," he said.

Then Olivia turned, caught up with Millie, and took the basket back.

"Cheer up, Olivia. We're lucky our parents can feed us. We may as well enjoy it," Millie said.

Drawing in a sharp breath, Olivia said, "I wish. No, I pray this Great Depression will end soon. Good grief, it's been long enough."

"From your lips to God's ears."

The two friends made their way several more blocks and headed south before reaching the piers along the Hudson River.

"Except for the fishy smell, it looks like a delightful spot for a picnic." Olivia set the basket down on the wooden planks.

Millie waved. "Come on. Not there. Not yet. Pick a boat, and let's pretend it's ours."

"You mean picnic on someone's boat? It's not right. And what if we get caught?"

"Don't be a scaredy-cat." Millie walked along the pier, reading the names on the sterns. *Sea Shadow. Cat's Meow. Over the Moon. One for the Coast. Mine for Now.*

Lagging behind, Olivia pointed. "That one. *Mine for Now.*"

"Wouldn't you rather pick *Mine Forever*?"

"Doesn't look like a choice."

Millie placed one foot onto a thirty-foot sailboat with an inboard motor, causing it to sway slightly. She reached out. "Take my hand."

"In marriage, mine forever." Olivia chuckled louder than she meant to.

"Shh, let's not get caught."

Olivia took Millie's hand and sang in a soft whisper, "Let me call you sweetheart. I'm in love with you."

Teasing back, Millie puckered her crimson lips into a kiss. They sat on the stern's bench and spread the contents of the picnic basket onto a red-and-white checkered tablecloth. Then together, they softly sang, "By the sea, by the sea, by the beautiful sea."

"I love weekends," Millie said. "And it's wonderful here on our boat."

Playing along with the charade, Olivia said, "Glad I gave our chauffeur, Charles, the day off."

Chuckling, Millie produced a block of cheese from the sack. "We'll have to slice this ourselves since we dismissed the servants." Searching the basket, she said, "Oh, shucks. I forgot to pack a knife." Millie stood and tried to open the hatch. She pushed harder, and to her surprise, it slid open. "Geez, I can't believe it's not locked," she said as she stepped over and grasped the railing. "Don't make me go down there on my own."

"Oh brother." Olivia gripped the railing and followed Millie down the steep steps. They rummaged through the galley for a knife.

Olivia paused. "Do you hear something? Anything? What's that sound?"

"Only water lapping against the boat." Millie held up a butter knife. "This will have to do."

Olivia picked up a newspaper clipping on the counter. "Look! *Mine for Now* won first place in a regatta."

Millie snatched the paper, and her eyes settled on two handsome young men with broad shoulders and beaming smiles. One wore a silly Popeye the Sailor Man shirt.

"I'll take the one wearing the captain's hat. You can have Popeye,"

Millie said, letting out a chuckle. "On second thought, Popeye is strong and has a sense of humor."

The boat listed slightly. Olivia reached for the clipping. "Did you feel that? We better get out of here." She dropped the paper onto the counter.

Just then the engine powered up, and the boat moved away from the pier and out into New York Harbor.

The girls froze. "Oh my God, we're trapped. Someone is taking the boat out. We're in trouble. Big trouble," said Olivia.

Millie's voice squeaked. "You and your big ideas to picnic on *Mine For Now*."

"It wasn't my idea."

"You chose the boat."

The boat picked up speed, rising and falling with the swells. Olivia held on to the edge of the counter with one hand and put the other on her hip. "I wish we had never boarded this trap. In deep trouble, we are. We're going to die out here. We're being kidnapped. Someone's going to kill us and throw our bodies overboard. No one will ever find us." Olivia's voice quivered. Her hand shook. "My mother will never know what happened or why we disappeared."

Millie held up a butter knife. "Don't blow your wig." She pointed to a lantern hanging on a hook. "Grab that. If he comes down the steps, hit him with it, and I'll stab him."

Olivia reached for the lantern. Her knees wobbled. The boat pushed farther out into the harbor, and suddenly the engine cut. Enormous work boots shuffled past the porthole, and the boat listed. Olivia gasped for air. A whimpering moan escaped her lips, and Millie tightened her grasp on the knife.

The man in the boots began to make his way down the steep steps. He held a jackknife in one hand and a rope in the other. Olivia dropped the lantern, her knees buckled, the color drained from her face, and her body melted into an unconscious heap on the floor.

The man with the knife turned to face Millie. Her knees wobbled, and her eyes widened. Olivia, out cold, lay on the floor of the boat.

The man exhaled then laughed. He shook his head. "Wasn't what I expected." He threw the rope to the side of the cabin.

"Are you going to kill us?" Millie asked, her voice shaking.

The man folded his jackknife before sliding it into his pocket. "Listen here. If you don't put down your weapon, I'll throw you over for bait." He grinned as he eyed them. "What are you doing here? I saw your little lunch spread out on the deck. It figures it would be a couple of harmless gals who don't know the meaning of trespassing."

Millie waved the butter knife. "Don't have a cow. We were looking for a knife to cut the cheese for our picnic."

"On a boat that doesn't belong to you?" The man stepped closer. "Well, look at that. Seems like one of you is already dead." He lifted Olivia, cradled her like a baby, and tapped her cheek, but she remained still. He held her in a way that raised her feet above her heart.

Olivia's eyes fluttered, and a broad-shouldered young man with strawberry-blond hair and sharp, stately features came into focus. His skin glowed as if it had been kissed by the sun. She found herself gazing into the deepest blue eyes she had ever seen and smiled.

Suddenly realizing the danger she was in, she struggled out of his arms, let out a shriek, and pushed herself away, nearly toppling over.

"Slow down, honey," he said. "Listen here, you and your friend are the trespassers. Not me. Now, are you going to share that picnic with me or not?"

"Don't look at me, pal," Millie said.

"Sure," Olivia said, her voice quivering. Her fingers brushed back her curls, and she smoothed out her dress.

"Good. I sure could eat something about now."

The girls traded glances and followed him up to the deck.

"I'm John Sullivan," he said.

"I'm Olivia, and this is Millie. Is *Mine for Now* yours?" She giggled.

"No, but you are," he replied with a hearty laugh before continuing. "It's not mine, but all the same, I get to enjoy it while I look after it for my friend Ryan. I'm out here when the timing's right, which is rare these days." John winked at Olivia.

Blushing, she turned her attention to the picnic basket, set a platter on the tablecloth, and unwrapped the salami and cheese. Millie sliced the cheese with the knife she was still holding.

John barely took his eyes off Olivia, who by now had a curious sparkle in her eye.

Millie turned on her dreamy look, batted her eyelashes, and asked, "Will your friend Ryan come out for a sail sometime so I can meet him?"

Even though Olivia wanted to go sailing, too, she would not have asked. Yet this time she was grateful for her friend's outgoing style.

"Perhaps I can convince him to accept your invitation to his boat." John chuckled.

Glancing at John's boots, Millie asked, "Do you work? Those boots aren't what I would expect someone to wear on this fine boat, and you might be due for a new pair."

A slight groan escaped Olivia's lips as she looked away from Millie.

"These boots get me a paycheck and get me to the top of the world and back down to sea level."

"Where's the top of the world?" Olivia asked.

"All you have to do is look up to see where I work." He nodded toward the Empire State Building. "Sometimes we'll raise three or more floors in a week. We're scraping the sky with the tallest building ever."

"You're not afraid of heights?" asked Olivia.

"Can't be. Sometimes there are harnesses or Derrick cables to hold on to. But no one's as brave as the Mohawk Indians. They're fearless, the way they walk the girders. Graceful as ballerinas. They glide as though they were on the ground. Anyway, we get paid extra to be brave and fast."

"Really?" Millie said. "Are you an Indian?"

"Nah, I just like watching them. That's all."

"I've seen photographs of the workers on the girders. Better than a circus act. I think the photographer is Lewis Hine," Millie said.

"Right. I was harnessed to a girder, high above the world, when he shot some photos. You might have seen me in some."

"Sounds like you have the best of both worlds," Olivia said.

"Yes, right now, I'm on the top of the world—at sea level. It doesn't get any better unless you have someone to hold your hand." John reached for Olivia's hand. She pulled away but not before feeling his touch. His hands—calloused. His touch—gentle. His smile—kind. The touch caught her by surprise, and something fluttered inside her. Before she looked away, she saw a sparkle in his blue eyes.

Millie put one hand on her hip and set her eyes on John. "Listen, fella. Are you playing hooky? Shouldn't you be in school? You look about our age. Maybe a year or two older."

John tightened the lace on his boot. "Since my father lost his job, I dropped out to help with rent and put food on the table. I would have graduated a year ago, but Mom and Pop need me. Maybe someday I'll go back to Fordham Prep and study literature and pursue my art hobby."

John pushed the throttle, motoring closer to the Statue of Liberty. "Now, there's a lady I'm keen on," he said then quoted from the poem by Emma Lazarus. "Give me your tired, your poor. Your huddled masses yearning to breathe free. The wretched refuse of your teeming shore. Send these, the homeless, tempest-tost to me."

Standing on tiptoe, Olivia reached her arm high as though holding the statue's torch. "I lift my lamp beside the golden door," she said, quoting another line of the poem. "Lady Liberty is my favorite."

John held a hand above his eyes to block the sun. "She's a beauty all right. I've painted her."

"That's swell. What else do you paint?" asked Olivia.

"Other statues. But after dropping out of school, there's not much time. Maybe someday. I'd like to paint the statues in Central Park."

Olivia sat on the stern's bench and swung her feet back and forth. "Why statues?"

A hearty laugh escaped John's lips. "They stay still, but you have to be quick before the light changes. Otherwise, you'll have to come back the next day at the same time. It also makes a nifty study to paint them in every season. I've painted Shakespeare once with snow on his noggin."

Wiggling her fingers, Olivia mimicked snow falling. "Imagine that. It would make a pretty picture with the fallen snow."

"I'd like to paint a picture of your beautiful face. That precious smile." John grinned.

Olivia blushed and peered back at Lady Liberty.

"If you like statues, I'm taking you to Central Park. Wait till you see the sculptures there."

"I'm not going anywhere with a stranger."

"I don't believe we're strangers any longer. Will you go, dollface?"

"Well... only if you promise not to jump out from behind Shakespeare or something else and scare me." Olivia smiled and turned away. "I'll think about it," she said, trying not to sound too enthusiastic.

"I promise I won't scare you."

CHAPTER 8

OLIVIA'S PARENTS

Olivia's mother, Gloria Hunter, set down her teacup on a dinner table set for three. She looked over her shoulder as if to summon a servant, but they were gone along with the grand Upper East Side apartment overlooking Central Park.

Instead of a view of the park, the lavish chintz curtains parted to a view of Manhattan's busy Amsterdam Avenue.

Gloria looked at her watch and turned to her husband, Alexander. Trying to disguise her shaky voice, she murmured, "It's not like her to be late. Especially when we are having black bottom pie for dessert."

Alexander Hunter folded his arms across his chest and regarded his only child's place setting. "If she's not here in two minutes, we can start without her, and she can go to bed without dinner."

Gloria stared at the empty plates.

After precisely two minutes, Alexander placed his dinner napkin on his lap. "You may serve us now."

Gloria led the couple in grace then ladled out small servings of Hungarian goulash. They had grown used to modest portions. They ate in quiet. Without servants.

After dinner, Alexander excused himself to the living room,

reclined in his overstuffed chair, and clicked on the radio. The jazzy piano music of Duke Ellington chimed in. He rotated the dial until the praises of a vigorous evangelist tuned in without static. He turned up the volume and lost himself in the words of the preacher.

An art collection, which had once adorned the Hunter's walls, sold for pennies on the dollar. The family's grandfather clock remained, marked time, and stood witness to the dark era of the Great Depression. The roar of the twenties ended with the stock market crash of 1929, and Alexander vowed not to go under. He maintained appearances. He wore creased trousers, pressed white shirts under suspenders, carried a cane, and kept his spats polished but was angry about his losses.

Gloria was grateful for what remained of their estate. She was glamorous and kept an outfit for every occasion, planned or spontaneous. Feathered hats matched her dresses, and gloves covered her milky-white hands. She continued to attend extravagant socialite parties, which provided rhetoric for the gossip columns. Visions of announcing Olivia's coming-out party and eventually her wedding played in her hopes. One day, she predicted, Olivia would walk down the aisle in the same wedding gown that Gloria and her mother had each worn.

Still, Gloria had another side. When she wasn't at a party, she helped in the soup kitchen, collected clothes for the impoverished, and even assisted in mending them. But her devotion to her husband and only child came first.

It had not come easily for Alexander to make the unlikely move to Amsterdam Avenue near 86th Street, which was still an affluent area but less so than where their prior Fifth Avenue apartment was located. Their two-bedroom, two-bath apartment had a dining room and a fair-sized living room. This New York luxury was more than a step down from the elegant twelve-room apartment they had left behind on Fifth Avenue.

Alexander continued to hold on to his import-export textile business, but he considered putting the furrier division to rest. His customers still wore chinchillas and fox stoles, but they no longer purchased them. As the rag trade diminished, the few who purchased mink now bought coats with mink only on the collars. Alexander had many adjustments to make. He laid off help but retained the few employees with family ties, especially his brother, who steered racks of furs in and out of doors along Seventh Avenue.

Gloria stood in the doorway, her forehead scrunched into wrinkles and her mouth twisted with determination. A long coat draped her arm.

The nine p.m. chime of the grandfather clock drew Alexander from the blaring voice of the high-spirited evangelist. He looked up at his wife. "Where is she? Where is our daughter? Her curfew passed hours ago. Who does she think she is? The queen of Sheba?"

Olivia's mother slipped on her coat. "I'm going to look for her."

"Sure, why don't you start at the Bowery and weave your way through every cross street lined with the homeless? You could be back before hell freezes over!"

The door was pushed open, and Olivia dashed in. The hair on her hatless head stood out in every direction. She inhaled deeply as her eyes searched her mother's and then darted to the angry look on her father's face.

Alexander glared at his daughter. "Who do you think you are walking in here four hours late? Your mother was worried sick. Where have you been, and who were you with?"

"I was with Millie."

Alexander's eyes narrowed on his only child. "Who else?"

"John."

Olivia's mother took a step closer. "Who is John?"

"He's nice." Olivia looked at her mother. "He really is. You would like him."

"What is his last name? How old is he? Where does he live?" asked her father.

"John Sullivan is twenty, lives in lower Manhattan. And he is working on the construction of the Empire State Building. It's almost done. He's amazing." Olivia turned to mother. "He's handsome too."

Alexander's voice rose. "Twenty? Twenty! And lives downtown! I don't care what he looks like. You are only seventeen. Now you want the company of a twenty-year-old man?"

"Daddy, I'll be eighteen this year. I've grown up."

"You're a senior in high school. You are not grown up. You live under my roof, and you won't see him again."

"But—"

"Go to your room."

CHAPTER 9

OLIVIA'S SECRET AFFAIR

O livia and John stole time together as often as possible. Since Olivia's father had forbidden the relationship, they kept their rendezvous secret.

When she and John took their secret to the pier, they felt as though they were the only lovers in the world. Little did they know, the harbor held more than one secret.

They regularly strolled along the sidewalks of New York in areas they were sure her parents would not frequent, and often made their way into Central Park. Once, when they stopped in front of a statue of Simon Bolivar, John handed his Kodak to a stranger.

"Will you please snap our photo?"

John and Olivia hooked their pinky fingers and smiled.

"She's as cute as a bug's ear," the man said, handing the camera back to John.

"I'm a lucky man," John said. "Thank you for taking the photo."

John picked a buttercup and held it under Olivia's chin. It caught the sun's rays and cast a golden glow. "You're sweet like butter." He tucked the flower in her hair and wrapped his arms around Olivia. Her heart fluttered in the warmth of his embrace. John tilted his head, and his lips met the full, sweet softness of hers. Each day, their fondness grew.

One day, while strolling, John asked, "Have you been to an automat yet?"

"No. What's it like?"

"You're about to find out." They held hands and headed to Horn & Hardart on Sixth Avenue. "It's somewhat like a cafeteria. Only you don't see the workers."

The young couple slid their trays along the counter until they reached rows of glass doors, which held items like sandwiches and desserts. John held out a handful of nickels. "Here. Put these in, choose your sandwich, and turn the knob. The glass door will open."

Olivia stared at the little door. "What fun! It's amazing, the modern inventions." Olivia chose a chicken sandwich, and John selected a ham and cheese.

"Sweetheart, take these coins for the tea. It's over there by the pies," John said. "I'll find a table."

John looked about and set the trays on a table by a window while Olivia went for their tea. She pushed the lever. Tea flowed, soaking the counter. "Oh no!" cried Olivia.

Laughing, John rushed over. "Silly girl," he said as he helped wipe up the mess. "Not quite like the service we had at Caffe Roma last week. But pretty nifty though, huh?"

John set each cup in place, pressed the button for the tea, and carried them to the table near a window.

Olivia looked out the window and saw the Empire State Building disappear behind a cloud. A chill ran up her back, and she shrugged.

On another of the couple's excursions, they returned to the pier where they first met and stepped onto *Mine for Now*. John showed Olivia how to cast off the lines. Then they shoved off and motored into New York Harbor.

Before long, John cut the motor, hoisted the sail, and tacked into the wind. He smiled at the sight of Olivia's brown curls spreading like wings in the breeze. She gazed high above at the towers and the graceful span of steel wires as they passed under the Brooklyn Bridge, which connected Manhattan to Brooklyn and the rest of Long Island. Olivia tilted her head back. *What course will the wind take us? What destiny?*

With billowing sails, they left the hustle and bustle of the city in their wake. Grateful for John's sailing skills, they ran with the dangerous and thrilling swift current of Hell Gate and headed to the Atlantic Ocean. When the wind eased, John drew in the sails and dropped anchor. And just like that, they were in a different world.

John pointed toward land. "We'll swim to the shore."

Olivia went below deck and changed into her bathing suit.

Their skin glistened in the sun as they dove into the coolness of the water and swam to the beach.

Waves gently rolled onto the shore then slipped back, leaving a layer of shimmering water. The birds pranced to and fro with the waves, pressing fleeting footsteps into the sand, reflecting the tranquility of a golden day. A soft broken ribbon of lime-green seaweed marked high tide. The couple walked along the shore, scooping up seashells. John showed Olivia how to dig for oysters and littleneck clams on the sandy beach. They put their collection in a netted ditty bag John brought from the boat.

"It's a different world here. It's like we went around the block and entered a magical place," Olivia said. Her full lips stretched into a smile.

John set the shells on the sand and wrapped his arms around her. Olivia's heart danced, and something stirred in him. He pressed his lips to hers. Their bodies swayed with the soothing ebb and flow. They lingered for a long time, not wanting the blissful state to end. Once again, Olivia's heart filled with a joy she had never felt before.

When the tide moved out, they waded in and swam back to the boat.

John wrapped a large towel around Olivia, then he shucked the oysters and a few littlenecks. They ate them raw and gave the empty shells back to the sea.

Turning a seashell over in her hand, Olivia envisioned her hope chest—a family heirloom that had been handed down to her. She planned to tuck away a couple of seashells in the chest so she could someday revisit this special time.

Olivia enjoyed the many excursions, especially the visits to Central Park, which became her favorite place. She delighted in her relationship with John. Olivia missed Millie, but by now Millie was busy with a new boyfriend of her own and had forgotten all about the boat.

While Olivia's senior year took much of her time, John's work on the Empire State Building limited the number of stolen meetings. Even the love letters they wrote to each other did not ease their desire to be together. Luckily for Olivia, the mailman arrived after school every day, and she could hide their correspondence from her parents. The letters kept them connected. Olivia cherished the letters. She tied them together with a pink ribbon and hid them away in her promise chest along with seashells of hope and a buttercup that she pressed into the leaves of a letter.

On one unforeseen overcast day, Olivia watched from her window as she hummed the song by the Marvelettes, "Please Mr. Postman." She spotted the mailman and flew like a falcon to the mail slot in the front door. She caught the letter before it hit the floor. Her hand held a letter she had written to John. Olivia caught her breath. A scarlet stamp on the envelope addressed to John read RETURN TO SENDER.

CHAPTER 10

KAYLEE BABYSITS

1964

Kaylee peeked out from behind the kitchen door and turned her ear on her mother's telephone conversation.

"No, the older girls, including Mary, have babysitting jobs tonight, but Kaylee's here... Yes, she's young, but your house is right across the street. I can see it from here... If Kaylee babysits and runs into something she needs help with, she can simply call me on the telephone. I'll run right over."

Mother hung up and called Kaylee in her come-here-now voice.

Kaylee stepped out from behind the door.

Mother jumped. "You scared me!"

"Sometimes you scare me too." Kaylee smiled.

"That's nonsense." Mother raised a wooden spoon, and Kaylee stepped back.

"You have your first babysitting job for the Murphys," Mother said.

Kaylee clapped her hands. She needed money for the adventure she planned to take with her older sister Mary. The adventure to find John, the writer of the love letters she had stolen from Sister Killian's drawer.

Mother looked into the pantry. "You'll have to give me all of the fifty cents an hour you are about to earn."

Kaylee bit her lip and looked down. "That's not fair!"

"The Murphys have three well-behaved children. They are so good that even Dad says they are almost invisible. This job should be easy."

That evening Kaylee trudged across the street. *My very first babysitting job and Mother wants the money. It's just not fair.*

The kids behaved as expected and went to bed at the appointed hour. Delighted, Kaylee drank Coca-Cola, ate Cheetos, and watched a television show of her own choice. "What a treat." She switched the channel to *Leave it to Beaver*. No one tried to change the channel or steal her chips.

After drinking all the Coke, Kaylee walked to the bathroom.

Wow. Look at all this makeup. If I put it on, I might get pretty.

She put black mascara on her thin eyelashes then tried the bright-red lipstick. She took the eye pencil and blackened under her eyes and even traced over her eyebrows. Studying her face in the mirror, she batted her eyelashes like a movie star. Finally, Kaylee yawned and lay on the couch, rubbing her tired eyes until Mr. and Mrs. Murphy came home.

"Kaylee," Mrs. Murphy said with wide eyes as she shook Kaylee awake. "Um, we're back. Were the children any problem?"

Kaylee looked straight at Mrs. Murphy's glaring face. She sat up and turned to Mr. Murphy, who grinned while handing her the babysitting money. The Murphys watched Kaylee cross the street to her home.

Kaylee immediately walked into the bathroom to check her new beauty in the mirror. Her mouth gaped, her eyes widened, her breath huffed. A crazed-looking creature stared back at her. The mascara formed full black circles around her eyes. Clumps hung from eyelids. Red lipstick smeared her chin like a bloody beard, and her hair stuck out like quills on a porcupine. *No wonder Mrs. Murphy had glared at me.*

"Boo," she said to her reflection. She could scare a ghost. Glad her mother hadn't seen her yet, she scrubbed her face until it was red then handed over the hourly pay—at least most of it. She stashed the rest in her pocket and guarded it with her hand. Kaylee said good night to Mother and went to her bedroom with yet another sin to confess.

Mary looked up at Kaylee. "Looks like you really scrubbed up. How was your first babysitting job?"

"Fine, until I became an actress and scared a ghost."

"Huh?"

"It doesn't matter. We have money problems."

"Huh? What?"

"I only have a little money, and we need more for our mission—to find John."

"I have some but not a lot," Mary said. "We'll have to figure it out. Good night. We have church in the morning. Oh, Mrs. Riley gave Mother some hand-me-downs. You might find something to wear to mass tomorrow morning."

The Reagans, like a proper Catholic family, never missed Sunday mass. The old woody pulled up to the church's parking lot, and eight Reagan children clambered out. A girl standing on the sidewalk pointed her finger, counting each one, so Kaylee pointed her middle finger and aimed it at the girl. She should count the Mackeys. They had at least four more in that family.

Joey turned Kaylee's wrist so the middle finger pointed up to the heavens. "That's how you do it." Then he went inside to perform his altar boy duties.

The Reagan family filed into their usual pew.

Father Cunningham stepped over to the altar's podium, and Mother sent Kaylee a stop-the-daydreaming look. The priest raised his hands, spreading his green-and-gold vestments like angel wings. "The gospel according to John."

John, Kaylee thought. That name kept popping up. Maybe God could send a miracle so they could find John.

"Chapter five. Jesus healed a man at a pool of water known as Bethesda, near the sheep gate in Jerusalem," the priest continued. "Paralyzed for thirty-eight years and with no one to help, he could not enter the healing waters. Jesus told him to pick up his mat and walk. The man did as instructed, and Jesus performed a miracle. Later, Jesus met the man in the temple and warned him of the perils of sin."

During the homily, Father gazed over his congregation. "What a world this would be without sin."

Kaylee glanced at Brenda. Kaylee wasn't thinking about a world without sin. She was thinking about how to get Brenda off her back.

After church, Kaylee looked forward to the drive home since Dad's habit was to stop at the bakery for fresh bagels and hard rolls with soft insides.

Kaylee and her siblings thought Dad looked like Dick Tracy, but Mother said he looked more like Cary Grant. Sometimes Dad wore a hat to cover his balding spot. He parted his hair on the side, letting it grow longer so he could fold it over his receding hairline. But when he was behind the steering wheel, with his window cracked open, that long piece of hair flapped out like a wounded bird's wing. The back seat shook with stifled giggles.

Dad was friendly to everyone, including the baker, who gave Dad a baker's dozen. On the ride home Kaylee asked, "How do you make so many friends? I hardly have any. How can I make more friends?"

"Watch," Dad said. He beeped his horn and waved to random strangers. "See, that one is friendly. He waved back." The children's laughter encouraged him as they eagerly watched for the strangers' responses.

"Beep on, wave on, beep on," Kaylee chanted.

"Drive on." Mother blushed then slumped in her seat.

Dad kept one hand on the steering wheel and patted Mother's knee with the other. He peered in the rearview mirror. "Not everyone is friendly. Some strangers won't wave back, not even if you beep again and add a big smile, and once in a while, you get an obscene gesture in return."

"What kind of obscene gesture?" Joey asked with a smirk while raising his middle finger at Kaylee and keeping it out of Dad's sight.

"The kind of gesture that would shock your mother," Dad said.

Kaylee reached for Joey's finger to twist it, but it was gone in a flash, tucked into his fist.

"Will the strangers come after us if they don't like the beeping and give us a gesture or even something worse?" Kaylee asked.

"Not when I'm around, they won't," Dad said.

"What if you're not around?"

"Then don't go driving and beeping." Dad smiled and adjusted the rearview mirror.

"Very funny," Joey said. Kaylee figured he was most likely scheming to test the theory, even though he was much too young to drive. They dropped the topic as the family's station wagon pulled into the driveway.

"Who wants butter on warm rolls with eggs, sunny-side up?" asked Dad.

CHAPTER 11

KAYLEE

Thar afternoon when the children were outside playing, Kaylee spotted Brenda Mullarkey. She stuck out her tongue and crossed her eyes. Kaylee returned the look and topped it off with the muffled sound of the Bronx cheer. Like a baby blowing raspberries, she pressed her tongue between her lips and gave a sharp exhale. A vibrating sound emerged.

Kaylee knew Brenda noticed the oversized, handed-down blue plaid coat she was wearing, the one Mary knew better than to accept. So Kaylee got Margaret Riley's coat, even though it was way too big.

Whenever Margaret outgrew her clothes, Mrs. Riley left a stack of hand-me-downs on the Reagans' stoop or handed them to Mother. "Chances are it will fit one of your girls," she would say.

Brenda Mullarkey and Margaret Riley lived next door to one another and a few houses from the Reagans. They went to the same early mass, and they had shared the same school bus stop every day for years.

Kaylee knew Brenda watched the neighbors like a hawk seeking prey. Brenda knew more than just the colors of Margaret Riley's clothes because of her regular inspections. She could guess when another round of hand-me-downs was likely to land on the doorstep.

That afternoon, Brenda pranced down the street, holding her hoity-toity nose high in the air far longer than usual. The purple satin ribbon, which dangled over her finger curls, came undone as she jeered at Kaylee. "Do you have anything on under Margaret's coat? What are you hiding? More of Margaret's clothes? What about her panties?"

Kaylee smiled to herself. *I'm hiding the money I found in Margaret's coat pocket. The money only I know about.* Kaylee counted on adding it to her babysitting money

Days later, Kaylee peered from the kitchen window and spotted Brenda promenading along the street.

"Look, Mother. It's that girl Brenda who picks on me at school."

Mother peeked out. "Would you like me to have a talk with her?"

Kaylee didn't expect this and surprised herself, saying, "Yes."

"Run out after Brenda and tell her I want to see her about something."

Brenda came in the house, which also surprised Kaylee. She was stunned that Miss Bratty, Miss Curly Goldilocks, Miss Know-it-All was standing in her kitchen, listening to Kaylee's mother question her behavior.

Mother's eyes darted from one girl to another. Brenda smiled sweetly but said nothing. Mother smiled back at her. Kaylee's jaw dropped.

"Now shake hands, you two, and get along," Mother said. At least for the moment, Brenda heeded the reprimand and held out a limp hand. Kaylee gave it a hard squeeze.

When Brenda left, Kaylee said, "Brenda might never pick on me again!" Under her breath, she mumbled a word known to be the equivalent of a female dog.

Mother pulled Kaylee by the ear to the bathroom sink. She pushed a bar of Ivory soap into her mouth and scrubbed out the curse word. One taste of Ivory soap was all Kaylee needed never to curse again—at least not in front of her mother. Kaylee rinsed out her mouth and scrubbed Brenda from her hands.

While Kaylee was tasting soap in the bathroom with Mother, Joey slipped outside. He whistled as Brenda strutted her way home. The sound of the whistle caught Brenda's attention. She jiggled her curls, looked around, and hesitated long enough for Joey to pull her into the Murphys' hedgerow.

Joey wanted to surprise Brenda and make it to first base. Even though he was younger and too big for his britches, she didn't argue and let him kiss her on the lips. When Brenda pulled away, Joey held her purple hair ribbon in his hand. She was off and prancing, and he tucked the purple ribbon in his pocket.

After the incident with Brenda in the kitchen, Mary and Kaylee decided to play far away from Brenda's house—as far as they could get where they still knew other kids to play with. They played hide-and-seek and then fell into a rambunctious game of ring-a-levio. Mary got tagged and thrown into jail, which was the Malones' front steps.

Kaylee tried to free her, but the sound of a loud whistle signaled dinnertime, and they raced for home.

One playmate, Kenny, yelled, "You can't quit just like that!" But even he knew Kaylee and Mary had no choice when it came to Dad's whistle. They called it quits for the time being.

Other signals rang out, and kids ran to the call of their names or in answer to the chime of a dinner bell. But it was the sound of the whistle that beckoned the Reagans home. No one else could whistle quite like Kaylee's dad. Any attempt to imitate it would be shameful. No one could come close.

Kaylee picked up a blade of grass, stretched it between her thumbs, and blew heartily. A high-pitched squeal emerged. Kaylee threw down the blade of grass and yelled to Mary, "I wish I could whistle like Dad."

"Well, you can't, and that whimpering whistle wasn't Dad's whistle!" Mary said as they raced home.

Everyone knew the source of the strong, singsong, two-note whistle. The first note, being the loudest and almost sweet sounding, called them home to dinner. The second one, short and firm with a sudden stop, shouted *now*.

"That whistle we heard was the neighborhood's relay since we're out of earshot. That's why it sounded different," Mary said, her breath huffing. It was as though the neighborhood had a set of eyes and ears all its own and knew where all the kids were. "We are two relay whistles away, so we better run like fire, you idiot," she said.

With both hands waving in the air, Joey pedaled by on his Schwinn. Baseball cards clicked in its spokes. "Git," he called out to Kaylee and swiped her shoulder.

"Jerk!" Kaylee shouted back.

"Shut up, both of you," Mary yelled.

"What's a git, anyway?"

"According to Grandma, it's an idiot, idiot."

"Grandma's from a different world," Kaylee said.

"England is a different country, not world, and our ally."

"What's an ally?"

"A friend, not a foe."

"Who's a foe?"

"Russia."

"Anyway, if I was going to be called names, you could call me Lucky," Kaylee said.

"Lucky!" Mary said, exaggerating the first syllable.

"Yep, Luckee," Kaylee said, putting emphasis on the second syllable. "After Lucky Strikes, the kind of cigarettes Louella's mother smokes." She struck Mary on the arm. "Imagine that," she went on, pointing to the O'Malleys' house. "They have a dog named Winston. Mr. O'Malley must smoke Winstons," Kaylee said.

"Idiot," Mary said.

"No, just Luckeee."

"Did you ever hear of Winston Churchill?"

"Is that a story about a dog that went to church?"

Mary shook her head. "Just forget it."

Kaylee kicked an empty soda can in Mary's direction. "It's your turn. I'll bet we can kick it all the way home."

As they rounded the corner, Brenda's brother, Marty, attempted to pelt them with rotten apples he collected from the old orchard nearby.

Fortunately, Marty had yet to receive pitching lessons from their neighbor Carter, who could throw the fastest ball in the neighborhood. And being too young to have played dodgeball, he didn't have a chance of hitting his targets. The girls made it home unscathed.

"Luckeee," Kaylee crowed. "Luckeee." She sang, "Olly olly home free," as if she had freed Mary from the Malone's jail.

CHAPTER 12

THE PRINCIPAL'S OFFICE

S ister Killian arranged the seating in her classroom according to test scores, from the students who had scored the highest to those who got the lowest marks. Kaylee sat in the dumb row by the window. It was the dumbest row in the whole class, and the whole school knew it. Goody Two-shoes Angela Marie sat in the first seat in the first row. And test grades gave snot-nosed teacher's pet Brenda Mullarkey a seat right behind Angela.

Despite the arranged seating, Kaylee cherished sitting by the window. The tall windows stretched to the high ceiling, allowing a bird's-eye view of the playground. Except for the teasing the assigned seating caused, Kaylee considered sitting there to be a reward, not the punishment Sister intended. Kaylee could look out at the swings and climbing bars and daydream. In her mind, she created a play about two lovers. She aimed to perform it in the basement of her house and charge the neighborhood kids a nickel for admission. Then they would have money to search for John, the lover in the letters.

Mary could be Olivia and dress up as a damsel in distress only to be saved by a tall, handsome Romeo. Kaylee grinned and pushed the thought to the back of her mind. She had more important things to consider at the moment, while guilt and confession gnawed and tugged at her heart.

I don't know what gets into me or why I am so impulsive. If only Sister would stop picking on me. If only Brenda would knock it off. If only I were pretty and smart. I have an idea from watching the Little Rascals. I'll put a comic book between the pages of my geography book, and when I get caught, Sister will send me back to the convent, and I can return the letters.

Kaylee put her letter-returning idea in place. She sat at her desk, pretending to read a geography book but reading a comic book instead.

The metal edge of the ruler hit her fingers hard.

"Dang," Kaylee cried out in pain.

"Get upstairs to the principal's office. *Now!*" Sister spewed, and spittle escaped through her clenched teeth.

Kaylee's face flushed red.

Oh no, not there. I need to go to the convent and put the letters back before I get caught. The letters are in my book bag. They'll be here—unguarded.

Her head pounded at the thought, and her heart sank. Her hands quivered. Kaylee grabbed her book bag and started toward the door.

"No," growled Sister. "Leave that here."

Kaylee dropped the bag and prayed Sister would not go through it. The entire class watched in dead silence as Kaylee made her way past the front rows of seats occupied by Goody Two-shoes Angela Marie and Bratty Brenda Mullarkey. Brenda, who was sitting at a desk reserved for students with perfect attendance, smirked.

True to form, Brenda bullied Kaylee by sticking her foot out, causing Kaylee to crash headfirst into the door. Scores of laughter rippled through the rows. Collecting herself, Kaylee glared at Brenda and stuck out her tongue. And for good measure, she pointed her middle finger at Brenda before she flew out the door and before Sister could dish out any more reprimands. Kaylee sauntered down the hallway, rubbing her head.

Kaylee sniffed a hint of tobacco as she entered the principal's office.

"You again," Sister Agatha said as she slipped her corncob pipe into the top drawer. She rose, cracked the window, and returned to her seat behind the oversized mahogany desk.

"You remind me of my very misunderstood self when I was your age. Feisty, impulsive, poor penmanship, difficulty paying attention. But all gets better with age." Sister opened another drawer and held out a piece of red licorice. "Enjoy," she said and pulled one out for herself. "Once Sister sent you here due to a misspelling. Do you remember how to spell ship?"

"Yes, ship is s-h-i-p. It ends with a p, not a t." Kaylee chewed the licorice and tried to forget about her book bag and what Sister Killian might do if she found the letters. Kaylee closed her eyes at the thought, swallowed the licorice, and prayed in silence. She prayed she would not get caught.

Sister tapped on her desk. "What current sin brought you back to my office?"

"A comic book. And it wasn't even funny."

Sister peered at Kaylee with puzzled eyes. "Care to elaborate?"

"It's just that geography can be so boring and comics, so much more interesting and entertaining—most of the time."

"Perhaps there is some truth in that, but save the comics for home. It won't get you promoted to the next grade, but the right knowledge will. Do yourself a favor and try to behave. Then you can come for a visit on your own accord."

"You're nice, and Agatha's a nice name," Kaylee said. "May I take Agatha as my confirmation name?"

Sister Agatha nodded. "That pleases me. It's a good name, means holy, also means lamb. Since you are much like a little lamb—well, when you want to be—it will suit you." But Sister Agatha said nothing about Kaylee being holy. Sister added, "You'll be a soldier of Christ, and the gifts of the Holy Spirit will increase for all who make their confirmation." Sister gazed at the clock, picked up a book of matches, and opened her desk draw. "Now, little lamb, go back to the classroom and try to please Sister Killian."

Kaylee headed down the long corridor, marching more like a Christian soldier going off to war than a little lamb looking for its mother. She entered the classroom to find Sister Killian reaching for Kaylee's book bag. Then, as if her prayer had been answered and the Russians were suddenly her allies, the siren for an air raid drill blared.

"So, we're under nuclear attack," cried Louella. "We're all going to die. My mother is going to have another baby. I want to live to see it."

"It's *just* a drill," Sister said as she and the children took cover. Kaylee giggled at the sight of Sister curling into a big black ball and hiding under her desk. Kaylee hoped she would roll out the door. She didn't.

Those seated in a window row moved away and crouched along the back wall with arms wrapped over their heads. The others crouched under their desks and waited. Louella shivered as she waited for the bomb to drop. But nothing happened.

The bell, signaling the end of the school day, rang like music to Kaylee's ears. The girls shuffled back to their desks and gathered their homework. By then, Sister Killian seemed to have forgotten about the book bag, and Kaylee breathed a sigh of relief.

After school, when Kaylee reached home, she stood before Mother. "When I'm confirmed in the spring, my confirmation name will be Agatha. My full name will be Kaylee Deborah Agatha Reagan. Doesn't that sound important?" She was about to explain that she'd chosen the name because Sister Agatha was nice to her, but Mother spoke first.

"Oh, that's wonderful!" Mother said. "Thank you for choosing the name Agatha."

Kaylee scratched her head.

That evening, when the Reagan family gathered at the supper table and after grace, Dad announced, "I'm glad you chose Agatha for your confirmation name, Kaylee. Your faith is strengthened." Mother looked pleased.

"Why does the bishop slap you when he says your confirmation name?" Kaylee asked.

Dad laughed. "To remind you to be brave in your faith, but he'll probably just tap the girls on the cheek."

"How hard did he smack you?" asked Kaylee.

"Hard enough," Dad said. "He kept smacking me, and each time he did, I added another confirmation name, so I became William Patrick Joseph James Peter Paul Maurice Edward Anthony Reagan."

Kaylee grinned, not knowing whether to believe him.

Later that evening, when Kaylee and Mary put on their pajamas, Kaylee said, "Mary, I think Dad got beat up at confirmation."

"You never know," Mary said.

"The other thing I don't know is why Mother and Dad are thrilled that I chose Agatha as my confirmation name."

Mary rolled her eyes. "It's Mother's middle name, idiot."

"You're the idiot," Kaylee said. "I didn't pick it after her. I didn't even know it's her middle name. Sister Agatha gave me a piece of candy, so I picked it after her."

"Why would she give you candy?"

Kaylee held her nose high. "Because she likes me."

"Did everyone get a piece?"

"No, never mind. I don't want to talk about it anymore," Kaylee murmured. She turned her thoughts to the letters, hid them under the mattress, and turned out the light. "Hey, Mary," Kaylee whispered, "How come you never get into trouble?"

"With a name like Mary, everyone thinks I can do no harm. Mary is the Blessed Mother. She's queen. Take a name like Theresa or Joan. Like Joan of Arc. They're saints," Mary said. "Besides that, my teacher wants to take us on our eighth-grade field trip and go upstate to Auriesville to see the shrine of North American martyrs."

"If I ever reach eighth grade, I hope we go someplace fun. We already have martyrs in class. I have a Theresa Rose and a Joanlee in my class. They both sit with Angela Marie in the first row, where the smart kids sit. That proves it. Do you think my name Kaylee is dumb?"

"No," Mary said. "But it didn't help that the Catholic school took you into first grade, even though you were too young for the public school kindergarten."

"Yeah, that figures. Must have been too many kids at home for Mother. I remember the first day of school when Sister Dominique said, 'Write the alphabet.' I had no idea what she was talking about.

What's an alphabet? I couldn't imagine. I drew a picture of what this alpha monster might look like. Everyone else was writing, and I was drawing. Sister Dominique grabbed her long pointer, which was longer than me, poked my hand, then tapped on the letters that wrapped around the room above the chalkboard.

"'This is the alphabet,' she said, enunciating each syllable and tapping the pointer with every beat. Then, when I picked up the pencil, she took it from my left hand and showed me how to hold it in my right one. It just felt funny. I sat there trying hard not to cry. I just wanted to move the pencil back to my left hand. But she wouldn't let me. I wanted to go home, but she wouldn't let me. I looked out the window instead."

"It's okay, but I'd like to see what the alpha creature looks like," Mary said.

"I'll show you." Kaylee turned the light back on and drew a big black blotch with hairy spider legs pointing in every direction. She drew a bonnet on its head, tied with a ribbon at the neckline. The spider had hairy legs and wore black shoes. An arm stuck out from the middle and held a ruler.

"Ugh," Mary said.

"Monsters aren't pretty." Kaylee leaned over to check under her bed.

"Everything okay under there?" Mary said.

"Okey dokey. Good night." Kaylee switched off the light.

Something quietly slid from under Mary's bed to Kaylee's. It growled and kicked at the bedsprings, causing Kaylee to wobble all over her bed. She let out a loud, piercing cry.

"What's wrong?" Mary gasped.

"The monster is here! Under my bed!" screamed Kaylee.

"But you just checked," Mary said as she reached for the light and looked under Kaylee's bed. "Thank God. It's only Joey."

Joey slid out, stood up, and flicked the dust bunnies from his pajamas. "Ha ha. That was a good one." He grinned then dashed out, slamming the door behind him.

"Don't get mad at him. He's just plain stupid sometimes," Mary said in her voice of reason.

"Okay. I'll just get even." And for the last time that night, the light went out.

CHAPTER 13

PATCHES THE DOG AND SHAKESPEARE THE TURTLE

K aylee cradled a turtle the size of a half dollar in her palm and gently petted it. Mary looked on as Kaylee stretched out her arm so Mother could take a better look.

"Don't come any closer, Kaylee!" Mother cried.

Kaylee took a step back, remembering the worms she had once brought in the house to show Mother.

Mother pushed away the pot of peeled potatoes then tightened her apron. "Stay back," she said.

"Mother, this will help you slowly get used to creatures. They're sweet and harmless." Kaylee repeated what she had once said when worms slithered through her muddy fingers. "Critters won't hurt you. Please let me keep him. Pretty please with sugar on top."

Mary rolled her eyes as she looked on the hopeless scene.

Kaylee pleaded, "If I raise him, I can earn another Girl Scout badge. I'll feed him. Clean out his little house. Then I can look smart. Teachers will have to admit I'm smart. I can show them all! Even the kids. Even Bratty Brenda."

"Don't call her bratty," Mother said.

"Okay, but she is worse than bratty. She is a bully."

Kaylee raised the turtle to her lips and kissed its shell. "Turtles are clean, not like worms, and don't eat much, and I don't think he'll need any shots from the vet. Can we keep him? Pretty please with extra sugar on top."

Mother gave a slow, unsure nod and shrugged. "Okay, don't lose him in the house."

Kaylee jumped for joy. Mary's jaw dropped.

"What will you name him?" Mary asked as she and Kaylee walked from the kitchen.

"John. After the man in the love letters."

"Not such a good idea. How about Shakespeare instead?"

Kaylee held the turtle up. "Why should we call him Shakespeare?"

"Dad loves to quote him, and he's Grandma's favorite writer. Besides, he's smart, like the poet, especially how he hides in his shell when Joey's around. He's a miracle turtle since Mother's letting you keep him."

Shakespeare tucked his head in his shell as Kaylee and Mary baptized him over the bathroom sink. Next, they filled his little glass house with rocks, twigs, and a small water bowl cut from a paper cup. Kaylee placed it on the floor by the television stand and followed Mary into the kitchen for the family supper.

After grace, Kaylee glanced around. Then, when no one was looking, she slipped one of her meatballs onto a plate under the table.

Joey leaned toward Kaylee and whispered, "Why are you hoarding food?"

Kaylee jerked to attention and glanced over to see Mother and Dad, who were occupied with their own conversation. "If you don't tell on me, I'll let you in on a secret, but you have to promise first," Kaylee said.

There was a long silence while Joey considered his options and Kaylee held her breath, staring at him. Popping an entire meatball in his mouth and chewing slowly, Joey mumbled, "I promise." Then, with his mouth still full, he opened it wide for Kaylee to see. "See food and eat it." He smirked, reaching his fork to stab another victim.

"Yuck! You're disgusting!" She tried not to laugh. "You better keep your promise. No tattletaleing."

Joey made a loud swallowing noise and burped. "I cross my heart and hope to die."

Kaylee sat back. "You've got your fingers crossed behind your back."

"That's just in case. Beside, how can you see behind my back?"

"Practice," Kaylee said.

After supper, Mary helped Kaylee with the dishes then they led Joey down the basement stairs.

Joey sniffed around. "What's that smell? Wet dog and pee?"

A whimper emerged from under the stairs, and a cardboard box moved all on its own.

"There's something alive in there! What is it?" Joey yelled as he ducked under the stairs to have a look.

"Be quiet," Kaylee said as she opened the cover of the box. A little black-and-white dog wagged his tail and licked Joey's face.

"Looks like he got in a fight with a lion. Where'd you get him?" Joey asked.

"We heard him crying from the basement window of that scary old empty house. You know, the one on the hill in the abandoned apple orchard. He looked like he was going to die. He was hanging from a rope tied around his neck. A cinder block was underneath him. He scratched up his paws, trying to reach it and take weight off his neck. He tried and tried to get away. There was blood on the cinder block and on the ground. That's how we found him."

Joey clenched his fists. "I'd like to punch the guy who did that to him."

Mary placed fresh newspapers in the box. "We hid him here to nurse him back to health."

Kaylee fed him a meatball and gave him water. Joey held him as Mary changed his bandages. "Why would someone be so mean and hang him from a rope and let him go hungry?" Kaylee asked.

Mary shrugged. "Evil sinners, that's who. At least he's getting patched up."

Kaylee patted his head. "That's what we'll call him—Patches."

"And his name matches his black-and-white spots that look like puzzle pieces," Mary said.

"I'll be right back." Joey ran up the stairs.

Mary cracked her knuckles, and for good luck, Kaylee rubbed her own knuckles on Mary's head. "Even though Joey crossed his heart, I hope he won't tell and I won't have to die."

Joey came back with socks and a soft pink blanket for Patches. He patted Patches from head to paw, making Mary smile. Patches licked Joey's face all over again.

"Ugh, dog lips," Kaylee said and grinned.

At night, five-year-old Liz cried for her blanket, and in the morning Dad yelled, "Where are my socks?" Dad left for work wearing dirty socks. He slammed the door behind him. Liz wore a sour face.

The school bus pulled away, and Mother went downstairs, carrying a basket of laundry. She froze at the sound of a bark, peeked under the stairs, and found a raggedy-looking patched-up dog wearing socks and sitting on a soft baby-blue blanket. Mother dropped the laundry basket. Her scream could have woken the dead. Kaylee's encouragement had not worked as Mother was still afraid of anything that moved and wasn't human. Mother shot upstairs, taking two steps at a time.

At the end of the school day, Mary, Kaylee, and Joey leaped off the bus. They ran to let Patches out through the basement door. Mother watched the culprits from the window above.

Mother sat up extra tall at supper like she usually did when she had something big to announce. "Who would like to tell your father where his socks are?"

Kaylee spilled her milk. She stood to reach for the empty glass, and a hidden plate of food fell from her lap and smashed onto the floor.

"Seems like you might have something to say," Dad said, looking at Kaylee. Kaylee wiped away the milk mustache above her lip and chewed her food with her mouth closed.

Mother looked under the table. "What's going on here?"

Kaylee swallowed hard. "Charity includes caring for the sick and injured. At school, our teacher said to help the underdog."

Joey burst into laughter, and Mary grinned.

"Get to the point," Dad said.

"Patches is an underdog, but he's getting better from the food and your socks."

"Who's Patches?" Dad asked.

"Does he have my blanket?" Liz asked.

Joey looked at Liz. "Shut up!" he said.

Kaylee explained how she and Mary had rescued a dog. She went on and on about caring for the sick and injured before Dad could interrupt her.

Dad considered Kaylee's remarks as he put his elbows on the table and clasped his hands in front of his mouth, the way he did when an announcement of some sort was likely. "You've done a good thing to help the dog. You'll have to find a home for him very soon since Mother won't get used to Patches. She doesn't need another mouth to feed either."

Dad slapped his palms on the table. "Now, find a home for the dog."

That evening Kaylee fed Shakespeare, handwashed a pair of socks for Dad, and hung them to dry. Liz got a dirty blanket back. Joey didn't get scolded for taking Dad's socks, but he never seemed to get scolded anyway.

Joey suspected Marty had hurt the dog, and two days later, Joey gave Marty a black eye, even though Marty said he didn't know a dog named Patches. Joey said he did. He just didn't know the name of the dog he'd hurt.

Kaylee and Mary drew pictures of Patches with Home Wanted written in large letters above the drawings. Kaylee said a prayer and pinned the posters to the telephone poles in the neighborhood. Days passed, but no one came forward to adopt Patches.

One afternoon, Mary played Beethoven's Fifth Symphony while her piano teacher, Mrs. Clef, waved her finger as though conducting an orchestra. "You sound as lovely as a concert pianist. You should be proud and delighted."

Mary smiled and held her head high.

Kaylee brought Patches to meet Mrs. Clef in the hope of finding him a new home. Patches was on the mend and bathed, so he didn't smell disgusting anymore, but some dirt had been mistaken for patches of color and remained on his coat.

Mrs. Clef had long gold hair and a big voice that matched her enormous body. She could be heard from here to kingdom come and had once sung in Carnegie Hall. She had high aspirations for Mary. But watch out if she hugged you as you could get lost in her arms.

Patches jumped onto her lap and nuzzled against her soft belly. Mrs. Clef hugged him until he was almost lost in her folds. She was already in love with the little dog. "I'll give him a temporary home until you find a permanent one. I know your mother is a city girl and never had pets, even though some city kids did. In fact, it's said pets are dirty little disease carriers." But Mrs. Clef herself probably didn't think so since she left with dirty little Patches.

After Mary's piano lesson, Kaylee left to feed Shakespeare, but he was missing from his little house. "Shakespeare! Here, Shakespeare! Here, Shakespeare!" Kaylee cried out.

"Idiot. He's not a dog. He's a turtle. He won't answer and come running," Mary said. Mary and Kaylee searched and searched for him. They looked everywhere, including Joey's bedroom, but he was nowhere to be found.

"He's dead. Gone forever. We have to bury him," Kaylee whimpered.

"How do we bury Shakespeare without his body? We can't have a proper funeral. Idiot," Mary said again.

"We can have a proper funeral if we bury his house."

Mary finally agreed, and the girls made the sign of the cross, said some prayers, and buried Shakespeare's house in the backyard. Next, Kaylee cut flowers from their neighbor's garden and laid them over Shakespeare's gravesite. She told Mary that stealing the flowers wasn't a sin since it was for a good cause. *It's not a sin,* she repeated to herself.

After the burial, Mary and Kaylee washed the dirt from their grave-digging hands. As they scrubbed the dirt from beneath their fingernails, Liz walked in, petting Shakespeare. Shakespeare the turtle.

"Where is Shakespeare's house?" Liz asked. "I've been looking for it all afternoon."

Mary and Kaylee's mouths fell open in unison. Kaylee glared at Liz.

Mary said, "Idiot."

"Go dig it up!" screeched Kaylee to Liz and handed over Mother's large cooking spoons.

Liz set the turtle down in the bathroom sink and made a run for it. Kaylee grabbed Mother's spoon and chased her. Liz let out a scream that would wake up even a dead turtle, but the turtle wasn't dead. Only his house was buried.

"If Dad hears you…" Mother's voice trailed off.

Kaylee put the spoon in Liz's hand and made her dig up the buried house. Then, after throwing a fit, Kaylee washed the house out, kissed Shakespeare on the shell, and brought him food and water. She was going to get a Girl Scout badge for this one.

CHAPTER 14

THE PLAY

Inspired by both Dad and the love letters, Kaylee and Mary kept busy making plans to put on a play. Grateful for Grandma Reagan's love of Shakespeare and all that she had taught their dad, they quoted lines and wrote some of their own.

Dad always had a quote from one or another of Shakespeare's plays. He was particularly fond of *The Taming of the Shrew* and often teased Mother: "Thy husband is thy lord, thy life, thy keeper."

Mother, a shrew in her own right, threw her head back and laughed. "There's small choice in rotten apples."

Dad took Mother's hand. "Sit by my side and let the world slip; we shall ne'er be younger."

Mother liked the Shakespeare line but barely had time to let the world slip.

Kaylee and her friend Louella spent the afternoon making up posters.

COME ONE
COME ALL
ROMEO AND JULIET
Starring Amazing Talent
Reagans' basement
After school Wednesday
Admission—five cents

They spent the rest of the day tacking the posters up on telephone poles.

On the day of the big event, Mrs. Clef dropped off Patches, freeing herself to visit her sister. Patches wagged his tail and licked Joey's face before curling up in his old spot under the basement stairs.

Joey collected admission as he guarded the basement door entrance and braced his long leg across the threshold. Marty Mullarkey was next in queue, and Joey looked him up and down.

"It's a nickel if you want to get in, but since you can afford more, I'm charging you double."

Red-headed Marty rubbed his freckled, spotted nose with a clenched fist. "You got a big mouth," Marty said. "And you won't get anything from me if you don't let me in for five cents. You don't even have chairs for the audience." Marty waved his nickel in Joey's face.

Joey knew if he didn't charge Marty more than a nickel, Marty wouldn't give him anything. Joey grinned and grabbed the coin from Marty's hand before Marty could change his mind. Louella ushered Marty to a spot near the back wall. Next in line stood Brenda Mullarkey and Eloise McCarthy.

Brenda wore her blond hair in two braids. Eloise wore angel wings left over from last year's Christmas pageant.

Joey kept his leg braced in the doorway and glanced at Brenda. "Hello, trouble," he said then turned to Eloise. "Hello, angel. Boys have to be at least ten years old to see *Romeo and Juliet*, but girls need to be only five. They mature faster." Joey winked at Brenda.

"But we're eleven. And we have the maturity of sixteen-year-olds." Eloise flapped her wings.

"Then it's ten cents for your mature age."

"We only have a nickel between the two of us, and you're lucky we're here," Brenda said. Joey knew this was most likely true and that it was probably Eloise's nickel.

"Two for one. Okay, you're in." Joey grabbed the coin, put it in his pocket, and lowered his leg just enough so they had to jump over. "Give 'em hell, little angel," Joey said to Eloise. Eloise flapped her angel wings and leaped over Joey's leg.

The basement buzzed. Kids sat cross-legged in their play clothes. A shower curtain hid the stage. The curtain bulged with movement in preparation for Romeo and Juliet's appearance.

A photograph of Simon Bolivar, from one of the love letters, inspired Joey. Mounted on his steed, the South American leader who fought for independence looked powerful and in charge, so Joey insisted on being Bolivar in the play, even though he had nothing to do with Romeo and Juliet. Joey borrowed Dad's old military coat and used burnt cork to draw himself a mustache. A large cardboard refrigerator box dragged from the McCarthys' trash became a house. Mary cut slits to resemble shutters on a window.

When the seating area filled up, Joey pulled a sword from the scabbard at his waist. He sliced the air above the heads of the audience members and, without decapitating anyone, drew open the stage's shower curtain. Then Joey mounted his rocking horse, which was attached to springs and hooked onto a metal frame. "Giddy up!" he yelled, the cue for Kaylee to begin. When nothing happened, he cried, "Shazam." Still nothing. Finally, he screamed, "Open sesame!"

Kaylee, who was playing Juliet, opened the window of the refrigerator box.

Kaylee poked her head out. A ring of flowers crowned her head. "Romeo, Romeo, where art thou?" Then, when Mary didn't appear, she asked, "Where are you, Mary?"

Mary, acting as Romeo and wearing Joey's cap and bed shirt, popped out from behind the box and genuflected. Then she played an imaginary piano and sang the notes of Beethoven's Fifth Symphony. "Da da da daaaaaaa." Her voice, disguised as a throaty baritone, rang

STRANGERS SAINTS AND SINNERS

out her lines. "What soft light yonder window breaks. It is East, and Juliet is the sun. Don't waste your love on anyone but me." Romeo threw a kiss to Juliet.

"Kiss her on the lips!" yelled Marty.

"I can't. She's my sister," Mary cried.

Joey raised a fist. "You want a knuckle sandwich?"

Then Mary forgot her lines, cracked her knuckles, and said, "Give a man a fish, and you feed him for a day, show him how to—"

The crowd hissed and booed. She began again, but before she could finish, Kaylee threw her crown at the audience.

Joey took a bow, pulled the curtain closed, held his sword high, and announced, "Intermission." Then he mounted his plastic horse, which Dad had assembled one year for Christmas. Joey took the reins and raised his sword as though he were galloping through a field of battle. With every bounce, he slid the horse forward and charged his way to the far side of the basement, where Dad had a small bar set with beer taps. Joey began pouring. Marty was the first to gulp one down. Then Joey served the audience.

"I prefer wine," Eloise said.

"Wait here," Joey said.

Marty took over the serving while Joey disappeared. Shortly, he returned with a paper cup full of wine and held it out to Eloise. Before she could take it, he pulled the cup back, took a sip, and licked his lips. "First thou shall kiss me here."

Marty clenched his fists. "She's mine."

"Drop dead, Marty," Joey said.

Marty grabbed the cup from Joey and spilled drops of red wine on his shirt. Marty drank the rest and landed a blow to Joey's gut. Joey clobbered him with his sword, and Patches ran like a wound-up banshee from under the stairs and bit Marty in the calf. Eloise and Brenda had finished a couple beers by then, as had most of the audience.

Brenda pulled darts from the dartboard. "Spread your fingers out over the dartboard. I'm an excellent shot," she said to Joey.

"When snowballs freeze in hell!"

"I'll do it!" Eloise said and placed her hand on the board.

Brenda took aim, but she missed altogether and landed a dart in Joey's bicycle tire, which he had parked in the basement out of Marty's reach. Luckily for her, Joey was back in a tangle with Marty, and Joey missed hearing the hissing of the tire.

Kaylee, who was still dressed as Juliet, opened the window of the big box and yelled, "Thus with a kiss, I die." She took another sip of beer and collapsed inside the box with a thump. The box fell over, and out she crawled.

By now, there was so much chaos that Mary entered stage right and said, "The End! Parting is such sweet sorrow that I should say goodnight till it be morrow."

Kids swayed in drunkenness and started yelling for their money back, even the ones who hadn't paid. Joey headed for the door with the cash, but suddenly Dad's car horn was beeping. Joey didn't want to be seen running away so gave a nickel to Brenda to open the garage door for his dad. Brenda took the money and was up five cents since she hadn't paid admission. She headed out to open the garage door for Mr. Reagan. Meanwhile, someone got sick and threw up in the corner. Joey held his nose. Then he took off.

Moments later, Mother descended the stairs. She surveyed the ramshackle room, sniffed the putrid stench, and yelled, sounding like the staccato keys Mary played on the piano. "Heavens to Murgatroyd! Is this what you call putting on a play? If your father sets his eyes on this—"

Before she could say anything else, Eloise threw up. By then, Brenda was bouncing on the rocking horse. A spray of vomit hit Brenda's braid.

Brenda shouted, "This is disgusting," and then fell off the horse and bumped her head.

Patches jumped and barked and peed everywhere.

There was a lot of commotion that evening in the neighborhood. Parents sent most of the neighborhood kids to their rooms, each parent accusing the other of something or other. Kaylee and Mary had to clean up a stinky, rotten, horrid, putrid mess in the basement.

The next day, most of the kids in Sister Killian's class put their heads down on their desks to make it through the school day. Sister appeared puzzled since there wasn't any known illness going around, but no one would fess up to what was ailing them.

CHAPTER 15

TRAIN RIDE

JOHN

On Saturday morning, Mary and Kaylee kissed Mother goodbye. "We're going out to play, then we're going on a picnic," Kaylee said as she packed peanut butter and jelly sandwiches and two apples into brown paper sacks. She added a couple of Oreo cookies to the bag and slipped a pack of red licorice into her pocket.

"Don't ruin this evening's dinner with candy," Mother said.

The two sisters hopped over little Liz's game of jacks. They scooted along on their secret mission to find John Sullivan and figure out why he had not answered the last of Olivia's love letters.

After paying for round-trip tickets, Kaylee and Mary took their seats on a train that would take them to Manhattan. Kaylee elbowed Mary and nodded toward a man seated across from them. The dirt on his torn clothes matched his dirty face and fingernails.

Kaylee leaned in closer to Mary and whispered, "Do you think he's homeless? Should I give him my lunch?"

The man locked eyes with Kaylee. Pee trickled down his pant leg and flowed in a steady stream in the girls' direction. "Ugh," Mary whispered. "Let's move. I feel bad for the guy, but there's something

84

creepy about him. Besides, the pee and whiskey stink to high heavens, and he could be dangerous."

Brave Mary motioned for Kaylee to follow her. Then Mary dashed to claim seats near the door. Kaylee stood to follow her, but the scruffy man grabbed her arm.

"You can have my lunch," Kaylee told him. "Just let go of my arm."

But the man held tight, narrowed his eyes, and grinned. A growl escaped through his clenched teeth.

Unwanted lessons from Joey flashed in Kaylee's mind, and she landed a well-placed punch to his shoulder. The stranger did not let go. Kaylee launched another surprise attack and landed a kick to his shin. Sneering, the stinky man let out a moan and released Kaylee's arm.

"How do you like them apples?" Kaylee said and slipped over to sit with Mary.

Mary took Kaylee's shaky hand. "No wonder Dad doesn't like us to take the train to Grandma's unless he travels with us."

"We don't see Grandma as much anymore. I miss her." Kaylee closed her eyes and thought about her family's move from their Manhattan apartment near where their grandparents lived to a house in the suburbs of the Hudson Valley.

Mother hadn't wanted to leave her parents behind and especially missed teatime with her English mother and the brogue of her Irish father. Dad had known he would miss regular visits with his Irish parents and that he would have to commute into the city for his engineering job, but he believed the suburbs were safer for children, and his friends agreed. So much of the Irish neighborhood moved, and the Reagans went with them. They said goodbye to their old apartment on the third floor of a five-story walk-up. They said goodbye to their old neighborhood of Inwood, Manhattan. And they had said hello to suburbia.

Instead of taking the train to school, the Reagan children rode a yellow bus. They moved into a ranch house. Since the house stood alone, no sounds of laughter or fighting escaped through attached walls, like they had at the apartment. As the children grew, Dad built an addition on the home, and then it was unlike every other house. Dad raised the roof and added three small bedrooms to the second floor, making a total of six bedrooms and two baths.

Clovers sprinkled the ample green yard, and the children pressed many of the four-leaf variety between pages of a book. Each year on Arbor Day, the Reagans brought free trees home from school. The trees sprouted and multiplied. Unlike most of the neighbors' yards, the Reagans' yard began to look like a young forest. Dogwoods, tulip magnolias, maples, and sycamores grew like the family they shaded. There was even one peach tree.

The Irish Catholic neighborhood was not as diverse as the trees that occupied it. Kaylee saw no difference between their Catholic neighbors and the few Protestant ones, except that the children attended different schools and went to different churches on Sunday. A few Jewish families also moved into the neighborhood and went to synagogue on Friday nights. Kaylee was in awe of the strangers. She didn't understand the difference between Catholics, Protestants, and Jews or why they boarded separate school buses. Kaylee pulled on Mother's apron strings and asked if she could go to the synagogue. Mother simply said, "No." When asked why, Mother didn't explain but mentioned Kaylee could play with any of the neighborhood kids.

The train rolled toward the city, and Mary mentioned Grandma's house.

"I want to visit Grandma when we are in the city. It's so great when she lets us take a big handful of pennies from the Tetley tin. The best part is going to the penny candy store," Kaylee said. Whenever Kaylee could, she loaded up on candy. "I like Bazooka bubble gum, candy necklaces, and Mary Janes, but mostly I like red licorice."

"How did I know?" Mary giggled.

The train screeched to a halt at Penn Station. The girls hopped out, and Kaylee followed Mary to the subway station.

A few Metro stops later, the doors slipped open, and the two sisters jumped over what Grandma called the gap and landed on the platform. They made their way up the stairs to the street and walked a couple blocks to the address on the envelope of the love letters.

Kaylee and Mary stood around waiting for someone to exit the apartment building so they could sneak in without a key or without one of the residents buzzing them in. Finally, they got their chance and slipped inside.

Mary eyed the return address on the envelope, read numbers on doors, and knocked. When no one answered, they knocked on another door and then another. Most doors slammed in their faces. No one knew John Sullivan. "Don't you dare bother me!" yelled one irate tenant.

"Let's get out of here," Mary said.

"Just a few more. Back this way." Kaylee dashed down the other side of the hallway, ignoring Mary. Mary chased after her.

"I told you this was a bad idea," Mary said.

"It was your idea," Kaylee said.

"You know it wasn't, idiot." Mary paused. "I only agreed because Aunt Betty lives in this neighborhood, and I remember how to get to her house. We've been there so many times. Besides, you said you would take my turn doing dishes for a whole month, so you owe me."

Kaylee made the sign of the cross, knocked on another door, and crossed her fingers behind her back.

This time, an old lady wearing a cornflower-blue housedress answered the door.

"Your dress is as pretty as Grandma's curtains," Kaylee said. The old lady accepted the compliment with a grin.

"Shush," Mary said as Kaylee was about to say more. "We're looking for our uncle, John Sullivan. My mother lost touch, and now that she's sick, she wants us to find him."

"She's not sick," Kaylee said.

The old lady widened her smile.

"And he's a priest," Kaylee said then added, "A Catholic priest," thinking that would add needed credibility.

Still smiling, the old lady said, "Well, I'm sorry about your mother. I do remember John." She placed one hand on the top of her head and tugged her hair toward the ceiling. The hair rose, exposing a smooth white skull. The old lady scratched her head with her free hand and replaced the wig. Kaylee's mouth dropped, and Mary's grin made one corner of her mouth turn up more than the other.

"I'm Kaylee, and my sister is Mary. How did you do that? Will you teach us your magic? How many tricks do you know?"

"I've got a few up my sleeve. I'm Martha," the old lady said. "I was about to have some lemonade. Why don't you come in and join me?"

The girls padded in behind her to the kitchen, and Martha put aside her paint-by-numbers portrait of a horse's face that was on the table.

"That's a pretty painting," Kaylee said.

"It's also easy. There is a code. You paint the color that corresponds with the number." Martha pointed to the numbers on the canvas and the numbers on the paint containers. "You see, it's easy. Would you like to try it?"

Before Kaylee could answer, Mary said, "We don't have time, but thank you."

"Anyway, I do remember John, but he's not a priest," Martha said.

Kaylee and Mary exchanged glances. Kaylee thought Martha seemed magical, and that was why she knew John.

"You girls should get your stories straight."

"We'll work on it," Kaylee said.

"Why do you really want to find him?"

Kaylee clasped her hands together. "He disappeared, and we want to know what happened to him."

Martha rubbed her chin as though in thought. "There has to be more to the story."

"He stopped answering love letters," Mary said.

"Well, well. Unrequited love. Now we have a story." She gestured to the kitchen table. "Have a seat."

While Kaylee and Mary sat, Martha stirred sugar into a pitcher of lemonade and poured it into tall glasses. She served the girls and joined them at the table. "Years ago, during the Great Depression, John and his family moved away because they could no longer make rent."

"Were you depressed?" Kaylee asked.

Mary cringed and scrunched her nose.

"We were all depressed, some more than others, but my family was luckier than most. We had regular meals, even though it wasn't always what we wanted to eat. But we ate. I worked in a sweatshop, and my husband worked for the *Daily News*."

"My dad reads the newspaper. I like to read the comics, and comic books, too. Especially funny ones." Kaylee grinned.

Mary rolled her wide eyes and pursed her lips like a fish. She held back on the you're-an-idiot part.

Old lady Martha chuckled and went on. "If my memory serves me, the Sullivans moved into a corner building about twelve blocks away. I'll write down the address for you. Their older relatives lived nearby and maybe still do. Your mother might know them. Ask her if she has family connections on that street."

"Right," Mary said before Kaylee could answer with the wrong words.

"You're welcome to use the telephone to call your mom. She might be worried about you two."

"No thanks." Mary glanced at a catlike clock with a wagging pendulum tail. "It's getting late, and we need to be back by dinnertime. We don't want to worry her."

Kaylee placed her hand on her head. "Wait. How do you make your hair come off?"

"It's a trick some folks learn without trying. Hopefully, you won't have to learn it."

Mary tugged Kaylee's hand. "Goodbye, and thank you for the lemonade."

Kaylee held out her left hand for the old lady to shake. Martha obliged with a bright smile and said, "You're welcome, and you know what? For a couple of Catholic schoolgirls, you sure have chutzpah!"

They strutted away as Kaylee fished train tokens and the address from her pocket and waved them in the air. Then she announced in a conductor-style voice, "Next stop—121st Street."

"We don't want to be late getting home, and that's our last token," Mary said dryly.

"So what? Come on, Mary. We got this far, and it will just cost more money to come back here. I have enough change to buy two more tokens to get us home, and that's it. Let's go. Now or never."

Mary moved her hand across her throat in a slashing motion. "Never."

"Let's flip a coin. Heads I win, tails you lose."

Mary agreed and lost the deal.

"You need to have your head examined. Enough is enough. Do you like searching for a needle in a haystack?" Mary asked, not expecting an answer.

Kaylee jiggled the coins in her pocket. "I would rather search for money in a haystack. C'mon." She walked swiftly in the subway station's direction before Mary could utter more refusals.

"All right," Mary said reluctantly as she caught up. She sighed. "But if we don't have any luck soon, we head back."

When they reached 121st Street, Kaylee and Mary continued to rap on doors and inquire about John Sullivan.

Finally, a very old man with a barking dog let them in. The small apartment opened into the kitchen. "Sit," he said, and so Kaylee sat at the kitchen table.

"Not you, idiot. The dog!" Mary blurted, not holding back this time.

"What are you girls after?" the man asked.

"My mother wants us to find her Uncle John."

"Your mother wants to find her Uncle John, does she? Well now, how old is your mother?"

"Thirty-three," Mary answered.

"And her uncle is about fifty? Well, is he an uncle on your mother's side or your father's side?"

"Mother's," Mary answered at the same time Kaylee said, "Father's."

Mary and Kaylee exchanged uneasy glances, regretting they hadn't taken Martha's advice to get their stories straight.

"Oh, Mary's right," Kaylee said.

The old man frowned. "What's her maiden name?"

"Lynch," Kaylee answered.

"O'Neil," Mary said.

The man's voice cracked. "Get out."

"Sorry. It's really Sullivan," Kaylee said.

A low male voice called from the living room. "Who's there?"

"Nothing to bother yourself with, John. Just a couple of rascals who need to leave," he said protectively.

As the older man opened the door to let the girls out, Kaylee rose and ran into the next room.

The man yelled, "Get back here, and leave my son alone."

Kaylee remained in the living room, and the old man huffed.

Mary heard Kaylee say, "Hi, John." That caught Mary's attention, and she walked into the living room too. The old man followed.

A man with a full, round middle sat in an armchair. His thin legs were propped up on an ottoman. His beard, white with flecks of red, covered a good amount of his pale face. His blond hair was full and thick with streaks of deep gold and hung carelessly across his forehead. John lowered his round spectacles and peered at the girls. Kaylee's eyes widened. *Could be St. Nick.*

Mary annoyingly asked Kaylee, "What are you doing? We're not welcome here. Come on. We need to get home now."

"Please lower the television," John said to his father.

The older man turned the knob on the television and turned around, watching the scene unfold before him. John turned his head to the girls.

"I'm Kaylee, and this is Mary." *Why doesn't he move much?*

"Seems you already know my name," John said.

"It's John Sullivan, right?" Kaylee replied.

"Why are you asking?"

Not knowing where to begin, Kaylee pulled red licorice from her pocket. "Would you like some?" she offered, avoiding Mary's disapproving stare.

John smiled and nodded. Kaylee pulled a piece from the bunch and accidentally dropped it on the floor.

"Butterfingers." She picked it up, kissed it up to God, and handed it to John.

John's smile widened. "I'll save it for later."

Kaylee turned to John's father.

"No thanks," he mumbled before she could say anything.

Kaylee turned to Mary, who waved her away.

"Now what's this all about?" John asked.

Kaylee put the remainder of the licorice back in her pocket. "May I have a seat?"

"Go on," John said, pointing to the couch. He motioned to Mary and his father. "Why don't you all have a seat while Kaylee here explains?"

Mary took a seat beside Kaylee on the couch. The older man shifted his weight but remained standing by the television.

"My name is Kaylee, and I go to St. Patrick's Grammar School and have something to say. I'm not sure how to tell you, but it all started with detention."

John's smile turned to a grimace as he propped himself up straighter. He stiffened his arms to scoot his back farther up on the pillow. Mary sat wordlessly staring at the man she believed to have written the letters.

"Go on," he said, nodding at Kaylee.

"I go to a Catholic school, and it's a sin to sign your own home-work notebook. I committed that sin."

Mary cracked her knuckles. "Skip that part, and just get to the point."

"That's what I'm trying to do." Kaylee went on, "I got detention, and after school, I was sent across the street to the convent. Well, and in a way to Sister Killian's bedroom to wait for Mother to pick me up."

The older man widened his stance and crossed his arms. "What does that have to do with your mother's uncle?"

"That's just it. He's not her uncle, but we're looking for an old boyfriend," Kaylee said.

"Whose old boyfriend?" asked the old man.

"Olivia Hunter's," Kaylee said.

No one said a word. Mary and Kaylee exchanged glances.

"What are you talking about?" John finally asked, his voice much louder and huskier, his color a little more ashen than a moment ago. He pushed himself a little taller.

"I found your love letters in her bedroom, a whole stack of them tied with a ribbon. Some letters at the bottom of the stack were stamped RETURN TO SENDER. The sender was Olivia. I think you're John—on the other end of those letters."

"If they were my letters, what would they be doing in a nun's bedroom? She must be holding on to someone else's letters," he said.

"Well, whoever she is, she wrote to you and searched for you. You didn't answer, and judging from the letters, no one would help her find you."

"How did you find me?"

"We went to the return address on the envelope. An old lady who lives nearby told us to try here."

"But Olivia didn't find me."

"One of your old neighbors told Olivia you disappeared and that she didn't know where you went. Olivia must have felt her love was lost forever. I think she didn't know what else to do, so she became a nun."

John looked at Kaylee. "This is unbelievable... impossible. You have an exceptional imagination, young lady."

Kaylee's face scrunched in puzzlement at John's frown. Her lower lip formed a pout, and Mary cracked her knuckles. Kaylee wished Mary would call her an idiot or something to break the silence. But nobody said a word.

John gazed upward. His mouth quivered. Finally, slowly he spoke. "It was a long time ago." He rocked forward and inhaled deeply as a softness filled his voice. "You see, I loved Olivia very much and planned to propose to her in a park a long time ago." He closed his eyes, lifted his arm, and covered his eyes with his sleeve.

The old man moved to John and handed him a handkerchief. "You don't need to tell them any more."

John cleared his throat, and the old man stepped back.

"Central Park," John said. "Times were tough then. I quit school to work on a construction site and help my family. I managed to save enough money to buy an engagement ring for Olivia. Then one day something changed all that. At work, the scaffolding collapsed beneath me. My legs were broken, but the doctors said it was worse than that. They said I could never walk again. I couldn't face Olivia. I didn't want her to know I had become half a man. That's how I felt back then… still do today."

Kaylee wiped away her tears. "But she loved you. She looked for you. She's lived all these years without knowing what happened to you. How sad. Will you see her if she finally finds you?"

"No. I wouldn't want her to see me this way."

"What if something bad happened to her instead?"

"Then it would be a different ending. But that's not what happened."

"Can you walk?" asked Kaylee in her bold and innocent way. Mary cringed.

"It took years of practice. I can walk farther with crutches, but it's not always easy."

Tears rimmed Mary's eyes. Kaylee rubbed her forehead. The room was thick with quiet.

Mary gazed at the clock and broke the silence. "If we leave now, we should make it home by dinner."

"One more minute," Kaylee said and pulled something from her pocket. "John, this is one of the letters stamped RETURN TO SENDER. It's never been opened. It was meant for you years ago."

John accepted the letter and began to read silently.

Dear John,

The thought of not being with you makes me gasp for air. Sometimes I don't know if the next breath will come. But it does, somehow it does…

John didn't finish reading the letter. He folded it and placed it in the envelope. Kaylee held her breath, but John didn't tell them what was in the letter. Instead, he slipped it into his shirt pocket.

Kaylee exhaled. "One more thing before we leave." She handed him an old photograph.

John took the photo and placed it face down on the table beside him.

Kaylee and Mary spent the last of their tokens and hopped onto the subway. They still had the tickets to transfer to the train. "We'll be back home by the time Dad whistles for us," Mary said.

The locomotion rocked them into a trancelike quiet as the train rolled away.

Kaylee thought about what would have happened if the scaffolding had not collapsed with John on it. Her mind was racing, and after a while, she elbowed Mary. "What if John were on a lunch break when the scaffolding broke? Do you think he would have spent all these years in an easy chair? Would Sister Killian still be Olivia Hunter? Or would she be Olivia Sullivan? Maybe they would have lots of children."

"Gosh, you sure know how to chatter," Mary said.

"Well, I'll bet they would have had grandchildren by now. I wonder how many? I wonder who my teacher would be. But, God." Kaylee paused. "Oh no. Did Sister Killian discover her letters were missing? If she did, does she suspect me? I need to find a way to return them."

Suddenly Mary gasped for air, and both her hands flew to her forehead. He eyes looked like they popped out of her head like an alligator's. "Oh no, this can't be."

"What's wrong?" Kaylee asked.

"We're heading in the wrong direction!"

"I thought you knew the way! That's why I invited you."

"Invited? You bribed me!"

"You wanted to find out what happened to the lover just as much as me."

"Shut up, Kaylee."

"No, you shut up. It's getting dark. Dark brings out the boogeyman in cities."

The train stopped. Kaylee and Mary jumped out and tried to cross

95

over to the platform heading in the opposite direction. "Dang," cried Mary as she grabbed the barred gate and rattled it.

Kaylee pointed to a sign and read, "Closed for maintenance."

"Are you sure you're out of money and tokens?" asked Mary.

Kaylee patted her pockets. "Only a couple of train tickets, which won't do us any good. No more of anything else, except licorice. Don't you know where we are?"

"Looks like Peter Rabbit's garden," said Mary.

"Very funny. Didn't Mr. McGregor kill Peter?"

"Shut up before I kill you."

Mary looked around and gestured to Kaylee. "This way."

They climbed the stairs, exited at the street level, and kept walking. Darkness settled around them as they walked down a strange block littered with garbage. Most of the buildings had boarded-up windows painted over with graffiti.

A car slowed as it passed the girls but kept moving before it turned and was out of sight. Kaylee held back tears. Mary shivered and reached for Kaylee's hand. They kept walking until Mary's foot hit a crushed beer can. It rolled into the gutter, making a hollow clanging noise.

Kaylee rubbed the back of her neck as though to wipe away a prickly feeling. "Mary, do you hear something?"

"Hear what?" Mary leaned in closer to Kaylee.

"Shuffling. Like footsteps."

CHAPTER 16

LOST

MARY AND KAYLEE

The sky darkened, streetlights flickered on, and somewhere a cat screeched. Kaylee rubbed the back of her neck and looked over her shoulder. "Mary, a man is following us. He looks like the man on the train. Do you think he is after us? To get even? For the punch?"

The girls quickened their pace, and the stranger matched their timing. Kaylee squeezed Mary's hand. "I'm scared. Let's run."

Kaylee dropped Mary's hand to take off running, but at that moment the man's arms wrapped around Mary. She shouted, "Run, Kaylee! Run!"

Kaylee eyed the man, and then she spotted an empty wine bottle lying in the gutter. She picked up the bottle, stood on tiptoes, and broke it across the man's head. Glass shattered, and the man dropped his hold on Mary. Something wet hit her face. The man released his arms and stumbled backward.

"Run!" shouted Kaylee.

She dropped the remainder of the bottle, and the two sisters sprinted until they turned a corner and ducked between two cars.

Kaylee wiped her face, smearing the stranger's blood on her hands and shirt. "I don't think he'll be coming after us."

"Let's hope not." Mary controlled her labored breathing.

Kaylee's voice trembled. "What are we going to do now?"

"We'll hide." Mary crawled under one of the cars lining the block. "I just hope you didn't kill him."

Kaylee followed. "Mother will kill me if I killed him."

Kaylee looked out from under the car. "What happens if the driver comes and rolls over us?"

"Then we'll get out from under here and run. Just don't kill him." Mary grinned.

"Yeah, if there is anything left of us." Kaylee's stomach growled. "I'm hungry."

Mary tapped Kaylee's pocket. "Eat as much of that red licorice as you want."

Kaylee split the last piece of candy with Mary. "Are we going to die under here?"

"If we do, they could bury us together."

"We share a room. We could share a coffin," whimpered Kaylee, her voice breaking.

"Sure can."

Glare from an oncoming car's headlights illuminated Kaylee's foot. Mary reached over and tucked her sister closer. "Pull your foot in, Kaylee. Someone might see us."

The car came closer. Slowed. Stopped.

The sisters held each other tightly.

While the girls cowered under the car, their mother was wondering where they were. She glanced at the clock again. "I'm worried about Mary and Kaylee. It's not like them to miss dinner." She turned to her son. "Joey, go back out and look for the girls." She then turned to her husband. "What if something happened to them?"

He tapped her hand. "Nothing bad happens in this neck of the woods. Remember, that's why we moved here."

Joey opened the door to step outside as a police car with the letters NYPD pulled up in front of the house.

Mother's mouth dropped open as she made her way to the door. A flashing light rotated from the car's roof and fell across Mother's face, causing her to blink each time it swirled. A moan escaped her lips. She placed a hand on Joey's shoulder to steady herself. Dad moved beside her. She reached for him and put one hand on her belly. A police officer emerged from the car.

"Oh God." Mother's voice quivered.

The policeman opened the car's back door, and Mary and Kaylee hopped out. Mother let out a sizable exhale as the girls ran to her. She threw her arms around them.

The police officer said, "I found them under a parked car. They have some explaining to do."

Mother looked at the blood on Kaylee's hand and gasped. "Does she need medical attention?"

"No, but someone else does, someone who got what they deserved," said the policeman.

"Does that mean he's alive? I didn't kill him?" Kaylee asked.

The officer paused for a moment and shook his head. "You didn't."

"Too bad. I was hoping to visit Kaylee in jail. She could watch me through iron bars as I chomp down red licorice." Joey chuckled.

Kaylee sent a punch Joey's way, but he was too quick, and her knuckles rapped against the door.

"Ouch!" she screamed.

"Enough," Dad said and thanked the police officer for his efforts.

Once the Reagans were all inside, Dad crossed his arms over his chest. "You two have supper. Then we'll sit in the living room. You both have some explaining to do."

Joey rubbed his hands together and hid behind the couch.

After supper, Dad grounded Mary and Kaylee for two weeks. They couldn't go out after school. They missed playing and running home to the sound of Dad's whistle, and Kaylee was stuck doing more dishes when it wasn't even her turn.

Joey said the two sisters had gotten off easy and suggested they take out the garbage, too, but Dad didn't buy it.

CHAPTER 17

TEN COMMANDMENTS

Sister Killian tapped the pointer on the Ten Commandments written on the chalkboard. The tip slid down to the seventh one. "Thou shall not steal," she said.

Kaylee looked up. Sister Killian glared at her.

Oh God, what would I confess to Father this time? Kaylee turned her gaze to the window, avoiding the piercing eyes of Sister. She couldn't help but think of John, the writer of the letters, sitting in his overstuffed chair with his feet up in the musty room. His voice resounded in her head. "How did you find me?" Kaylee wondered if Sister remembered the sound of his voice or what he had said the last time they were together.

Kaylee thought Mary was a lot luckier since she didn't have to look at Sister Killian every day. Mary didn't have to worry if Sister figured out who had stolen her letters. That was only fair since Mary wasn't the one who had taken—well, stolen; no, borrowed—the letters. Kaylee reminded herself she meant to put them back.

Really, I only borrowed them. I would not keep them. It's just that now, every time I sin, Sister Killian sends me to the principal's office instead of to her bedroom in the convent—her bedroom with the drawer and the key. The key to putting them back.

Kaylee felt a sharp poke on the back of her head. "What!" Kaylee said.

Sister slapped the ruler into her palm. "I said stop daydreaming and do your work unless you want to share your thoughts with the rest of the class."

If only she knew. Kaylee picked up her fountain pen and applied it to her paper, but she didn't know what to write.

"Did you forget the answer to what is the seventh commandment?" asked Sister.

Kaylee wrote, "Thou shall not steal."

"Write it one hundred times," Sister said. "Next time, you'll pay attention. And when you complete the assignment, go to the principal's office."

Kaylee was grateful to serve her punishment during the school day instead of after school, when Sister made her wait in the convent during detention, causing her to miss the bus ride home and causing her mother to have to pick her up. So instead of sitting in the convent, she sat in Sister Agatha's office, missing lessons and eating red licorice. But she was still scheming to come up with a way to return the letters. By now, Kaylee had missed so many lessons she failed most of her tests, except for spelling. Sister Killian continued to seat students from the smartest to the dumbest, according to test scores. Kaylee still sat in the dumb row by the window and worked herself down to the last seat—the dumbest seat in the whole class. Goody Two-shoes Angela Marie sat in the front seat in the first row. Snot-nosed teacher's pet Brenda Mullarkey sat right behind her.

Upon returning to the classroom, Sister pointed to Kaylee. "Stand and recite verbatim the answer to what is Catechism."

Kaylee had memorized this for homework and knew how to answer. "Catechism is the teaching of religion. It begins with the Apostles' Creed and ends with another prayer."

"You left out the other prayer, the Lord's prayer. Stand in the back corner of the classroom and face the wall."

Sister gave the test for math and geography to the rest of the class. Since Kaylee remained standing, she couldn't take the test, so she got a big fat zero. The only girl who used to be dumber than Kaylee was Louella. Louella had been held back a grade. Kaylee thought Louella should be in the first row since she already had all this learning last year, but maybe Louella wasn't good at test taking either. Maybe Louella was more brilliant than everyone thought. It was just that her lazy eye made her look stupid because you couldn't always tell who she was looking at when she spoke. Kaylee couldn't decide which eye to stare at, so she just stared at Louella's big nose.

Kaylee couldn't stop thinking about whether Sister Killian had figured out who had taken the letters. *Maybe she knows, but then maybe she doesn't know.* Kaylee wasn't the only one to get rapped on the back of the head with the ruler. Sister walloped Louella when she was replacing a cartridge in her fountain pen. The ink splattered here and there. Some drops showered Sister's hand, and a couple reached her face. Half the students in the class cracked up, so they had to fold their arms and put their heads down on the desk.

After what seemed like a week, Sister said, "Pick up your heads and take out a piece of paper. Write one hundred times *I shall not laugh in class.*"

Kaylee wondered if Louella had any ink left to write anything a hundred times. Containing herself, Kaylee held her breath until she sounded like a tire hissing hot air.

"All you little sinners are going to confession," Sister Killian said. "You will march to church in size order from shortest to tallest."

"Hey," Kaylee whispered to Louella. "I get to be the chief leader."

"So be quiet, or you'll lose the chance."

The only time Kaylee got to be at the head of the class was when she was first in line. The only positive attribute of being the youngest student in class was she was also the shortest. It made her the leader of the pack—today.

Sister patted Angela Marie on the head. "Put on your beanies."

The little beanie hats sat on their heads like upside-down bowls. The smart girls in the first row pushed bobby pins into them. It kept them anchored from the wind and from falling off when they bowed or genuflected.

Kaylee led the procession across the street as a gust of air blew Peggy McCarthy's beanie away. Louella broke ranks and chased it, but it slipped through the grate of the sewer, causing a cacophony of giggles and mumbles of disgust.

Bratty Brenda brushed her hand over Peggy's hair and messed it up. "Don't worry. We'll find you something to put on your head." Girls always had to wear something on their heads in church. Boys didn't. Other than on the school bus and sometimes on the playground, church gatherings were one of the few times the girls in Sister Killian's class encountered boys during the school day. Once they reached fifth grade, the girls and boys at St. Patrick's were separated. The boys occupied the upstairs classrooms, where the Brothers commanded attention with the help of whips and paddles.

The students filed into the pews, sat, and waited for their turns to confess their sins. The smell of incense lingered from an early-morning mass that Father Halligan conducted in Latin. Somehow, Peggy made it inside the church without her beanie.

A white object originating from Brenda passed from hand to hand like a baton in a relay and made its way down to the girl sitting next to Peggy. She took it and used a bobby pin to secure the object to Peggy's head.

The snickers started on the girls' side of the church then rumbled like a wave over to the boys. Kaylee looked around to see what was so funny. She poked Louella, who was sitting nearby because she wasn't tall either.

"What's that thing on Peggy's head? I've seen that thing in the bathroom cabinet. What's it doing here?" Kaylee whispered.

Louella turned her gaze to Peggy. "It's a sanitary napkin." She muffled a laugh with a cupped hand. Kaylee didn't giggle because she didn't know what a sanitary napkin was.

"Sanitary must be a thing to keep you clean," Kaylee said.

Louella grinned. "So, in a way, it is."

Sister approached Peggy. "Get that thing off your head!"

Peggy removed it and looked at the object in her hand. Tears rolled down her cheeks.

Peggy turned and smacked the girl nearest her across her face. "I'll bet your friend Brenda is behind this," she screeched between clenched teeth.

Peggy could be an ally if we needed one, mused Kaylee.

Sister held on to the end of the pew, reached over several heads, and pulled Peggy's hair. "Be quiet."

"Ouch!" Peggy cried.

Chuckles rippled throughout the pews, especially in the boys' section.

Brother Peter raised his finger to his lips and announced, "Extra penance for your disruption. Kneel and pray five Hail Marys."

Father Cunningham sat like a caged lion in the middle enclosure of the confessional booth. Nearby, Father Halligan sat in the middle of another one. Each booth had three compartments, enabling the priest, who sat in the middle, to turn to the next sinner by sliding one screened window closed and turning to open the opposite one.

Kaylee hoped to confess her sins to Father Halligan because his penance was lighter and he didn't ask questions. But when it was Kaylee's turn, he was occupied with other sinners. As if doing them a favor, she gestured to some of her classmates to cut in line so she could fall into place for Father Halligan's confessional, but they were on to her. Kaylee slipped into the empty confessional booth, kneeled, and waited for Father Cunningham to finish with the sinner on the other side of him. Soon the small window slid open, revealing a dark screen and a silhouette of Father's head. She couldn't quite make out his face, and she hoped he couldn't see hers either.

"Bless me, Father, for I have sinned. It has been two weeks since my last confession," Kaylee said and froze.

"Go on, my child," Father said.

"I committed forgery."

"What do you mean? Usually, the word forgery is in reference to counterfeit money."

"Counterfeit? You mean you can make fake money? Is it hard to do?"

"What a terrible question." Father paused. "Now confess what you forged before you commit another sin. Honesty is the best policy."

"I signed my mother's name in my homework notebook. I got into a fight with my brother, Joey."

"Is there anything else you would like to confess, my child?"

"Yes. I stole something, and that's everything. I'm ready for my penance."

"Slow down, child. What did you steal?"

Kaylee didn't answer.

"I'm waiting," Father said.

Kaylee didn't enjoy making up lies in the confessional, but she hadn't expected Father Cunningham to ask what she'd stolen. Wasn't it enough to confess she stole something?

"A piece of red licorice," she lied. She must have stolen one at some point or another, she thought, so it wasn't a lie. At least not a new one.

"For penance, you must say three Our Fathers and ten Hail Marys."

"Thank you, Father." Kaylee blessed herself with the sign of the cross and left the booth before Father could change his mind and give out more penance.

Kaylee prayed. "Can you forgive me for telling a lie in the confessional booth?"

She recited her penance quickly and saved some for her nighttime prayers so it didn't look to the other students as though Father had given her too much penance, which would be evidence of too many sins. She sat down as if she were done praying and glanced around to see who was still kneeling. Brenda was already sitting and caught Kaylee's eye. Kaylee squinched her eyes and stuck out her middle finger.

Sister Killian entered the confessional booth and closed the door behind her.

CHAPTER 18

THE MILKMAN

Mother wiped her hands on her apron. "Mary, please set the cereal boxes on the table, then go outside and check the milk box to see if Norman delivered the milk for breakfast." Mother looked over her hungry flock of school-age children sitting at the table. "We don't have time to cook eggs. If Norman is still about, invite him in for tea."

Joey watched from the kitchen window as Mary stepped outside and waved to Norman. The milkman put the parking brake on in the milk truck, left it running, and followed Mary inside as he carried a rack of milk bottles.

Except for a milk belly and an eagle beak, Norman stood like a skinny, tall pencil. He wore a milkman's cap with a shiny blue visor. On Sundays, when he was a church usher, he wore a checkered brown suit. Purple dots spotted his tie.

"Give me that," Joey said, grabbing the bottle of fresh milk from Mary. He poured the top layer of heavy cream over a bowl of Lucky Charms and set the bottle on the table. Not a trace of cream remained. Kaylee poured the smooth white liquid over Cocoa Puffs while Courtnay, Mary, and Liz drenched their Frosted Flakes until they were soggy. The three youngest children—Lucy, Orla, and Emma—played with their oatmeal.

Mother stood at the counter, gestured for Norman to sit, and poured him a cup of tea. "Norman, wouldn't you agree Father preached a wonderful message during last Sunday's sermon?"

Norman sat, took off his hat, and placed it on his lap. "He reminded us to obey the Ten Commandments and—"

"Hey, Norman. How much money do you get passing the collection basket around during mass?" interrupted Joey.

Norman ignored Joey and recited the commandments.

Hmm, thought Kaylee. She would bet that was where Joey got his candy money.

Joey reached for a spoonful of Kaylee's Cocoa Puffs, but she pulled the bowl away just in time. That was when Joey waved the stack of Sister Killian's letters in her face.

"Give me that!" Kaylee shouted.

Joey put his face an inch from Kaylee's and opened his mouth before swallowing his chewed-up food.

Kaylee looked at Joey the way Mother looked at wiggling worms. "Ugh, you're a pig."

"What's that in your hand?" Mother asked Joey.

"They're mine," Kaylee said.

"Love letters," Joey said, looking at Kaylee through squinty eyes. "I found them under her mattress."

Mother set her teacup on the saucer, put her hands on her hips, and turned to Kaylee. "Where'd you get them?"

Kaylee crossed her fingers behind her back. "I found them in church, next to the hymnals."

"They belong to someone, and that someone should have them," Norman replied.

"They belong to Olivia," Kaylee said.

"Who's Olivia? And don't talk with your mouth full," Mother replied.

"I don't know. Could be she's a saint. Could be she's a sinner."

"I'll take them." Norman reached across the table and grabbed them before Joey could resist. "I'll put them in the lost-and-found box at church."

"Holy cow," Kaylee said to the milkman. She had to get them back to Sister Killian. But how?

"I'm not amused," Norman declared and slipped the letters into his pocket. "Thanks for the tea." Peering out the window, he rose to leave. "Oh, good God! Oh, God help us!"

"What?" Mother asked, her voice shrill.

Norman dashed out the door with his cap and the letters in hand. The school-age children ran out after him, leaving Mother behind with the youngest ones. He watched as his truck picked up speed and rolled down the hill with a kid behind the wheel.

Norman ran as fast as he could, waving his arms. His hat blew off his head, but he held on to the letters. "Watch out! Get out of the way!" he yelled.

A bunch of neighbors ran outside and yelled, "Get out of the way. Watch out!"

Kaylee, Mary, and Joey chased Norman as the truck flew through the bushes in the Murphys' yard, crossed the street to take out the O'Learys' white picket fence, then barreled through the Mullarkeys' yard before coming to a stop in the Flannerys' hedges.

Kaylee and Joey reached the truck before Norman, who was out of breath. Marty Mullarkey crawled out of the truck, crawled through the bushes, then scampered off.

"Ya better run fast, Marty," yelled Joey, cheering him on and ratting him out all at once.

That night, the neighbors argued over who should fix the fence, Norman or the Mullarkeys.

The next day Mr. Mullarkey showed up with a cigar in his mouth, a tool belt around his waist, and a shovel in his hand.

Meanwhile, Kaylee couldn't wait to go to church on Sunday so she could get to the lost-and-found box and get those love letters back. Only two more days. She paced.

* * *

On Sunday, as the family entered the church's vestibule, Kaylee headed for the lost-and-found box.

Mother caught her by the hand. "This way," she whispered.

They made their way up the center aisle, genuflected, piled into the pew, and waited for mass to begin.

Joey and another altar boy led the priest in the procession from the sacristy to the altar. Kaylee leaned into Mary and whispered, "The little stinker looks like a saint."

Mother gazed at the two girls and pointed at Father Cunningham.

The priest raised his hands. "According to the Gospel of John, Jesus healed a paralyzed man at Bethesda in Jerusalem. You, too, can heal by believing in Jesus and the Gospel of John." Then he preached the eighth commandment—Thou shall not bear false witness. His voice commanded, "'False witness.' What does that mean? It means lying, equivocating, deceiving. If you commit those acts, you break the eighth commandment."

The corners of Kaylee's mouth turned down. Mary cracked her knuckles.

Kaylee leaned close to Mary. "How can I equivocate if I don't even know what it means? But I think I can sound it out, maybe even spell it," she whispered.

"It's like lying, only in a roundabout way. Like not telling the whole truth."

"I'm tired of commandments," Kaylee said to Mary.

Mother turned toward them and placed her index finger in front of puckered fish lips, but something distracted her.

Two-year-old cousin Willie J. Reagan recognized Joey and broke away from his mother. The toddler made his way to the altar to pay Joey a visit. Mary and Kaylee grinned and clapped their hands in delight at the scene. Willie J.'s big brother, Frankie, chased after him, but quick little Willie J. saw him coming. He crawled under the altar next to the priest's feet and peeked out. His flaming-red hair fell over his eyes and brushed against the altar's skirt. He pushed his hair away, rubbed his eyes, lay on his belly, and propped his little chin in his hands. Then he waved his feet back and forth and picked his nose.

Kaylee and Mary chuckled uncontrollably, and Mother shot them a "stop the giggles" look. The congregation swayed in their pews and angled their heads for the best view. Father Cunningham raised his arms then collapsed them by his sides.

Kaylee glanced around to see who was watching and spotted Brenda Mullarkey. Brenda stuck her tongue out at Kaylee. Kaylee returned the gesture, allowing her tongue to linger just a little longer, and then crossed her eyes.

"Where's your hat? How did I miss this? Don't you even have a mantilla or a chapel veil?" Mother handed Kaylee a tissue with a bobby pin. "Put this on your head."

"I can't wear that. Brenda will make fun of me. I left my chapel veil here last Sunday. I bet it's in the lost-and-found box," Kaylee whispered.

Mother turned her attention to the scene at the altar. Joey hopped up and down, grinning when Frankie approached. Frankie grabbed Willie J.'s feet and dragged him out from under the altar.

Kaylee slipped past Mother before she could stop her. She made her way to the vestibule, pulled a chapel veil from her pocket, and placed it on her head. Kaylee rummaged through the lost-and-found box.

Oh no. What if Norman didn't put the letters in here? What if Father Cunningham found them and placed them somewhere in his bedroom? How will I get into his bedroom? What am I going to do?

She fumbled around and prayed to St. Anthony to help her find the letters. Finally, she reached under a pile of scarves, and lo and behold, there they were, next to a pair of rimless granny eyeglasses. She could read them with these glasses, Kaylee thought, hoping it wasn't a sin that the letters had been found but not by the person who had lost them. She slipped the letters into her pocket along with the spectacles. She returned to the pew, sat beside Mary, and put on the eyeglasses. "I look smart, right?"

Mary chuckled behind her cupped hand. "Maybe, but you might see better."

"See these?" Kaylee said and slid the letters out from her pocket, just far enough for Mary to have a look. "It's a miracle," whispered Kaylee.

"Why do you want them back?" Mary moaned. "I was hoping to be done with this."

"What if someone else finds them and then finds John?" Kaylee whispered, lowered the eyeglasses over her nose, and grinned.

"Ridiculous." Mary giggled.

Mother threw them one of her looks and shot an elbow into her oldest daughter Courtnay's side. The poke picked up thrust as it rippled through the sisters, starting with Courtnay then Liz then Mary until it landed in Kaylee's side.

"Ouch! That hurts!" Kaylee screamed.

The priest looked up from his prayers, and Mother threw Kaylee a "Wait till we get home" look. When the moment passed, Mary whispered in her lowest possible voice, "We already visited John. We're done with this."

Father Cunningham ended mass with a blessing.

The family piled into the car and waited for Joey to complete his altar boy duties and whatever mischief he could get into in the short time after mass.

"Kaylee, go see what's taking Joey so long. And next time, you will remember to wear something on your head!" Mother said.

Kaylee entered the vestibule and spotted Joey leaving the washroom, holding a bottle of sour water—otherwise known as pee or urine. He walked over to the holy water fountain, poured it in, and hid behind a column. Soon Norman appeared, dipped his fingers in the fountain, and blessed himself. Norman wrinkled his hook nose and sniffed his fingers. His jaw dropped, and his mouth turned down. A disgusted scowl crossed his face. He returned the collection basket to its place and rushed to the bathroom.

"Gross!" Kaylee whined and punched Joey.

"If you tell, I'll kill you," Joey threatened.

"Not if I kill you first," Kaylee said, adding, "Jerk!"

"Shut up!"

"Jerk."

Joey chased Kaylee to the car, calling, "Shut up!"

"Jerk," Kaylee said, timing it so she could get in the last word before climbing back into the car.

When they reached home, Kaylee ducked through the large access doorway at the back of the bedroom closet and entered the attic. She surveyed the rows of insulation and hid the letters under a loose pink fluffy mound. Joey would never find them there. Then she brushed off tufts of the itchy pink stuff and scratched her arms.

A putrid smell hung in the air. Kaylee searched like a bloodhound for the source. Her nose led her to a moldy, rotten old Easter egg. Holding her nose, she picked it up and headed back through the closet door and into the bedroom. "What's this doing here?" Her outstretched hand carried the rotten egg as she headed toward Mary.

Mary waved her arm. "Get rid of it! Get it out of here! Go!"

"Who put this in the attic?"

Mary held her nose. "It had to be Joey since he helps Mother hide the eggs on Easter eve," Mary said in a nasal voice.

"What a jerk." Kaylee threw the egg out the window and peeked out.

Rosemary, the next-door neighbor, stopped bouncing her ball in the driveway and bent over the rotten egg. "P U, it stinks," she yelled.

Joey stepped over to examine it.

Joey would know where the rotten egg had come from. Kaylee backed away from the window, wiped her hands on her blouse, and headed to the attic to move the letters farther to the back.

CHAPTER 19

THE PILLOW FIGHT

Kaylee tucked her report card into her book bag and grimaced. Like the love letters, it was out of sight but not out of mind. Her head hung as she rode the school bus home.

How am I supposed to get good grades if I always have to stand in the back of the classroom while my classmates ace tests I'm not given a chance to take? I get an automatic zero. It's not fair.

As the school bus chugged along, Kaylee, with her stomach in knots, had a death grip on her book bag. Forging a signature in a homework notebook was one thing, but signing a report card was out of the question. Dad always signed them, not Mother, and Kaylee had never practiced Dad's signature. Besides, her brother and sisters would have report cards that needed to be signed. If Kaylee didn't show up with one, it would be a dead giveaway that she was hiding it.

After dinner, Dad sat in the living room, put down the newspaper, and reviewed the collection of report cards. He set Kaylee's aside. Beginning with the oldest, he called each of his children to his side, patted them on the back, and said, "Good job."

"Kaylee Reagan. Come see me!" he shouted.

Kaylee stood before him. Her lips turned down at the corners, and she tucked her clammy hands deep into her pockets.

"What do you have to say for yourself?"

Kaylee shrugged.

"I'm waiting."

Kaylee opened her mouth wide enough to catch a fly, but nothing came out.

Dad tapped the report card on the coffee table as if he were getting ready to shuffle a deck of cards. "You have poor grades and a D for effort. Yet dumb you are not. When you set your mind to something, you can do anything. You're smarter than most, including the neighborhood boys." Dad tapped his finger on the table. "You're the only girl I know who can sew, climb a tree, build a fort and even an igloo. Why don't you show that in school like you do in Girl Scouts?"

"Dad, Girl Scouts is different. There's no dumb row or dumb seats. It's not like school, where they make you stand in the back and miss a test. Besides that, my classmates pick on me."

Dad raised an eyebrow. "Turn your other cheek, and give it a shot. You can do this, Miss Skinny Bones. Smart, you are. Maybe smaller and skinnier than the other kids, but smarter." Dad placed his finger under Kaylee's chin and raised her head. She wiped a tear from the corner of her eye. "How can we help you improve your grades?"

"Will you take us to Palisades Amusement Park or Coney Island if my grades improve?"

"Study. Get decent grades, and I will surprise you and the rest of the family with something you've never seen before and may never see again. Not in your lifetime."

Kaylee smiled. "What is it, Dad?"

"If I tell you, it won't be a surprise, but believe you me, you'll be thrilled."

Kaylee threw her skinny arms around Dad's neck.

Kaylee went to her room, took out her books, and tried to forget about the surprise so she could concentrate on her homework. But the words had lives of their own. Sometimes o's looked like a's, and some letters disappeared.

Before bedtime prayers, Kaylee crept into the attic to retrieve Olivia's letters. Mary was on her bed, reading *Teen Magazine*, when Kaylee slipped back into the bedroom.

Kaylee put on the spectacles she had pinched from the church's lost-and-found box and glanced over Mary's shoulder. "Man, oh man, I can see the shape of words so much better."

Mary closed the pages of the magazine and looked at her. "Maybe you needed glasses all along."

When she finished her homework, Mary listened as Kaylee read a love letter.

To my darling Olivia,

I've enjoyed taking the endless stairs at work. It gives me extra moments to think of you and brings me closer to heaven. But since the elevator works again, there are no long pensive climbs.

We are close to finishing the one hundred second floor of the Empire State Building. In more ways than one, I'm at the top of the world. On a clear day, it's easy to see our favorite place—Central Park.

When we return to the park, we'll stroll beyond the pond, past the statue of Zeus. Then we'll make our way over to the Bethesda Terrace, where an angel perched high atop the fountain looks gracefully over the waters. There, in the center of the park, is where I want to speak to you about our future.

It has been the longest week ever without seeing you, and since I must work this coming weekend, it will be two endless weeks before I see you again.

Oh my darling, you are always in my thoughts. When I close my eyes, your soft touch and the lovely scent of your hair are with me. I can't imagine my life without you.

"I do love nothing in the world so well as you"—Shakespeare

Sincerely, with affection,
John

Kaylee spread her arms wide like angel wings, looked to the heavens, and moaned, "Oh, my darling."

Mary held a lock of her hair below her nose as though she had a mustache. Then she pursed her lips, inhaled deeply, and pressed a palm over her heart. In a singsong voice, Mary quoted Shakespeare. "Oh, sweet love, I do love nothing in the world so well as you." Then she collapsed on the bed, pretending to faint.

Kaylee held her arms high, like Father Cunningham, and in a ghostly voice said, "I'm St. Olivia, and you shall kneel before me and ask for forgiveness for not answering the last of my letters."

"I don't think there is a St. Olivia, but any saint would put these letters back. No, a saint would never have taken them in the first place." Mary pointed at Kaylee. "Saint, you are not."

"Why would I want to be a saint? They all get tortured." Kaylee stuck out her tongue and rolled over like a dying dog.

"No, they don't."

"They do too! Take St. John. He got his head cut off." Kaylee tilted her head to one side and swiped her fingers across her neck. "The painting of his bloody head is in the convent. And look at St. Joan of Arc. She got burned at the stake."

"She's the only one I can think of who got burned."

Kaylee exhaled. "If I'm not a saint, I must be a sinner."

"We're all sinners, some of us worse than others. There are degrees of sin." Mary tapped one index finger on the night table, mimicking Dad. "Take original sin or mortal sin. Those are the bad ones."

"Like if you kill me?"

"Ha ha," Mary said. "That's sacrilegious."

"Sister is sacrilegious. She took away Gladys Dunn's desk, so Gladys had to stand all week."

"Why?"

"Louella said her parents didn't pay the money they pledged to the school."

"Does Sister Killian know that Gladys's father lost his job? Her sister is in my classroom. She has a desk."

Kaylee wagged her finger and bared her teeth. "Your teacher isn't mean like mine."

"Because we're good. Not like you."

Kaylee grabbed her pillow and flung it at Mary. Giggling, Mary tossed it back. Kaylee threw it, and Mary jumped, catching it in midair. The laughter caught little Lizzy's ear, and she scooted in. Before long, the three youngest girls peeked in then returned with their pillows in tow. Lucy, Orla, and Emma jumped on the bed, and then Joey joined them. He beat the girls with their own pillows. Feathers floated like snowflakes and coated the bedroom. Kaylee sneezed, brushed feathers from her hair, and spit one out. Then Joey grabbed Kaylee's pillow and flung it so hard he knocked little Liz off the bed. She landed with a thump and let out a piercing scream that could wake the dead. Liz lay on the floor, her arm twisted in the wrong direction.

Everyone was screaming in horror when the door flew open to reveal Dad. At the sound of his whistle, no one moved, as if playing a game of freeze tag. "What in God's name is going on here?"

Mary drew in a sharp breath. "Joey threw the pillow, but I don't think he meant to hurt Liz." With that, Mary saved Joey's bottom, but Kaylee figured Joey wouldn't get in trouble anyway.

Dad scooped up Liz and left the bedroom.

Kaylee pointed her finger at Joey. "You're a sinner."

"You're no saint."

"I'm holier than thou," Kaylee retorted.

"Drop dead."

"No, you drop dead."

"Drop dead," Joey repeated. Kaylee fell to the floor and played dead. Joey held her down, and Mary tickled her until her stomach hurt from laughing.

Nighttime prayers brought a hush over the Reagan home. When most of the lights flickered out, Kaylee whispered to Mary, "I miss Grandma. Why did we move from the city?"

"Too many sinners there, that's why. Remember the time when Aunt Betty got mugged in the elevator? Dad didn't want to take any chances it could happen to us. So now, Dad has to commute into the city every day. And when Mother needs the car, she gets up early and drives him to the train station. It's funny she had to learn how to drive. I thought Mother would kill us when she backed out of the driveway and hit the telephone pole," Mary said.

"Yeah, Mother wanted to know who moved the pole."

"It's worse when it snows. Then Mother has an excuse to hit things," Mary said.

Kaylee stuck her thumb out. "Or when she picks up hitchhikers in case she needs to be pushed out of a ditch."

The girls giggled. Then the house took one more deep breath and settled into the quiet. It was long into the night before Dad returned from the hospital with Lizzy's arm set in a cast.

CHAPTER 20

THE SPELLING BEE

KAYLEE

S ister Killian stood tall. She picked up the bell and wagged it like a dog's tail, but not a sound emerged from its metal dome. She turned the bell over. "Who removed the clapper?" Her flushed, scowling face demanded an answer, but not a single soul gave her one. Not a single sound was heard.

A loud flatulence emerged from a whoopee cushion as Sister sat down with a huff. Broad grins turned to giggles, and the girls squirmed in their seats, except for Angela, whose eyes widened.

Sister stared the class into quiet then stood and examined the deflated cushion. "Who did this?" she rumbled as if someone might be stupid enough to fess up.

Sister wrote on the blackboard *Not Funny*, which made it even funnier. As she underlined the words, the chalk skipped on the blackboard, emitting a sharp, screechy squeal causing the girls to cringe.

Louella held her hands over her ears. "Ugh."

Sister tried to ring the bell again. Then her face reddened as she slammed the clapper-less bell on her desk. She stood before the class, holding a worthless bell, looking like Kaylee's idea of an under-the-bed monster.

Sister picked up the pointer and tapped it over the words *Not*

Funny. "Each and every single one of you will take a sheet of paper and write these two words—one hundred times."

Louella and Kaylee exchanged glances and cupped their mouths to suppress giggles.

Sister paced the classroom like a brewing storm. She repeatedly slapped her palm with the foot-long ruler, the one with the metal edge, marking each word as she spoke. "When completed, place it on my desk."

Sister slowed her pace, looked at the clock, and took several deep breaths. "Then line up along the wall for the spelling bee."

When the students finished, they stood with their backs to the wall and faced the center of the room.

"When you hear the word, say it, spell it, say it. If you're unsure of the word, you can ask to hear it in a sentence. If you misspell it, sit down. Otherwise, continue standing. The last pupil to remain standing wins the spelling bee."

After three rounds, Kaylee couldn't believe she was still standing. She had come a long way since she'd misspelled ship, ending it with a T instead of a P. Kaylee looked at her classmates. Even Brenda Mullarkey had taken a seat by then, but the words were growing more challenging, and it was Kaylee's turn once again.

"Sincerely," Sister said. Kaylee hesitated. "Miss Kaylee Reagan, it's your turn!"

I remember the word from the love letters. Mary taught me how to divide the word into syllables and sound them out.

"Sincerely, s-i-n-c-e-r-e-l-y, sincerely."

Sister eyes narrowed. "How do you know how to spell that word?"

"There's sin in sincerely. It's the first syllable." Kaylee smiled, and her classmates giggled.

"There must be more to it than that," Sister said.

"My mother makes us write thank-you letters at Christmastime to our aunts and—"

"You better be careful," Sister interrupted.

"But I end my letters with sincerely. Please let me finish explaining."

Sister folded her arms across her chest. "Spell opportunity."

"But I already went."

"Spell it."

"Opportunity, o-p-p-o-r-t-u-n-i-t-y, opportunity."

"Little wonders never cease." Sister added the word Shakespeare to the list of words she wanted Kaylee to spell, and Kaylee spelled it correctly.

"How do you know how to spell Shakespeare?" Sister asked.

"I had a pet turtle named Shakespeare. He got lost once. I thought he died. Keeled over."

More snickers.

"Spell John," Sister said.

Uh oh. She knows. Kaylee shivered, remembering she learned how to spell the other words while reading Olivia and John's love letters.

"Can you use it in a sentence?" Kaylee asked.

A wave of chuckles rippled throughout the classroom.

"It's a boy's name," Sister said. "You don't need to hear it in a sentence. Spell it!"

Kaylee rubbed her temple. "John, J-o-n, John."

"Wrong! Sit down," Sister growled.

Kaylee sat, exhaling a long, slow sigh of relief but disappointed she had forfeited her chance to win the spelling bee. *I could have shown them all, including Brenda Mullarkey. Dad would have been proud.*

Kaylee peered out the window. Next time she got detention, she hoped Sister would send her back to the convent so she could put the letters in the bureau where she had found them. But if Sister already knew they were missing, she would know Kaylee had taken them and later returned them.

There must be a better way. Maybe tomorrow I'll put them in her desk drawer during recess when no one is looking. Perhaps I'll give them to her and say, "Look at what I found on the bus." Maybe not.

On the way home from school, Kaylee decided she'd better get those letters and do something with them. But what?

Before bedtime, Kaylee made her way into the attic to retrieve the letters. She searched frantically, but they were missing. Who could know the hiding place? She could still smell the rotten egg, which stank worse than pee and reminded her of Joey. Kaylee closed her eyes. The vision of Joey and Rosemary bent over the rotten egg leaped into her mind. Had the rotten egg given Joey a clue where to find the letters?

Later that night, when all the lights went out, Kaylee crawled like an inchworm into Joey's bedroom and slid the closet door open. Joey stirred, and Kaylee froze. When he settled into stillness, Kaylee searched his closet, but instead of finding letters, she found several communion hosts, wine, and a clapper. She examined the clapper. It looked like the missing part of Sister Killian's bell. She curled it into her fist, hid the wine and host in the other corner of the closet, and continued her search. Finally, Kaylee found the letters in Joey's book bag. What was he planning on doing with them?

Suddenly, a firm hand wrapped around her arm. "What are you doing?" Joey demanded.

Kaylee punched Joey. "These letters aren't yours."

"They aren't yours either."

"Well, I found them. Finders keepers, losers weepers. What were you planning on doing with them anyway?" asked Kaylee.

Joey made a fist. "Give them to the boys at recess. Save one for the church's bulletin board and the Ladies Auxiliary. Make an airplane and fly it into your classroom window. But first, I'll write your name all over them. Now hand them over."

"Yeah, right. I'll kill you before I hand them over to you. And if you try to take them, I'll rat on how Norman blessed himself with your rotten holy pee water."

"Prove it."

"I found your smelly holy-water bottle, and I'll give it to Mother if you don't bug off."

Joey only squeezed her arm tighter.

"Let go. Just you try to find the communion host and wine that were in your closet."

Joey loosened his grip and turned his gaze to the closet.

"I swear I'll give them to Mother along with the pee bottle,"

Kaylee threatened. "You're going to help me break into Sister Killian's bedroom so I can put these letters back."

Joey let go of her arm, grinned, and went to check the corner of his closet where Kaylee had found the things he'd taken. After coming up empty, he hummed like a bee. "A break-in. Hmm. Could be fun." He rubbed the nape of his neck. "Breaking into a convent... interesting, but a break-in is to rob something, not to deliver something."

Kaylee knuckle-rubbed Joey's noggin. "Don't get any big ideas. There's nothing you would want from a nun's bedroom."

"Well, you found something. We'll see. I'll help you if you give me back my host and wine and keep your big mouth shut about the pee."

Kaylee pointed to the other corner of the closet. "You'll find them there."

Joey rubbed his hands together as though he were scheming a plan and turned to Kaylee. "You don't want to get caught with that clapper. Sister Kill will kill."

Kaylee clutched the ringer in her fist. She guarded the letters, slipped out of the bedroom, and closed the door.

CHAPTER 21

THE BREAK-IN

KAYLEE AND JOEY

One afternoon, when a storm threatened and the last school buses pulled away, Kaylee and Joey crawled out from beneath the schoolyard's bushes. They looked both ways before dashing across the street to the convent's garden. A few leaves rustled in the wind above the statue of the Blessed Mother Mary.

Kaylee pointed. "That's Sister Killian's room. I remember seeing the statue from her window."

The matchbox-sized bedroom occupied the first floor of the two-story redbrick convent. A row of plain, white-framed windows lined the side of the convent and appeared to have glaring eyes. Stained glass marked the last of the windows near the back where the chapel sat. Several bushes ran along the base of the building.

Joey glanced at the redbrick building. "The window is too high up."

"No kidding. That's why you're here. Get down, and I'll climb on your shoulders, then you can straighten up." Kaylee balanced on Joey's shoulders, and he stood tall enough for her to reach the windowsill.

"It won't budge." Kaylee slid from Joey's shoulders.

"It's probably locked."

"No, I unlocked it when I was in detention. I'll bet it's still unlocked."

"What now?" Joey asked.

"I'm going to lace my fingers together like a stirrup and hold them tight." Kaylee demonstrated, and when Joey was ready, he placed his foot in her hands and hoisted himself up. Joey cupped his hands against the window to block the afternoon sun.

"It's dark and hard to see," Joey said, "but something is moving."

"Ouch." Kaylee moaned at the effort of holding up Joey and broke her clasp.

Joey fell, almost knocking her over. They scooted behind some bushes and waited.

"See if the coast is clear," said Joey.

Kaylee climbed back onto Joey's shoulder and, this time, pushed the window open and climbed inside. Then she leaned out. "Throw me the letters."

Joey threw them, but she missed the catch.

"I hear footsteps. I gotta hide," she said in a loud whisper then closed the window and slid under the bed just as the bedroom door opened. Kaylee clenched her teeth and lay as still as a statue. Her eyes followed the hemline of a big black habit swaying over shiny black shoes as someone paced the room. The shoes stopped inches from Kaylee's head. Kaylee held her breath until the shoes turned and made their way to the window.

Stay still. Don't panic. Mother will kill me. She'll lock me in the confessional booth for life. No red licorice.

The shoes marched their way over to the bed and turned. Then the bed sank to the tip of Kaylee's nose. Kaylee bit her tongue, squeezed her eyes shut, and prayed. Suddenly the bed sprang back, and the black shoes went out the door. The door closed behind them.

Kaylee slid out from under the bed, opened the window, and yelled to Joey. "Hurry!"

"Ya mean Sister Killian didn't kill ya?" Joey tossed the letters to Kaylee, and she caught them on the second try.

She found the key in the night table drawer and was about to put the letters in the locked drawer of the bureau when she heard footsteps coming down the hall.

"Shucks," she whispered. Kaylee tossed the letters on the bed, threw the curtains out the window, and slid down them. The rod tore from the wall, slamming against the windowpane. The glass shattered, and shards flew. Joey paused long enough to throw Brenda Mullarkey's purple hair ribbon onto the windowsill.

Kaylee and Joey raced off like squirming bottle rockets, rounded the side of the convent, and hid. After a few seconds, they peeked around the corner then bounded like hellfire was leaping at their heels. Kaylee huffed as their pace quickened. It took more than an hour to scoot home. Panting, they shot in through the kitchen door only moments after Dad's whistle sounded.

"Why are you two out of breath?" Dad asked.

"Playing a game," Kaylee answered.

"What kind of game?"

"Hide-and-seek," Joey answered.

Dad raised an eyebrow. "How do you get winded playing hide-and-seek?"

"It was more like tag," Kaylee said, trying to calm her breathing.

Dad raised his eyebrow and eyed them, but before he could say anything else, the smoke alarm sounded.

Joey covered his ears. "Supper's ready."

Mary rolled her eyes. They all smelled burnt meatloaf and knew the baking dish that held it would have to be soaked to come clean. "I'll do the dishes for you tomorrow if you do them for me tonight," Mary told Kaylee.

Kaylee sniffed the air. "No way," she said and turned to pick up a ringing telephone.

But Joey grabbed it first. "Hello, who is this?"

Kaylee leaned in to listen.

"This is Sister Killian. Is this the Reagans' residence?"

"Wrong number," Joey answered and hung up the phone.

CHAPTER 22

SISTER KILLIAN ~ THE CONFRONTATION

Sister Killian's fingers grasped the telephone. "Good evening," she said as she wound a purple ribbon around her hand. "May I please speak with Mrs. Mullarkey?"

"Speaking."

"This is Sister Killian. There has been trouble in the convent garden. It occurred after school. Does Brenda know anything about it?"

"What kind of trouble?"

"Trouble with a capital T. Now please ask Brenda what she knows about it."

"Why would she know anything? She came right in to do her homework after getting off the bus. I signed her homework notebook to confirm she completed the assignment."

"Which assignment was that?" Sister asked, using the question as a test.

"The one on catechism."

"Which one exactly?"

"The one on the sacrament of Confirmation."

Satisfied, Sister said, "I'm glad Brenda is diligent." Without saying goodbye, Sister hung up the phone. But Sister Killian had not finished with her calls.

At the Reagan house, Kaylee was collecting dinner plates from the cupboard while Mother juggled utensils as the telephone rang. Mother lifted the receiver and raised her shoulder, holding the phone against one ear while whipping lumps from the mashed potatoes. "Hello, this is the Reagan residence."

Sister Killian's voice squawked loudly enough that Kaylee could hear her through the earpiece. Sister yapped about trouble and wanted to know if Kaylee had gotten off the bus at the appointed hour.

"I believe she did, but I was busy preparing for this evening's meal. Hold on." Mother cupped her hand over the mouthpiece and turned to Kaylee. "Did you get off the bus this afternoon?"

Kaylee placed the dishes on the kitchen table and crossed her fingers behind her back. "Of course," Kaylee said. "Same as usual. How else would I get home?"

Mother set down the potato beater, wiped her hands on her stained apron, and held the receiver to her ear. "Yes, Kaylee came home as usual after school." The sound of a forceful click shot through the line, causing Mother to drop the phone.

Mother set a dish of meatloaf on the table and took off her apron. "Everyone sit and say grace before supper gets cold."

After grace, Mother turned to Dad. "Sister Killian called on the telephone earlier."

Joey slurped his milk.

Kaylee cleared her throat and, looking at Dad, said, "Did you have to rescue anyone from stalled elevators today?"

"Not today, but yesterday was a serious situation that could have gone very wrong."

With her eyes wide, Kaylee asked, "Why? What happened?"

"Three kids snuck into an elevator shaft and climbed around the floors," Dad said. "Two stupid boys, up to their old tricks, tried to impress a girl. This time they climbed ten floors. Then the girl looked down and screamed. People in the elevator pressed the alarm, and the firemen came to determine whether to evacuate the building."

"Geez, I wish I was there to see it," said Kaylee.

"I wish I was there to climb in and save the girl," said Joey.

Dad smiled then continued, "I led three firemen up the shaft to rescue the kids."

Mother took a deep breath. "I don't like that part of your work. An engineer should not be a rescuer. Westinghouse should hire a rescue crew. Those city kids put both themselves and you in danger. Sneaking into places they have no business being." She shook her head. "My kids would never do such a thing."

Joey and Kaylee exchanged glances.

"I'm beginning to feel glad we moved to the suburbs." Mother scanned the dinner table. "Make sure you eat your vegetables. People are starving in the world."

Kaylee didn't punch Joey or kick him under the table, and Joey didn't attempt to steal food from Kaylee's plate, but he was eyeing Liz's plate.

Their little sister had gotten a lot of attention since breaking her arm. Autographs and corny, dumb sayings like *hard arm, soft heart* had been written on Liz's cast, and Joey had drawn a picture of a pitchfork and a face with horns sticking out of its head.

Liz also got a lot of help from everyone, but none of it affected Joey. Not in the least. Liz got out of clearing the dinner dishes, and that old cast created more work for the rest of the girls.

Mother, hopefully having forgotten about the call from Sister Killian, put extra food on Liz's plate. Liz was beginning to grow dimples and to look chubby.

"She can have my vegetables," Joey said.

Mother sent an "eat your vegetables" look at Joey.

"Nice try," said Kaylee.

The following morning in school, Kaylee slipped the clapper from Sister's bell onto Brenda's desk. Sister drilled the students on honesty before turning to the religion homework. "Recite verbatim the definition of confirmation."

Kaylee stumbled over her response, reciting only the gist of the answer. Then Bratty Brenda answered correctly. Sister Killian instructed Kaylee, "Following lunch, you are to remain in the classroom during recess while the rest of the class goes out to play. Understood?"

Kaylee swallowed hard and bowed her head. *I'm in for a big one.*

While the children played outside, the ticktock of the clock boomed in the classroom. Kaylee glanced up at the clock's pendulum. It was as though a disapproving finger wagged back and forth with every tick and pounded at her thoughts. *If only I had studied catechism, I would be out to recess, playing with the rest of the class. I'd be a saint and not a sinner. If only…*

Kaylee laid her head on her desk.

"Sit up!" Sister's words knifed through Kaylee.

Kaylee sat up.

"Straight!"

Kaylee pushed her shoulders back and stuck out her small chest.

"Where were you after school yesterday?" Sister quizzed her.

"Playing with my brother Joey."

"Did Joey help you break into my room at the convent?"

Kaylee rolled the question over in her mind. *I helped him. Good thing she is asking the wrong question.* "No."

"Did you remove something from my bureau while in detention?"

"Like what?" Kaylee asked, hoping Sister would say something other than letters so Kaylee could answer no.

Sister glared. "Letters."

Kaylee cringed and crossed her fingers. "No."

Sister held out the Bible. "Swear on it."

Kaylee's mouth quivered. She said, "I wish I never took them."

Dead silence.

"How dare you?" The three words slithered from Sister like a hiss from a snake. Then her words came louder. "How could you?" And louder. "How could you commit such a deceitful sin? You'll have detention every day for a month of Sundays, and I will hold you back."

Kaylee would repeat the fifth grade. Sister would note it on her report card when it was issued at the end of the school year. Everyone, except for Kaylee, would be promoted to the sixth grade. Even Louella.

"You won't have a single friend," Sister told her.

Kaylee held her breath. To fight off a scream, she bit her tongue. She pressed her thumbs into fists and held herself back.

"You will have to repeat the entire year!" Sister seethed through clenched teeth as her lips moved in an exaggerated motion, forming the syllables to every word.

"Take it back, or I won't tell you," Kaylee said in a guttural voice, holding back her anger.

Sister's hands trembled. She glared at Kaylee, walked closer with furious steps, and raised her voice. "Tell me what?"

Kaylee looked into Sister's eyes and quietly said, "I met John."

"You did what?" Sister's voice trembled.

Sister bent down, meeting Kaylee eye to eye. "What are you talking about?" After a long pause, Sister brought her voice down an octave. "How could you possibly meet John? How do you know who he is? Or where he lives? Impossible!"

Silence followed. Sister moved to her desk, sat, and dropped her head into the palms of her hands. She pressed her elbows together on the desktop and narrowed her eyes at Kaylee. "How did you find him?"

"We had tea with a strange lady. I mean, a lady who was a stranger."

"Who are we?"

"Me and my big sister took the train to the address on the envelope. John wasn't there, but we met an old lady wearing a blue dress. It was very blue. The dress looked like my grandma's curtains. She made us tea and did magic tricks."

Sister pursed her lips and rolled her eyes. "Go on."

"That strange lady gave us an address where she thought we might find John. We went there."

Sister thumped her desk with her palms. "What else?"

"There was an older man who knew John. It was his father. And then we met John. He didn't move much."

Sister's voice sounded too quiet. "What do you mean?"

"He did move—I mean, his arms and head and all—but he didn't stand up when we came in or when we left. You know, like most people do. Anyway, I think they do, and—"

"Adults don't need to stand up for children," Sister interrupted before Kaylee could add that crutches had been leaning against the wall.

The toll of the bell signaling the end of recess distracted Kaylee. Sister's hands trembled, and for the first time, Kaylee felt compassion for Sister Killian.

"I'm sorry," Kaylee said. She went to the coat closet, removed a piece of paper from her pale-blue coat pocket, and placed it on the desk in front of Sister Killian. "This is the address the strange tea lady gave us to find him."

Kaylee took her seat as the classmates entered. Sister said nothing, and an odd stillness fell over the classroom. The schoolgirls exchanged puzzled glances.

"Take out your history books and read the next chapter quietly to yourselves," Sister said. "A quiz will follow."

The afternoon remained quiet. It was a different quiet. There was no quiz.

CHAPTER 23

THE SUBSTITUTE

On a foggy morning a week after the confrontation, the school bus pulled up in front of St. Patrick's. Kaylee wiped the condensation from the window and peered out as bells in the tower beckoned students to class. A stranger, clothed in a dark-blue dress, walked from the convent with a suitcase in hand. Something about her was familiar, but Kaylee couldn't put her finger on it. The stranger got into the back of a taxicab.

Children scampered off the bus, splashed, and stomped through oil-slick rain puddles and headed to their classrooms. Sister Killian was nowhere to be seen.

Instead, a substitute teacher announced, "Sister Killian will be away for a while, and I, Mrs. Baxter, shall fill in." She wrote her name on the blackboard.

Whispering and giggling among themselves, the children hung their coats. They filed into seats, but not their typical assigned ones, except for the girls in the smart row, who refused to go anywhere else. Kaylee kept to the last row but moved up a few seats for a better view of the playground.

During roll call, classmates took on new identities. Some chose names depending on whose seat they occupied. Giggles followed. Kaylee became Louella, except she didn't have long, braided hair.

Louella became Molly because she was smart, Sharon became Elizabeth and so on. Brenda stayed Brenda, and Angela Marie stayed Angela Marie. The lively babble of chatter rose. Everyone seemed more alert in their new roles. Finally, the children stood for morning prayer and finished with the Pledge of Allegiance.

Mrs. Baxter distributed a history quiz, and Kaylee wrote Brenda Mullarkey's name at the top of the paper.

Kaylee made sure she answered all the questions wrong, including those she knew. Mrs. Baxter corrected the quizzes during recess and found three sheets of paper with Brenda Mullarkey's name. Not a single paper contained either Kaylee's or Louella's names.

After recess, Mrs. Baxter announced, "Apparently, three Brenda Mullarkeys exist in this classroom. Two Brendas flunked, and one had a 98 percent. Will the real Brenda please raise your hand?"

Brenda raised her hand and proclaimed, "Mine is the one with the 98 percent grade."

"I don't have papers from Kaylee and Louella. The two of you, please stand."

Kaylee stood with her chin up and her shoulders back and glanced at Louella. *I might have a new ally.*

"Both of you will miss recess tomorrow when you retake the test. Now I'll repeat roll call. You will raise your hand and answer 'here' at the sound of your real name, but keep your new seat. Please copy the homework assignment from the blackboard."

Kaylee leaned forward and squinted, as usual.

"Kaylee, please move your seat to the front center of the room, where you will see the blackboard better."

Kaylee dragged her feet as she moved to the front of the classroom.

Later that afternoon, Mrs. Baxter addressed a note to Kaylee's parents suggesting they have her eyes examined and handed it to Kaylee to take home.

After school, Kaylee invited Louella to play, but Louella had other ideas. "So, Kaylee, let's show them and study for the test. We can ace it. Then the teacher will promote both of us to sixth grade."

Kaylee nodded. "Try to remember all the questions that were on the test."

"If we get good grades on the test, let's become blood sisters," Louella said.

With high hopes of acing the test, Kaylee reviewed the homework that evening. First, she put on the eyeglasses she had pinched from the church's lost-and-found box. She couldn't help remembering Mother's hushed moans about money, so she tore up the teacher's note about getting her eyes checked.

The following day, Kaylee wore the eyeglasses and received 100 percent on her test, as did Louella. Kaylee was off to a new start with a new grade, a new smile, and a pat on her back from Mrs. Baxter.

"You could have told me you have spectacles," Mrs. Baxter said.

"I didn't think of it."

"You look smarter with them specs on," Louella said.

"I am smart. At least my dad says I am," Kaylee answered, relieved Mrs. Baxter did not assign seats according to test scores.

I'm turning over a new leaf like Dad said I could.

In the evening, Kaylee asked Dad to please sign her test paper, even though a signature wasn't required. Dad patted Kaylee on the back, the second pat she'd gotten that day.

"We have a new teacher, Mrs. Baxter, and she's nice," Kaylee announced. "I've seen her in church but didn't know who she was."

Mother looked at Kaylee. "I know her. She's on the Ladies Auxiliary committee. She is nice."

"She's smart too. She remembers all our names even when we tried to fake her out, like when we switched seats."

Mother raised her voice. "You did what?"

"It wasn't just me. It was everybody. She ain't forgetful either."

"Isn't," Mother corrected.

"Isn't what?"

"Not *ain't* forgetful. *Isn't* forgetful."

Kaylee smiled. "Oh, that, too, and she doesn't have favorites either."

Kaylee went to her bedroom, placed her test on her bed for Mary to see, and thought about her classroom. Someone was missing, and that someone was Sister Killian. An image of Sister's face flashed in Kaylee's mind. Surprised to find herself wondering about Sister, she closed her eyes and pictured Mrs. Baxter's clothes on Sister Killian. Kaylee's eyes widened.

Was the woman I saw leaving the convent Sister Killian? Wait until I tell Mary.

* * *

The next day, Mrs. Baxter announced she would present a film on menstruation. "If you know the meaning of the word menstruation, please raise your hand."

Three girls raised their hands. The hand of Angela Marie—Miss Know-it-all—stretched high.

"Yes, Angela," Mrs. Baxter said. "Please explain."

"It happens once a month when the full moon makes girls bleed," Angela said.

The students in the class looked about wildly, moaning and grumbling. Then, for a moment, the ticktock of the clock was the only sound that could be heard.

"I suppose there is some relationship to the moon. Both have a monthly cycle," Mrs. Baxter observed. "It means a girl is on her way to becoming a woman, and someday she'll be able to have a baby." Some schoolgirls blinked away surprise and giggled, but most moaned and shivered. Kaylee looked at Angela. She couldn't imagine bleeding. Anyway, how did Angela Marie know so much?

"She must be a bleeder," mouthed Kaylee to Louella.

Louella stared at the crucifix with the blood on the wounds and raised her hand. "So how much do you bleed, and where does it come out?"

Kaylee lifted her arm and pointed. "Your armpit."

Brenda held her nose. "P U, you stink."

Kaylee shot a spitball and hit Brenda in the head.

"You won't get away with that!" Brenda yelled.

Kaylee looked around and raised her shoulders.

Mrs. Baxter surveyed the class, and Brenda raised her hand. "Brenda, would you like to add to the definition, or do you have a question?"

"My question is, do boys bleed?" Brenda asked.

The other students chuckled and squirmed.

Kaylee gloated. Miss Know-it-all didn't know it all.

Mrs. Baxter rang the small bell on her desk. "Quiet, class. Boys don't bleed, at least not when it comes to menstruation."

The janitor wheeled in a film projector. "All set to roll."

Mrs. Baxter pulled down the window shades and the screen, which covered part of the chalkboard. Louella raised her hand.

"You can ask more questions after the movie." Mrs. Baxter turned off the lights.

The film flickered and rolled. Pictures of fallopian tubes, ducts, and ovaries flashed on the screen. Next, a flat voice explained a monthly cycle in vague detail, then an image of a sanitary pad appeared. The sanitary pad looked like the one Peggy had on her head that day in church.

"So you bleed from your head!" Kaylee whispered to Louella.

Louella grinned. "I guess we'll find out for sure."

The narrator also said that when a woman becomes impregnated, the menstruation cycle stops until sometime after giving birth.

Kaylee wondered how women got pregnant. Did their babies just appear like the Virgin Mary? The only thing Kaylee had figured out from watching the film was that impregnated meant pregnant, and that led to birth.

At the end of the film, the students seemed more puzzled than they had before the movie began. The classmates chattered and whispered to one another.

"Quiet, girls," Mrs. Baxter said.

Kaylee raised her hand.

"Yes, Kaylee. What is your question?"

Kaylee didn't know why Mrs. Baxter thought she always had a question. Maybe she had something smart to say—like Angela Marie.

"Do birds and bees have anything to do with how girls get pregnant?" Kaylee asked.

Mrs. Baxter hesitated. "Your mother will fill you in on the details."

"Yeah, she should know since she's pregnant. Again. The stork visited your mother. Not just any bird or bee," Brenda said in her squeaky, sarcastic voice.

Kaylee tried to hide her shock. She couldn't believe her ears, but something told her not to call Brenda a liar. When Mrs. Baxter turned away, Kaylee pointed her middle finger in Brenda's direction.

"Yeah, it has something to do with that." Brenda smirked.

With what? Kaylee didn't understand the meaning of the middle finger. She just knew Joey used it a lot, and he could count on a reaction when he did.

"Pay attention, girls," Mrs. Baxter said. "Some of you will mature faster than others. Therefore, we view the film in the fifth grade. When I was a little girl about your age, my friend began her monthly cycle. She was so frightened by the blood she cried out, 'I'm dying.' Today, you'll learn to know better. When menstruation arises, you will comprehend its meaning."

Louella leaned close to Kaylee. "So, I don't understand for sure, but if this happens to me, at least I'll know I'm not dying."

"I guess it's going to hit all of us. Too bad it can't happen to boys, especially Joey," said Kaylee.

Kaylee raised her hand. "When is Sister Killian coming back?"

Mrs. Baxter shrugged and said nothing. Kaylee hoped that meant Sister would be away a while longer.

Later that evening at the super table, Kaylee looked from her mother to Dad. Joey wiped his milk mustache with his napkin and reached for more milk.

"You better learn to share," Kaylee said.

"Why? You're the one who should share."

"Mother's pregnant," Kaylee said.

Mary dropped her fork, and Joey dropped his jaw.

Joey turned to Mother. "Pregnant?"

"We were going to tell all of you sooner than later," Mother said.

"But can we afford another kid? We already have too many," Joey said.

"Well, which one would you like to put back?" Dad asked.

Joey looked around the table until his eyes rested on Kaylee.

"Don't look at me, you jerk," Kaylee said.

"I would put back Kaylee."

Kaylee glared at Joey. "You should go back to where you belong."

Dad tapped his palms on the table. "None of us can truly imagine life without any one of you. That is how it will be with the new baby," Dad said.

CHAPTER 24

NYC

OLIVIA

Sister Killian, grateful for the hiatus granted by Sister Agatha, arrived on the doorstep of the Leo House dressed as a layperson. She knew she would find comfort and be welcomed at the Catholic guesthouse, situated in Chelsea on Manhattan's west side. Sister checked in as Olivia Hunter.

In the chapel of the guesthouse, Sister Killian joined the small congregation for daily mass. She listened to the sermon on healing powers, inspired by the gospel according to John. "Jesus healed a paralyzed man at the pool of Bethesda," the priest said. "The man, cured after thirty-eight years, carried his bedding away."

Sister had listened to many sermons before. But this time a sense of peace washed over her, and she wondered if there was a particular message for her in the sermon. After mass, she lingered and knelt in prayer before the statue of the Blessed Mother Mary. Then, with rosary beads threaded through her fingers, she made the sign of the cross, genuflected before leaving the chapel, and found a seat in the quiet courtyard. A cardinal alighted on the statue of Our Lady of the Travelers as if recalling its designer, Sister Mary.

Sister Killian closed her eyes in reflection as the sun warmed her face. Light filtered through the small canopy of leaves, spreading a light of lace upon the welcoming statue.

* * *

Sister Killian's thoughts drifted to a time when she had known John. Why had the last of her letters been returned? Had John married? Did he have children? Grandchildren? Who did he live with? Who did he love? Who loved him? If he had a wife, what was she like? Did he still work in construction? Or had he gone back to school?

Sometimes Sister dreamt about John, but when she was awake, she would not allow herself memories of a time when she was happy. It would be too difficult to relive the memories and endure not knowing what had happened to John. She recalled his last hug. She closed her eyes. Her memory shifted to John's gentle touch as a wave of emotions pulsed through her. She believed she would never experience the love of a man again.

Olivia's thoughts continued to drift. It was 1931. The taxicab's horn rang out like a death sentence, calling Olivia to leave the only home she knew. Olivia's mother embraced her at the threshold. She held her mother, her heart heavy with the knowledge she might never see her again. Mrs. Hunter called to her husband, but he did not come to embrace his daughter one last time.

Her father's harsh words haunted her. "Never come back. You disgraced us."

Olivia was pregnant.

Her father had disowned her, and her mother watched their only child walk away with their unborn grandchild.

Olivia's heart pounded as she tried to understand the banishment. She got in the cab and stole one last glance at her home before the taxicab pulled away. Her mother stood in the doorway, her hands over her heart. Sadness showed in her weary eyes and her deep frown. The turned-down corners of her mouth tugged at Olivia's heart. Olivia leaned over and held her stomach. The baby within kicked. A tear dripped down Olivia's cheek.

The cab delivered her to a place where unwed mothers gave birth, a place where the family's name would be spared, a place of untold stories, a place run by the Sisters of Charity. Sadness was in the air. It was in the cries of infants. It was in the eyes of the young, unwed mothers. It was in the waiting.

The pregnant women had one thing in common, but friendships did not form. Perhaps it was a time they wanted to forget. There was little comfort in knowing that they were not alone. Time passed as unborn babies grew in the bellies of mothers, mothers who would not get a chance to mother.

With each passing week, Olivia's belly swelled. Finally, a baby boy entered the world with a cry. Without giving Olivia a chance to hold him, the nuns took him from her.

Later that night, Olivia slipped into the nursery, scooped the infant into her arms, and held him close. The Sisters who kept watch did not pull the baby from her, as Olivia had expected. Perhaps they feared that the new mother's tears would turn into wails that would wake the entire nursery. A soft smile graced Olivia's face as she counted her baby son's fingers and toes and inhaled his sweet baby scent.

She slid the blanket away to reveal the infant's arms and whispered, "John, you have a pretty little birthmark. It looks like a tiny hand on your forearm. The hand of God is watching over you."

Her swollen breasts ached with a longing to care for her son. Then two nuns approached and stood side by side, as if forming a solid wall against her.

"It's time for us to do our work and feed the infant," one nun said.

Olivia, who knew she was holding her baby for the first and only time, looked upon his sweet, tiny face. Tears rolled down her cheeks and trickled onto her swollen breasts. A whine escaped her tightened lips as she slowly and gently placed the baby boy into the Sister's arms. With a sinking heart and extreme fatigue, Olivia cradled her belly, still round from giving birth. Her breasts let down as she heard her baby's cry. The Sisters turned away, her new baby boy in their care. Olivia headed for her bedroom.

Alone on her bed, tears slid down Olivia's face like rain. Olivia wanted to know her son, to nourish him, to watch him grow, to watch him take his first step, hit his first baseball, to celebrate all his birthdays, and know that someday he would have children—her grandchildren. She had named him John Sullivan, after his father.

It wasn't long before the nuns told Olivia to pack her things. It was time for her to go. But, not knowing where to go, she lingered and forced herself to be of use to the nuns so she could see who would take her baby away.

Olivia's mind raced. Who was going to take on her motherly role? Who would hold her son's hand and watch him take his first step? What woman would be granted that joy? Would she be kind to him? Would she take him to the playground? Would she know his favorite color, his favorite food? What she wouldn't know was who the baby resembled, whose eyes he had, or who had given him blond hair.

Before long, a young couple arrived. Olivia clenched the windowsill as she watched them leave with her baby. She watched until they were out of sight, like her own mother had watched Olivia on the day she left home. She closed her eyes to emptiness and sorrow. So much sorrow.

One by one, she watched the other babies leave. One by one, she watched their birth mothers leave without them, their wombs void. New mothers-to-be arrived regularly. Olivia remained, made herself useful, and cared for the expectant mothers and the children born to them. She became a new mother over and over again.

Olivia held on to the memory of her own mother and imagined her standing in the kitchen. She could almost smell freshly baked bread and butter cookies. But then she remembered the day she had left her childhood behind. Her mother's mouth had quivered, and her head turned down as she grieved the loss of her daughter, the loss of her grandchild. Olivia could picture her father, the stubborn set of his jaw, the emptiness in his eyes. Yet his powerful will had kept the family's good name intact, a will against shame. She had wondered what her parents would tell others about her whereabouts. She had thought that perhaps they would say she went away to college, but she wasn't sure how long they could keep her secret or what lies they might conjure up to maintain the farce—the secret.

While at the foundling home, after Olivia had given birth, she had awakened to the sound of someone knocking at her bedroom door. She uncurled herself from a fetal position, pushed herself up from the floor, and smoothed out her dress. A pang of hunger stabbed at her. "Who is it?" she asked.

"You missed dinner again. You must be hungry. Come to our table," a sister said. And a new family had taken root.

After the birth of her baby, Olivia had spent long days in the small chapel of the hospital, praying. She prayed to God and the saints who stood in concrete memory of their goodness and holiness. There, among the cold, solid statues, she found warmth in the little chapel. She found warmth in the rows of candles burning before the Blessed Mother Mary, each lit in hope of an answer to a prayer. Olivia lit a candle. A slotted box beside the candles held coins offered by those seeking answers or relief. Freshly lit candles flickered. Others melted until their flames died out, sending up prayers on the wings of angels.

In the lonely, empty sanctuary of the chapel, she prayed and prayed and knew one day she would become a nun. Her old world had been snatched away. Gone forever. She pushed into a new world, a convent world, a world where she could bury her heart. A current of amnesia and dreams swept away the past. As each day drifted by, she became more absorbed in her new life. Each day brought a deeper indoctrination. Before long, the nuns accepted her into the sisterhood, but not without Olivia confessing her sins. She said her penance. She made her peace.

She had taken her vows. She had vowed to lead her life as a nun. Her new name was Sister Killian.

* * *

Olivia blinked as her mind returned to the present. A lifetime of longing was hidden somewhere below the surface of her consciousness. It was time to pay John a visit. It was time for Olivia to reveal something to John—a secret she had been harboring for over thirty years. And perhaps it was time for John to reveal his truth.

CHAPTER 25

OLIVIA AND JOHN

Sister Killian turned the paper over in her hands. Despite Kaylee Reagan's poor penmanship, she had been able to decipher John Sullivan's current address. With a deep, sharp inhale, she knocked on the apartment door. Her freshly ironed, plain gray dress fell below her knees and matched the color of her simple laced shoes. She took a step backward, stood still, and waited.

Finally, a voice called, "Who is it?"

"Olivia Hunter." She had started to think of herself as Olivia again. Yet she was startled to hear herself say her name from another time, perhaps because she was no longer dressed as a nun—or because she was about to confront her past.

John took a moment to answer. "C-come in," he stammered. "It's open."

Olivia entered with a slow, timid gait and crossed into the living room, a room that held a musty scent and appeared even darker in contrast to the bright outdoor sun. Olivia's hands were trembling. She squinted, resting her eyes on a man reclined in an oversized chair, his feet up on an ottoman.

John's head jerked up. He stared as if an apparition had appeared before him as their eyes met for the first time in over thirty years.

John's breathing paused, and Olivia watched the color drain from his face. Then a gentle, hazy softness seemed to pass over him.

John's blue eyes held a sparkle. "Is it you? Or am I dreaming?"

"Yes, John. It's me," Olivia said, her voice soft and gentle.

"Please sit down." John's voice quivered. He motioned to the couch across from his chair.

Olivia moved to the couch, sat, and scanned the room before fixing her eyes back on John. The tune "Misty" by Johnny Mathis drifted from the radio. A ray of light filtered through the curtains, revealing a room of faded floral wallpaper, yellowed by age. A television, topped with rabbit ears, sat on a metal stand. A full bookcase stood beside it. Across the room, within John's easy reach, the neck of a floor lamp perched over a side table. On the table rested the *Daily News* and a telephone. Crutches leaned against the small table. Above the lamp, Raphael the archangel gazed over the room from a framed painting.

"My God, you are still as beautiful as the day—" John stopped speaking.

Olivia parted her lips, but no more words came. Her mind battled with the past as a flood of emotions washed over her. Her eyes remained fixed on John. A touch of gray streaked his blond hair at the temples and peppered a blond beard. He seemed larger yet smaller all at once. Olivia took in the crutches that were within John's reach. She took it all in— his legs propped up on the ottoman, his stillness, the dusty wheelchair tucked into a corner of the room.

John broke the silence. "I thought I'd lost you forever until a little girl named Kaylee and her sister surprised me with a visit. But I wasn't expecting this. You are here."

Olivia took a deep breath. Anger and an old, familiar ache pinched and gnawed at her insides. She looked at her hands folded in her lap and, without preamble, asked, "What happened? Where have you been? When the last of the letters were returned to me, I tried to find you. You wrote we would once again meet in Central Park, that it would be special. What happened to all the times we shared, the wonders, the magical places we went, the way we felt? All the times I visited the park only to find you were not there." Olivia paused. "I thought I tucked all these memories away, but here they are rushing at me again as though it were yesterday."

The room fell silent.

"Why are you reclined here in this dark, sad room?" Olivia asked. "Why did you stop seeing me? What happened? Didn't you love me?"

"Oh, I loved you." John's voice sounded far away. "It was because of my love for you that I stopped seeing you."

Olivia stiffened. "I don't understand."

John faltered. "As you see, I am only half a man. Even though some feelings have returned, the accident left me paralyzed from the waist down. My legs no longer carry me the way they once did. I couldn't marry you."

Olivia gazed at John's legs. "What happened?"

John took a long, deep inhale. "The scaffolding beneath me collapsed and…" John rested his hands on his legs and looked down. "The doctors told me I wouldn't be able to walk again or father a child. I wanted to marry you, ask for your hand, give us children." John gazed back at Olivia. "Yes, I wanted to propose. I had everything planned." John looked away as his eyes glazed over. "I was planning to get down on one knee beside the Angel of the Waters—the statue atop the fountain at Bethesda Terrace, the fountain in the heart of Central Park. But I could not get down on my knee. As you can see, I could not give you children. You deserved a better man, a better life."

After a long pause, John continued, "It was hard on my parents too. I fell into a coma, and since I was the breadwinner at the time, we could no longer make rent. We moved."

"That's the reason for the returned letters," Olivia said. "I didn't know what happened. You could have told me."

"I'm sorry, Olivia. By the time I woke from the coma, my life had changed drastically. I woke to a new life. I was paralyzed. My parents and I had moved to a more affordable apartment. It was not a sight for your eyes. Knowing you and your kind heart, you might have settled for half a man. A man unable to father a child. I wanted you to be free to live a better life."

Olivia hung her head. Tears welled in her eyes, her chest tightened, and her breathing slowed. She was motionless. Silent. Then the tears came. Olivia caught her breath. She searched for words. Finally, she leaned in and whispered as if in confession, "John…" She cleared her throat. "I don't know how to tell you."

John frowned, looking confused. "Tell me? Tell me what?"

Olivia swallowed, her voice barely audible. "John, you do have a son. We had a son. John, we did have a child." She kept saying it, as if convincing herself as well. She hadn't confessed to anybody outside the church.

The room fell silent until a wail emerged from John. It was a sound Olivia had never heard from a man. Then he just sat for a long time. Finally, his eyes fluttered, and a faint smile played on his mouth. "I dreamed we had a child… a long time ago." John's jaw quivered as he wiped away his tears. "Why did you keep him from me all these years?"

Olivia's mouth dropped open then stretched tight. As if looking for an answer, she turned her gaze to Raphael the archangel.

"What's he like?" John asked. "I want to meet him. I want to meet our son. He must be quite the man by now."

Olivia turned back to John and stared. "I-I don't know where he is." Her words stumbled out.

John shook his head as if to clear it. His lips did not move.

"I only knew him briefly before they took him from my arms," Olivia said.

John sat back, closed his eyes, and waited for Olivia to begin. Olivia turned away, not knowing where to start.

"When my pregnancy became apparent… when I began to show… when I could no longer hide it, my mother questioned me. By then, your letters had stopped, and my letters to you came back in the mail stamped RETURN TO SENDER. My mother looked woefully upon these returned letters. It was as if the letters were stamped with a broken heart. My broken heart. You were gone. I did not know what to do, then my mother confided in my father. My father scorned me. 'Get out!' he yelled."

Olivia paused and bent her head. Her father's words still rang in her ears. "You have disgraced yourself and the family. Get out and never come back. You don't even have a boyfriend."

She continued with her story. "Then he said, 'Why don't you have an abortion? You should terminate the pregnancy.' My mother and I would have nothing to do with that sinful back-alley crime. My mother would never allow it. Abortion is murder in the eyes of the church. And the possibility of openly keeping the baby wasn't a choice. We didn't discuss it. I tried to ask about keeping the baby, but my father was too angry. He told me to stay in my room until I left the house. We never saw each other again."

Olivia pushed herself to stand, wrung her hands, and paced. "Then they sent me away to a home for wayward pregnant girls. The Catholic nuns ran it. I gave birth and stayed for a long time." A bead of sweat broke out on Olivia's forehead. "In a way, I never left. Most of the other girls went home after giving birth, their secrets kept. Everything was taken from me. I hid the letters. I hid it all—you, my baby, my parents, my home… and myself. I had no place to go. You were no longer part of my life. The only thing I had to hang on to was faith. With faith, I became a nun. Yes, a nun. And for whatever reason, faith brought us here to meet again."

John opened his eyes and leaned forward, his expression puzzled, as if not knowing where to start. "If you are a nun, as you say you are, where are your clothes—the habit that nuns wear? Kaylee, the youngster who paid me a visit, mentioned a convent, but I thought she had you confused with someone else."

"I teach at a Catholic school. It felt too strange to come to you dressed in the clothes of a nun."

"It doesn't matter what you wear, Olivia. I love you. I have always loved you. I never stopped loving you. You are a saint for your endurance and for coming to me now."

Olivia moved to the window, leaned on the sill with both hands, closed her eyes, and hung her head. John remained silent as though he sensed she had drifted to another time, another place. Olivia's hands gripped the windowsill as they had some thirty years ago at the foundling hospital.

Olivia stood motionless. In her mind's eye, she was watching a man and a woman leave with her baby. She watched until they were out of sight. Olivia threw her head back and gasped for air.

The curtains of John's window fluttered with the breeze, bringing Olivia back to the present. She turned back to John and moved closer. Olivia's stomach churned in the recalling of that lost time as her thoughts wound back to the time of the Great Depression. Olivia told John of the hollow, numbing void that haunted her after giving the baby up for adoption. She told him of how much she had missed raising their son—his first steps, his first words, his first day of school. Olivia went on about how she would have loved to be with him on the playground and push him on a swing. She told John that each year on their child's birthday, she went into a church, lit a candle, and prayed for all his birthday wishes to come true. It was the only day of the year Olivia consciously went back in time. She prayed their son would have a happy life with loving parents but did not know if that had happened.

"I was practically homeless after our son was born," Olivia said. "As time passed, my only choice, it seemed, was to join the order of the Sisters of Charity. I did. I could never love another man after you."

John shook his head. "The paths we choose. We do our best to make the right decisions with each turn of the page. Yet there are still chapters to be written and new choices to be made."

Olivia wrung her hands. "Sister Agatha granted permission for this visit. At least for a short while, but I feel I must return. In the meantime, I am lodging at the Leo House, where I can take time to think and pray. I have much soul searching to do as I fully consider whether to return to the convent or leave it for good. By leaving forever, I will have broken my vows. Yet if I wait too long, I'm not sure they will take me back. I don't know if I can or want to go back. And I want to see my mother."

John offered his hand. Olivia moved to take it but thought twice and pulled away. Their pinkies caught for a moment like they had years ago. They gazed at each other, and tears welled up in their eyes. "Oh, John, the life we could've had."

They both closed their eyes, each giving in to a flood of tears. The shifting light of the day played across the room, bringing calm into its quiet haze.

Finally, John opened his eyes. "I want to meet my son. *Our* son. I had a dream a long time ago that I would have a little boy, and the hand of God would look after him. God would bless him. In my dream, a birthmark in the shape of a little hand marked his arm. But I was convinced it was just a dream. Impossible to be true."

Olivia leaned closer. "But it is true. God did stamp such a mark upon his arm."

John took her hand and clenched it so she could not pull away.

Olivia turned to John. "I realize now how much you, too, have missed. Perhaps you were spared the agony of knowing." Olivia hesitated. "If… If the scaffold had not collapsed, life would have been so different. If only…"

John squeezed her hand and interrupted her thoughts. "We can't go back and change what happened, Olivia, but we'll move through this, even after all these years. Now let us try to find him."

Olivia placed her other hand over his and looked into the eyes of the only man she had ever loved.

"I'll search for our son."

CHAPTER 26

OLIVIA'S ENCOUNTER WITH A PRIEST

Olivia made the long walk from the Leo House on West 23rd Street to the Foundling Home on East 68th Street.

She shifted her weight from one foot to the other and knocked on the door of the place where she had given birth over thirty years ago. She waited.

A deeply set dark eye peered through a crack before the door swung open. A man wearing a cassock stepped out onto the step, closing the door behind him. A white square in the center of the collar, under his chin, marked a priest's vestment.

"How can I help you, my dear?" he asked.

"Father, this building used to be a foundling hospital."

"I'm aware of the history. The hospital expanded, and in 1958, it moved across the street to Third Avenue. Now how can I be of assistance?"

"I'm looking for adoption records. Can you tell me? Are they stored here?"

"What year was the adoption? The one you are looking for?"

"Nineteen thirty-one."

The priest opened the door and motioned Olivia to follow him into a small office. "Have a seat."

Olivia sat and folded her hands in her lap.

"Was it you who gave up a child?" the priest asked. "Or maybe you are inquiring for a friend, as so many visitors say."

"Y-yes," Olivia sputtered. "I gave up my child. I want to find him."

"Even if we had the documents, the file would be closed, sealed for good."

Olivia sat still and fixed her eyes on a crucifix mounted on the wall.

"You're lucky the orphan trains stopped running by then."

"I… I don't understand."

"They sent scores of children on trains to homes stretching from here to the south and out to the west. By 1929, the practice ended. After that, most of the children stayed here in the New York area. It was easier to maintain supervision."

Sighing, Olivia momentarily closed her eyes. *My son missed being sent away on an orphan train by only a year or two.* A vision of a couple walking away with her infant baby flashed before her. *Maybe he is here in the city.*

The priest stood and waited until Olivia turned back to him. "I wish I could help. The child would be in his thirties now. Let me think." After a pause, he said, "Think of all the facts you know, write them down, then organize your search, remembering he may not want to know you. Or maybe he is looking for you as well."

"There are millions of people in this city, not to mention the suburbs," Olivia said.

"I wish I could be of more help, but it's a good place to start. Know he may not be interested in knowing you. God be with you, my child."

Olivia was grateful he didn't ask more questions and wondered how many women had knocked on this door and had been given the same advice. She wondered if any of them found the child they had given birth to, a child not raised by the birth mother, a child given up for adoption.

Olivia thanked the priest and left. By the time she reached the Leo House, a thought came to her as if heaven sent. She sat at the small desk in her room and listed all the facts she remembered. The baby's birth date—December 14, 1931. His weight—seven pounds, two ounces. His coloring—short locks of strawberry-blond hair, blue eyes. Name given at birth—John Sullivan.

Olivia closed her eyes and recalled touching and counting his teeny fingers and toes. She had slid his little sleeve up and had seen a small birthmark in the shape of a tiny hand. John dreamed of the same birthmark. A little hand stamped upon the baby's arm to hold him, guide him, and watch over him. It must be the hand of God, Olivia thought. She added the words *birthmark in the shape of a hand* to the list of memories that might help her find her baby.

A vigorous rap on the door pierced her thoughts. She set the pen down and opened the door to find a Sister of the house.

"Good afternoon, Olivia." The nun looked her over and smiled.

Olivia hesitated.

"That is your name? Olivia?"

Olivia gave a stiff nod.

"Well… Olivia, Sister Agatha phoned for you." She handed a note to Olivia. "Here's her number. She mentioned something about deciding. Please call her when you can. God bless you."

"Thank you. Is that all for now?" Olivia asked.

Sister nodded.

Olivia closed the door and leaned against the back of it. "Olivia… Olivia," she whispered, listening to the sound of her long-lost name.

She folded the paper with the phone number, opened it, folded it again, and paced restlessly about her small room. *I must decide. Do I return to the school as a nun, request an extended leave to look for my son, or return to John?*

Olivia looked in the mirror then walked to the bed, picked up her rosary beads hanging on the post, and knelt. Her prayers began with the sign of the cross, followed by the Apostles' Creed and the Lord's prayer. Olivia grasped the beads tighter. "Hail Mary full of grace, the Lord is with thee… now and at the hour…" Olivia stopped. *Yes, I am a sinner. I am also a mother.* Olivia stood.

If I find my baby—no, an adult male; a man—will it be more confusing for him to see me as a nun? A nun who took vows, who devoted her life to poverty, chastity, and obedience. Will he want to see me? And what about John? Will I ever see him again if I go back to the convent? How can I choose to break a promise, a vow I made to God? How do I turn away from a family that took care of me when no one else did? I'm so angry, even mean at times. No, I cannot decide now.

Olivia clasped her hands. Something else weighed heavily on her mind. She needed to visit a couple more people, but she wasn't sure she was ready.

Before supper that evening, she called Sister Agatha, asking for her patience.

A few days later, Olivia scoured the phone directories of New York City's five boroughs. Of course, there were many Johns. It was ridiculous that she didn't know his last name. She found a detective agency and called, but they did not search for adopted children.

Olivia returned to John's apartment. She needed more ideas.

Peter and Gordon's "A World Without Love" drifted from the radio. Olivia smiled at the sight of John's living room that appeared much brighter, fresher, and somehow cheerier than before. The curtains billowed over an open window, drawing in the sunny day's fresh air. "Your clean-shaven face suits you," Olivia said as she inhaled the long-lost, and once familiar, scent of Old Spice aftershave. She took in John's crisp blue shirt that brought out the deep blue of his eyes, the same blue eyes she had adored so many years ago.

A whistle from a tea kettle sang from the kitchen. "May I help you with that?" asked Olivia.

"Thanks, but no. I'm handling more things myself these days. Both times you visited, my father's been out walking the neighbor's dog. He's getting up in years, and I must become more able." John reached for his crutches and hobbled his way to the stove. "Tea? I remember you like yours with honey."

"Yes, please. And yours, with milk."

John set the teapot into a cozy and poured in the steaming water.

Olivia moved it to the table and found the teacups in the cupboard. She held one at eye level. "What a pretty rose pattern."

"They were my mother's favorite." John set down his teacup on a saucer. "It was near the end of the Depression when we lost her. She was quite thin at the time and unable to fight off pneumonia."

"I'm sorry for you and your father."

John nodded. "He, of course, took it hard, and to make matters worse, he had to look after me. My cousins chipped in. It was their way of thanking us in return for all the times we fed them during the Depression. They're well, and we see them now and again."

"I'm glad you still have some family," Olivia said.

John set out scones he said his father had bought from the bakery. They sipped their tea.

Olivia set her cup on the saucer, cleared her throat, and said, "I met a priest when I went in search of the hospital where I gave birth. He told me the adoption documents remain sealed, but he gave me an idea, which led me to place an advertisement in the classified section of the *New York Times*." Olivia passed the news clipping to John.

John read the ad aloud. "I suppose there's hope, but I wonder who would even see such an ad."

"I have my faith," Olivia said.

John leaned back in his chair, set his hands on the table, and gazed upward.

"Your thoughts?" Olivia asked.

John gazed back at Olivia. "I was thinking about the wonders of raising a son. I can only imagine what he must be like today."

"I can see him in my mind's eye," Olivia said. "I especially imagine him every December 14, on his birthday, each year growing more lovely than the year before. I'll bet he has your sense of humor, and oh, your smile." Without thinking, Olivia reached out to lay her hand over John's.

"Your curly hair and my smile," John said.

Smiles fell across both their faces. John gently brushed Olivia's dimples with the back of his hand. Then he straightened his posture, but the corner of his lips turned down. "Who would read such an ad? What if we don't find him?"

"People in search of lost loved ones will read it," Olivia said. "The priest remarked that from 1854 to 1929, some two hundred fifty thousand children were put on orphan trains and sent across the country to be adopted. Unfortunately, records were sketchy, as was any supervision. If our child had been born only a couple of years earlier, it would be much more difficult to find him. We should be thankful."

"Even so, it still seems nearly impossible," John replied.

"Yes, but if God wants us to find him, we will."

CHAPTER 27
TOLLING OF THE BELLS
KAYLEE AND LOUELLA

C louds of white dust rose over the playground as Kaylee clapped chalkboard erasers together. Some of the chalk dust settled onto her uniform, and she mused to herself.

Uniforms are not so uniform, but I wish my crumpled mess looked better. Look at Brenda Mullarkey's uniform. The pleats on the skirt of her jumper are crisp and dance when she moves. Mine are rumpled. Threadbare. And I don't have a nice haircut or a pretty ribbon to go with it. Even my bowtie is wimpy.

Kaylee looked down at her worn shoes.

If I can't get new ones, I'll polish these. And I can make my beanie stay on with bobby pins.

Kaylee brushed off white patches of chalk dust from her uniform.

Wait, I'll leave some dust to show I got to do a nifty chore. I'm the queen of eraser clapping.

She smeared a bit more of the white dust from the erasers into the threads of her uniform.

This is good dust. I'm a chosen one, one the teacher likes.

Kaylee slowed the pace of her run during recess so the remaining dust would not blow from her uniform. She showed off her emblem of good behavior a while longer.

But if I run slower, I'll have to be it *until I tag someone else.*

Brenda shouted as she ran by. "The new teacher picked you to clap erasers because she doesn't know how stupid you are!"

"Shut up!" Kaylee called back and raced after her. "Tag, you're it," Kaylee said as she tapped Brenda on the back. She ran with the wind, and the wind blew away the dust.

It was not often a teacher chose Kaylee for a prized chore. Chores were an honor. Well, at least the right ones were. One of the hardest chores was to open the tall window using a long pole. It took careful coordination to place the L-shaped metal part into the keyhole at the top of the window and slide it open.

Following recess, Mrs. Baxter, the substitute teacher, said, "Louella McDermott, please open the window."

Kaylee smiled with pride that her friend Louella was the newly chosen one. Grasping the pole, Louella held it steady with both hands, carefully reached up, and aimed for the L-shaped keyhole. A proud smile spread across her face. Just then, a spitball hit Louella squarely in the ear. One hand let go of the pole to rub away the sting. The pole wavered out of control and smashed through the windowpane, shattered the glass, and scattered a thousand pieces in and out of the classroom.

"Dang. So, dang," Louella said and gasped.

The sound of the glass shattering caused Kaylee to burst out with laughter. Mrs. Baxter flashed a disapproving look her way. Kaylee turned in time to see Brenda hide her pea-shooting straw under a book. She'd get Brenda for that.

Mrs. Baxter continued to allow the students to sit where they wanted. Once again, Kaylee chose the second row. Mrs. Baxter handed out the corrected tests. "Good job," she said as she placed Kaylee's on her desk. Kaylee was beginning to get grades that would have earned the seat she now occupied.

"Sister Killian would be surprised," Kaylee said.

"What did you get?" Brenda asked.

"For me to know and for you to find out," Kaylee said.

Brenda reached to grab the paper from Kaylee, but Kaylee pulled it away just in time. The only thing Kaylee disliked about her seat choice was sitting too close to Brenda Mullarkey, who was still in the first row. Brenda stuck out her tongue at Kaylee.

Kaylee rolled her eyes. "Cat got your tongue, Brenda. What about your mouth? The one that shot a pea through the straw hidden under your book?"

Brenda didn't answer. She slyly maneuvered the straw into her desk and did not bother Kaylee for the rest of the day.

Kaylee grinned. She was gaining ground. Kaylee also beamed at her newfound attention from the substitute teacher. But it still wasn't always easy to keep the sins she would have to reveal at confession to a minimum. She liked how her eyeglasses helped her to see the chalkboard and made her look smart at the same time. Yes, Kaylee was enjoying sitting in the second row, and lately she had not been in trouble.

Mrs. Baxter looked at the clock. "It is time for lunch. Kaylee, you have earned the honor of helping the Sisters sell candy after lunch."

Someone in the first row moaned.

Kaylee ate her lunch faster than usual. She especially liked that she would be rewarded with a couple pieces of free candy for her help, but she always craved more than a few pieces. After lunch, Kaylee joined the Sisters in the main foyer, where the candy was for sale. She eyed the red licorice and remembered she had snatched an extra piece the last time she helped. She had promised herself she would pay for it and was running in arrears.

If I take only one as a reward, I'll be even. But I must have more. I just have to.

"I could steal another one," she said when Louella came by.

"So, you'll have to tell the sin in confession," Louella said.

Kaylee stared at the candy. "That's not a real terrible sin to tell."

Louella rubbed her knees then clasped her hands together in prayer. "So, you'll get extra penance."

Kaylee eyed the red licorice. "What if I didn't plan the theft but just grabbed it on impulse? Then it might be forgiven."

"Yeah, but you might get caught and lose your chance to ring the bell."

Kaylee scratched her head. "You're right. I guess I'll hold off on committing this sin. I wish I could ring the big bell upstairs in the boys' classroom." Just to pull on the rope that hung through the ceiling from the bell tower would be a thrill. Kaylee unconsciously stuffed a piece of red licorice into her mouth. Realizing her mouth was full, she chewed quickly to hide the evidence. She wiped her mouth with the back of her hand and slipped a piece to Louella. Louella chewed it like a horse.

"It's not fair that only the boys get to ring the big bell," Kaylee said.

Louella swallowed the red licorice. "So, that's the best ringing of all. At the beginning and the end of the school day but especially at the end."

The boys in fifth through eighth grade, who were taught by the Brothers, occupied the second floor of St. Patrick's School. On occasion, when the second-floor windows were open, the smack of the Brothers' belt resounded in the air and could be heard in Kaylee's classroom. Sister Killian used to rub her hands together and grin, saying things like "Spare the rod and spoil the child." But with Sister gone, Mrs. Baxter simply closed the windows.

Kaylee knew she wasn't supposed to play near where the boys entered the school or under the windows of their classrooms, but she and Louella planned an adventure. It was the middle of the week, during recess, when Louella pointed to the bushes bordering the boys' entrance that led up to the second floor.

"Over there!" Louella yelled to Kaylee. The girls ran from their playmates and crouched low behind the bushes.

"So, okay. Nobody's watching." Louella pulled her mother's sewing needle from her pocket and unwrapped it. "Let's do it."

Kaylee sucked in her breath as Louella pricked her finger with her mother's sewing needle. "Ouch!"

Louella pricked her own finger, and they touched their fingers together.

"To blood sisters!" Louella said.

"To bloody sisters!"

Louella pulled on her earlobe. "So, maybe we should pierce our ears next. We could thread this sewing needle and sew a loop right through our earlobes. You have to pull it through and push it around every day so the hole doesn't close up. Then we can get real earrings."

"It might hurt," Kaylee said.

"You freeze your earlobes with ice first."

"My mother told my big sister she couldn't get hers pierced until she's emancipated."

"Whatever that means," Louella said.

"Maybe it has something to do with getting pregnant," Kaylee said.

"I don't know 'cause my mother doesn't have pierced ears."

Kaylee scratched her head. "Mine neither."

A few drops of blood trickled down Louella's finger. "So, glad it's not menstruation blood."

"Me too."

Louella pulled two of her mother's Lucky Strike cigarettes from her knee socks, placed one in her mouth, and handed one to Kaylee. "So, dang," she said, "I forgot the matches." They pretended to inhale and blow smoke rings.

"My mother had the baby," Louella said. "It's a girl born early and weighs five pounds. She has the littlest fingers I ever saw. My mother is always trying to feed her more milk. My father wants my mother to quit smoking, but Mother doesn't think it would make any difference. She says she likes it too much."

"Maybe it's why she has a cough." Kaylee looked at her unlit cigarette and smashed it under her foot.

"Let's go," Kaylee said. They crept through the school's side entrance that was used by the boys and went upstairs on tippy-toes.

Louella peered around the corner. "Coast is clear."

With fingers smeared with blood, they softly padded into one of the boys' classrooms—the one with the rope. The one with the bell.

"So, you get the first pull," Louella said.

Kaylee grabbed the rope, pulled hard, and held on. It lifted her up high.

"Let go!" Louella yelled.

Kaylee screamed as she crash-landed with a loud thump.

"Come on. We got to get out of here," Louella said.

"Oweeee." Kaylee rubbed her leg. "I can't move. It hurts."

Just then, Brother Maurice ran into the classroom with a paddle in hand. His mouth fell open. "Girls!" he yelled.

Kaylee left the school in an ambulance.

* * *

"Hello," Mother said, picking up the telephone and smearing it with flour. She pushed the hair from her face with her forearm.

"This is Brother Maurice from St. Patrick's School. Come and get your daughter in the emergency room."

"Oh my God! What happened?"

"She has a sprained ankle. She's lucky she didn't break her leg."

"Kaylee. Right?"

"Yes," Brother Maurice said. "Kaylee has some explaining to do."

Kaylee's mother had heard that before. The sound of Brother Maurice hanging up the phone followed his pronouncement.

Mother arrived at the emergency room, spoke with Brother Maurice and the doctor, then silently wheeled Kaylee to the car in the wheelchair the hospital provided.

"Get in. Start explaining," Mother said.

"Why do you have to be pregnant again?"

"That's not an explanation, and we already went over this."

"Well. Why?"

Mother's knuckles tightened on the steering wheel as they pulled away. "Why would you ask me that?"

"Brenda Mullarkey says you'll never stop having kids. She says we can't afford another kid."

"It's none of her business."

"How much will a new baby cost?"

"You can't put a price on a baby. Now tell me how you hurt your ankle."

"Just swinging a rope, and I didn't let go when I should have."

"Was it a jump rope?"

"Something like that," Kaylee said, relieved they were almost home. Then the car swung into the driveway, just missing Joey's bicycle. Kaylee took a deep breath, pushed the car door open, knocked over the bike, and hobbled into the house.

CHAPTER 28

IN SEARCH OF A SON

MELINDA AND BETH

Thirty-year-old Melinda Spoleto sat in the office of the New York Times, fluffed up her fiery red hair, and gazed into the small circular mirror of her compact. She blotted away a smudge of Romance Red lipstick, closed the makeup case, and scanned the classifieds. Careful not to smear her freshly painted scarlet fingernails, she puckered her lips and blew on them.

Melinda, responsible for editing the paper's obituaries, secretly longed to be a gossip columnist. *If only I had the connections, I could write a column.* Melinda pulled her red lips into a smile and turned the page. Something for which she had been on the lookout caught her eye. Her jaw dropped. With a sharp inhale, she picked up the telephone.

Farther uptown, in Manhattan, Melinda's pregnant friend Beth Abbott answered her telephone on its tenth ring.

"Hi, Beth," Melinda said before Beth could say hello.

"Hi, Melinda."

"There's something you need to see. I found an advertisement in the classifieds."

Beth laughed. "Oh, come on. I thought you had a new boyfriend."

"It's not like that. A man didn't write this ad. A woman wrote it."

"Really? What's going on? What are you searching for?" Beth asked.

"I'm not."

"Well, why are you reading the classifieds?"

"It's part of my job, but this is about you."

Beth giggled. "Did the *National Enquirer* get us mixed up?"

"No, not this issue."

"Okay, then what in God's name are you talking about?" Beth asked.

"I've seen the most interesting post in the newspaper. I always check the classifieds in case something intriguing for you and that handsome husband of yours turns up, and today it did."

"Okay, Sherlock. Stop beating around the bush. What's going on? What have you got?"

"A description of your Harry. Someone is looking for him."

Beth laughed. "Looking for him? He's not wanted by the police, is he?"

"Listen, Beth. Harry's birthday is December 14, right?"

"Yeah."

"Just double-checking. Remember, you mentioned if you and Harry ever had a child, you would be interested in knowing about Harry's biological parents and their medical history? And don't you want to know what kind of people they are? Are they loving? Are they—"

"I can't worry about that. It may seem odd, but Harry wants nothing to do with people who gave him away. I tried to persuade him, but he's not budging. Harry will be angry if I meddle."

"But—"

"But nothing. Look, if they were loving parents, how could they give him up?" Beth interrupted, making it sound more like a statement than a question. "I don't know how anyone could do that. And for whatever reason, I'm no longer interested in any medical history. Besides, there must be many men fitting Harry's description. After all, New York is a big place. I'm going to hang up now so I can finish dinner preparations before he gets home from work."

"Just listen to the ad," Melinda pleaded. "In search of a man born on December 14, 1931. Name at birth—John Sullivan. Seven pounds, two ounces. Strawberry blond hair. Blue eyes—"

"Sounds like it could be thousands of people. It's a coincidence. Got to go. Talk soon."

"Wait!" Melinda yelled. "It goes on."

"What now?"

"Just one more thing. The ad mentions a small birthmark in the shape of a hand." After a moment of silence, Melinda embellished the ad with a bit of a white lie. "I am looking for my son, who was taken from me."

Melinda heard the phone drop.

"Are you all right? Are you all right?" Melinda's voice squeaked, like a broken record. "Beth? Beth, are you there? Oh my God, are you all right?"

"I'm here, Melinda. I had a stabbing pain, and I dropped to the floor."

"Maybe it's a contraction. You're in labor!"

"For a moment, I thought it was a contraction, but it's too soon. It was just a scare—a false alarm. I think I would know if I were in labor. Anyway, this is unbelievable. It sounds like you found Harry's mother. It doesn't seem possible."

"Isn't John the name you chose for the new baby if it's a boy?" Melinda asked.

"Oh my God. I'll have to talk to Harry about this. I'm afraid to phone him at work. He'll worry and rush home, thinking it's time to deliver the baby."

"What is that swishing noise? Did I hear you moan?" asked Melinda.

"Not now!" Beth screamed.

"What's wrong?"

"It's my water! It gushed out like a river bursting through a dam."

Melinda held the phone with both hands. "Stay put. I'll call Harry for you, then I'll rush right over."

* * *

That evening, Beth gave birth to a healthy, beautiful baby boy with blue eyes and tufts of blond hair. Beth held him tenderly and stared in amazement, hardly believing the amount of love filling her heart. He looked like Harry. She held her new baby for a long time until the nurse came in.

"Get some rest," the nurse said. She gently took the newborn from Beth's arms. "He's going to the nursery. I'll bring him back later for his feeding."

Beth watched the nurse stroll away with the infant and could not imagine how anyone could give up a baby. She closed her eyes and thought about Harry, and her heart swelled with love for him. *There's much love to go around.*

Soon Beth opened her eyes to see Harry staring at her in awe. "I didn't want to wake you. They wouldn't let me see you until now." Harry took her hand and looked into her eyes. "He's beautiful, and he's ours." Harry bent over and kissed Beth on the cheek. "And now I have two treasures."

Beth smiled. "Around here, they keep the fathers at bay, but it sounds like the nurse let you visit him."

"I had to slip the nurse a five-dollar bill for a peek at him. And that peek was through the nursery window."

Harry removed his loose tie and sat beside his wife's bed. Blond swatches of hair hung over his forehead. His broad shoulders filled the chair.

Beth thought of the conversation she'd had with Melinda. "He's beautiful, but does he look like a John? Or maybe we should call him something else."

"He looks like a John to me, like a little angel," Harry said. "Why? Is there another name you had in mind?"

A nurse peeked in the room. "Visiting hours are over."

Harry rose and kissed Beth. "Is there something you don't like about the name John?"

"No, not really. Anyway, the nurse needed a name for the birth certificate, so I gave it to her. It may not be too late. We can catch her if you want to change it."

"I'm happy to stay with John."

* * *

The following day, Beth heard a knock on the door of the hospital room.

"Hello, Beth. It's me." Melinda poked her head in through the partially opened door. "May I come in?"

Beth scooted up in bed. "Hello, Melinda. Come in. Did you see the baby?"

Melinda came into the room and set a vase of daisies on the bedside table. "I had a peek at him through the glass window of the nursery." Melinda grinned. "I'll take him if you don't want him."

Beth smiled. "Can you imagine giving him away? I don't know how anyone could give up a child."

"Women have their reasons. It can't be an easy decision."

Melinda took a seat. "Did you tell Harry about the advertisement in the newspaper? His mother, you know, looking for him."

"No. I have caring for an infant on my mind."

"When will you tell him? When the baby is grown?"

Beth rolled her eyes. "Either then or on my deathbed. Besides, it's none of your business."

Melinda stared at Beth. "Guess not. But it is Harry's."

Just then, Harry entered the bedroom. "Hi, sweetheart." He leaned over, gave Beth a kiss and turned to Melinda. "Hello, Red. No need to stop your conversation. Where were you two?"

Beth cleared her throat. "Melinda was just leaving."

Melinda stood and looked at Harry. "Congratulations. She's all yours." Melinda stepped out and closed the door behind her.

"Sit down, Harry." She needed to tell him what Melinda had found in the newspaper. "I've been thinking about... John's name."

Harry interrupted. "We settled that. No need to worry."

CHAPTER 29

HARRY'S PARENTS

LOIS AND DAN

A week passed before the hospital released Beth and baby John. Once home, they soon fell into a comfortable routine.

One evening, when Beth sat on the couch beside Harry, their pinkies touched. Beth said, "Harry, I have to tell you something." She turned to face him as the buzzer rang.

Harry moved across the room to press the intercom button.

"Surprise! It's us!" Harry's parents sang in unison as their voices blurted through the speaker.

Harry pressed the button to buzz them into the building and turned to Beth. "What is it you were about to say?"

"Oh, it's not important. I'll tell you later."

Harry's father, Dan Abbott, a tall, lanky man wearing a fedora and a bow tie, entered the apartment first. He had a bulbous nose, which didn't seem to match the long lines of his face and the narrowness of his cheeks.

Harry's mother, Lois, followed behind her husband. Both had arms full of gifts. She wore her usual pearl necklace and matching earrings. Her long, straight nose complemented her high cheekbones. The brim of her olive-green hat tilted up on one side and matched her pencil skirt.

"Looks like you must have pressed the buzzer with your elbow." Harry grinned as he helped with the packages. "For the first time, come and meet baby John."

"John?" Lois asked.

"John," Harry repeated.

Lois tilted her head and tugged on her pearl earring as if trying to recall something. "Oh my, my," Lois said.

Oh my, my, my, thought Beth.

Dan removed a bottle of champagne from the paper sack and pulled out the stopper. A cork flew, and champagne bubbled over. Harry's father filled the glasses and raised his. "To new baby John." Champagne glasses clinked.

Beth took a sip from her flute and handed it to Harry. "Will you finish this?"

Harry took the glass and smiled. "You know I'd be glad to."

Lois picked the baby up from the bassinet and gently rocked him in her arms. Then, touching her cheek to his head, she looked at Beth. "Why don't you finish your champagne? You're not pregnant any longer."

"I'm nursing him, so it's not a good idea," Beth said, suppressing a frown.

"I have the best feeding solution." Lois handed the baby to her husband. She opened her bag of goods and removed baby formula. Then she held it up, rotating her wrist like a beacon. "This will give you freedom, and I'll be able to look after him so you can run out. More and more mothers are using it."

Beth's jaw quivered, and her temple pulsated. She glanced at Harry with raised eyebrows, but Harry cast his head down and sat in silence.

"That will not happen," Beth said as she took the baby from Dan.

Dan looked from Harry to Lois, cleared his throat, and asked, "Who would care for more champagne?"

"I would," Lois said, holding out her glass.

Beth took the baby to the bedroom for his feeding.

The visit ended with unopened gifts.

After Harry's parents left, the apartment appeared more quiet than usual.

"What was it you wanted to tell me?" Harry asked.

Beth inhaled sharply and put one hand to her temple. "On the day John was born, Melinda gave me some interesting news. Unbeknownst to me, she had been searching for your birth parents since I got pregnant."

"Why? What business is it of hers?" A muscle throbbed above Harry's jaw. "How dare she! How dare she!"

"Just because you don't like her—"

"Who said I didn't like her? It's just that she sticks her nose in everyone else's business and makes a calamity louder than a wood-pecker. She likes gossip."

Beth hesitated. "Melinda thought our child should know his real grandparents, or at the very least, we should learn of their medical history."

Harry raised his voice. "I don't care what Melinda thinks. How would she go about such a thing anyway?"

Beth grinned, trying to make light of the situation. "Melinda poked her nose in the newspaper and found an ad." Beth picked up a book and shook it. A news clipping floated like a leaf from the pages and landed on the couch. Beth reached for it and handed it to Harry, who read the ad. Harry froze.

"I know you never expressed a wish to find your parents, but there may be some truth in what Melinda says. Maybe our son might be very disappointed someday if we denied him an opportunity to know his biological grandmother."

"Well, I'm not interested and never was interested in knowing anyone who gave me away. And I never will be."

"Aren't you the slightest bit curious?"

"Not in the least. I have loving parents who took me in when someone else gave me away. My parents are my parents. So why should I care about someone who wants to meet me after thirty-two years? What would have changed? It's ridiculous. My mother is not someone who placed an ad in a newspaper years after giving birth to me. That woman is thirty-two years too late. She gave birth and abandoned me. I have a proper mother and a real father. They are the ones who took care of me and love me. Now let's leave this one alone."

Weeks passed quickly for Beth as she cared for her new baby boy. Melinda came to visit, bringing red carnations and a soft blue blanket fringed in red. The scent of the flowers mixed with the new baby's talcum powder and dirty diapers.

Beth held up the blanket. "You made this. It's sweet. Thank you."

Melinda sat down. "You're welcome. There's something I have to tell you." Melinda studied her hands and paused.

"Okay. I give up," Beth said. "What are you trying to say? It's not like you to beat around the bush."

"I spoke with the woman who placed the ad in the paper."

"What ad? What woman?" Beth asked, wanting to forget the way Harry had reacted when she told him about the ad. And especially not wanting to relive it.

"The ad in search of Harry."

Harry's harsh words resounded in Beth's ears. "What business is it of hers? How dare she?"

"I'm sorry," Melinda continued. "I felt you might like to know. You should know."

Beth frowned. "It's not your place to say what I should or shouldn't know."

Melinda started to say more, but Beth thought of Harry. Her husband had been firm about this. She didn't want to upset him. "Get out!"

Melinda sat stiffly. Her voice shook. "I've never, ever seen you like this before." Melinda picked up her purse and turned toward Beth. "How could you let this go unanswered? It's not like you. What are you so worried about? You're so close to knowing the mother of your husband, the grandmother of your son."

Beth stood up. "You need to go. It's time for the baby's feeding."

CHAPTER 30

OLIVIA REVISITS JOHN

For several weeks, Olivia stayed at the Leo House, where she spent time reading the Bible, praying, and thinking—knowing her decision about whether to leave the convent must come soon. Often, she walked to John's place, where they drank tea and got to know each other again. On this day, Olivia readied herself and dressed in a simple dress adorned with yellow and orange sunflowers. She wore a white kerchief and dotted her lips with Blossom Pink lipstick.

Sunlight spilled into John's living room, and curtains fluttered in the breeze. "Don't Let The Sun Catch You Crying" drifted from the radio. John rubbed his freshly shaven face, which held a hint of Old Spice.

Olivia smiled at his crisp new clothes. "You look spiffy."

"You look lovely," John said.

Something caught Olivia's eye, and her mouth gaped. An exquisite painting of the Statue of Liberty leaned against the wall. It was as though Lady Liberty's eyes followed Olivia as she moved about the room. The light in her crown shone like the torch she held high.

Olivia moved toward the painting. "We circled her the day we met.

And here she is, alive with hope." Olivia narrowed her eyes on the statue's face.

John grinned. "She towers over the harbor with a four-and-a-half-foot nose. Her mouth is three feet across."

"She's magnificent."

"Until she gets a cold, watch out," said John laughingly.

Olivia rubbed her nose and giggled. "God bless you," she said to the statue.

John braced his arms, grasped his crutches, and rose. "There's more."

He unveiled a large stack of paintings. "This is just a sampling. I took up painting again sometime after my accident." He smiled at Olivia. "What else was I supposed to do anyway?"

He gently flipped each painting, revealing one at a time. "This group are images from Central Park. Sometimes a friend drove me there so I could paint *en plein air*. At times, I took photographs and painted from the images. Here is Simon Bolivar, and here is one of the Falconer. This is Bow Bridge. Cleopatra's Needle. Shakespeare." John went on, flipping through one after another. Each painting was exquisitely finished, and each was marked with the graceful swirl of his signature in the lower right corner.

"There's more. We store some at my cousin's place, where they have more room. But this one is my favorite." John removed a linen draped over a painting.

Olivia gazed at a portrait of her young self with a backdrop of a boat's billowed sail set against an azure sky. The wind spread her curls like wings of a bluebird, and her eyes glistened with love. Her lips were slightly parted. Tears welled in Olivia's eyes.

"You're still beautiful."

The artistry of John's work silenced Olivia. They stood in the quiet for some time until she spoke. "Your work is amazing. It comes from the heart."

"I've had time to study. Books on the subject became my mentor, and well, this"—John pointed to his legs—"gave me the time. I stopped painting for a while, but seeing you again makes me want to pick up the brush once more."

After a brief silence, he put his hands on his stiff legs. "Now let's have our tea."

John pushed his crutches under his arms and moved to the kitchen.

"May I help?" Olivia asked.

"No, I need to do this." He flexed his muscles and smiled. "Even now, I'm getting stronger."

John served tea—his with milk, hers with honey—just like their old ritual. They sipped in the soothing warmth and made small talk.

John placed his cup on the saucer. "Is there much progress in finding our baby? I mean, our son, a grown man. I imagine him with your green eyes and dimples. Maybe he has my thick hair. Maybe it's blond, with a touch of gray." He grinned.

"I bet he's tall and handsome like you," Olivia said. "Every time I pass a young man on the street, I can't help looking into his eyes. Searching. They probably think I'm strange making eye contact." She giggled and straightened at the sound of her own laughter. "Me, who has lived my life as a nun for the past thirty-odd years, looking at men."

John raised his eyebrows and peered at Olivia over his spectacles.

Olivia clasped her hands together. "I haven't exactly found him, but there's some news, and I keep praying for more. There's a woman named Melinda who answered my ad in the classifieds. She told me she knows our son. He's married and has a newborn baby."

John raised his head, and his eyes widened.

"He and his wife are not interested in meeting either of us. But Melinda is keeping my phone number in case anything changes."

John's head fell, his eyes cast down. "Do you know if the new baby —our grandchild—is a boy or a girl?"

Olivia's face lit up. "A boy. There's more. His name is John."

John moved his hand to his forehead, raked his fingers through his hair, and exhaled. "If only—" His words stopped short.

After some time, Olivia spoke. "Sister Agatha telephoned me and wants to know where I am in my search. She said she isn't sure what

I'm looking for but prays for me, hoping I will find it. Perhaps we never stop searching for something."

John took her hand. "Perhaps not. I wasn't looking, and here you are. I found you again. You came back into my life. I loved you once. That love never went away. I still love you," he said, his voice comforting. Soothing. Olivia felt an old stir in her heart yet pulled her hand away.

"I'm a cripple and have no right taking your hand just now," John said. "I'm sorry."

Olivia wasn't expecting this. She wasn't expecting anything and didn't know what to say.

A breeze ruffled the curtains. John sat back and looked pensive. "Let's go out," he said.

"Where?" Olivia asked, eyeing the crutches and feeling unsure of anything these days.

"Central Park. Don't worry. We'll take a cab."

A little later, Olivia held the door as John climbed into a cab and placed the crutches beside him. Before long, the taxi pulled up to an entrance to the park. Olivia braced the crutches as John rose and steadied himself.

"We'll turn to the right, where the way is easier, and find a bench to rest on," John said. He hobbled into the park, and soon they sat within view of a statue. In front of them rose the figure of a military man mounted high on his steed. Front hooves were poised in the air as though ready to charge forward, yet frozen in time.

"A stranger took our photo in front of this noble hero, Simon Bolivar," John reminisced. "He liberated many South American countries from the Spanish empire."

A calm settled over Olivia as she recalled the moment the photo had been taken. She closed her eyes. "I do remember this statue, but something is different. I guess I don't remember it so clearly. I thought it was on a hill."

"You're right. It was on a hill. They moved it. It's still gallant, only in a different place," John said.

Olivia smiled. They stood and strolled along the tree-lined path, stopping at Gapstow Bridge to watch the ducks. Then they slowly made their way to the fountain at Bethesda Terrace.

"This is where I had planned to propose to you." John tapped his leg. "I wanted to get down on one knee. Now I can't even get down on two." John took a deep breath. "I'm sorry. I didn't mean to... I want you to know the earnestness of my feelings. Even with the Depression, I had saved for a ring." John's hand went to his pocket. "Once there was a gold band with a diamond hidden in my pocket." He gazed at the sky. Shakespeare's words ran through him. "'The course of true love never did run smooth.'"

Olivia caught her breath. "How different things would have been."

The clicking sound of hooves drew near, and the couple turned to see a horse-drawn carriage halt and release its passengers.

"May we pet the horse?" John asked.

"Sure," the driver said.

Olivia patted the side of the horse's face. The horse nuzzled her shoulder and whinnied. An unexpected laugh escaped her.

John grinned with delight. "I missed the sound of that."

"The sound of a horse?"

John chuckled. "The sound of your laughter."

Something inside Olivia said, "Me too."

Just then a bluebird fluttered by. Joy was in the air.

It was evening when Olivia returned to her room at the Leo House, and one of the Sisters summoned her back to the telephone.

"Hello, this is Melinda," said the caller.

CHAPTER 31

THE MEETING AT THE DINER

Beth set baby John in his bassinet. He looked like the picture of health as the family settled into their new routine. The telephone rang for the tenth time.

"Hello," said Beth as she picked up the receiver.

"Hi, Beth. It's me," Melinda said. "Please don't hang up."

"You should be sorry for what you did."

"I'm sorry. No, not really sorry, but I do feel bad. Horribly. But come on. You have to be at least a little curious about Harry's birth mother," Melinda said.

"Well, the truth is, I am. I've been thinking about it, but Harry will hear nothing of it."

"I'll set up a secret meeting. Then you can decide if you want to have any involvement or even tell Harry at all," Melinda said.

"It's risky. If I agree to the meeting and decide to do nothing from there, will you let this go?"

"I promise."

Days later, Beth and Melinda formed a plan to meet the woman who claimed to be Harry's biological mother. Beth struggled with the idea of leaving baby John with her mother-in-law to babysit while she and Melinda secretly met Olivia.

Harry's mother, Lois, held the new baby in her arms. "I'm excited to babysit John. Where are you girls off to?" Lois asked as she rocked the baby boy in her arms.

"Oh, just to get out a bit with Melinda. A change of scenery and fresh air will do me good."

"Would you like the baby and me to come along?" Lois asked.

"Oh, goodness, no thanks." Beth's voice was shaky and a little tight. "Melinda wants to surprise me with something, but she didn't say what."

Lois turned expectantly to Melinda, but Melinda ushered Beth outside before she could say any more and closed the door behind them. "We've been friends long enough for me to know you're not good at keeping secrets," Melinda said.

"My mother-in-law would have a conniption if she knew where we're going," Beth said in a huff as she tried to keep up with Melinda.

Melinda rubbed her hands together. "This is going to be good." They strode five more blocks, inhaling the scents of chestnuts and hot pretzels wafting from the stands of street vendors, until they stopped in front of a diner.

"Wait here," Beth said.

Melinda reached for the door handle. "I'm coming in with you to meet her."

"No, wait here."

"Oh, come on. I can't miss this. You might need me. You could kick me under the table to signal me to speak up or something —anything."

"Maybe to shut up." Beth grinned. "But you might be right."

She held the door open for both of them, and the smells of sizzling hamburgers, freshly baked apple pie, and greasy French fries whirled around them. Beth recognized Harry's mother instantly. Harry had the shape of her face, her eyes, and even her full lips.

"She's over there in the third booth," Beth whispered, without pointing.

"How do you know it's her?"

"Just look at her. She's Harry's mother."

The woman rose as they approached. "I'm guessing you're Beth, and you are Melinda," she said as they exchanged handshakes. "I'm Sis... I mean, I'm Olivia."

Melinda and Beth exchanged curious glances. They sat across from her in awkward silence. Beth, grateful for Melinda's company, tried to speak but only stiffened, cleared her throat, and wiped her forehead.

A short, heavyset waitress approached them. The cracking of her chewing gum inadvertently relieved some of the tension. She pulled a pad from her pink apron pocket and a pencil from the bun at the top of her head. Her wide hoop earrings swayed with the gesture. "What can I get you, pretty ladies?"

Olivia broke the silence with orders for tea and glanced at Beth, who nodded.

Melinda set her hands on the table. "I'll have my tea with apple pie. You can add a scoop of vanilla ice cream if the pie is hot. You know, pie a la mode with a cherry on top."

The waitress strode away, taking notes. The tune "I Will Follow Him" by Peggy March drifted from a nearby jukebox.

Olivia began. "Thank you for meeting with me. I'll get right to it. It was thirty-two years ago. I was unmarried, became pregnant, and at the age of eighteen, I gave birth. When my pregnancy became apparent, my father disowned me, and my mother was forced to follow his wishes. He demanded I leave home at once and not return. With the clothes on my back and a small bag, I landed on the doorstep of a foundling hospital run by the Catholic Sisters of Charity. My mother had told me they looked after wayward girls. Sinners. Girls who got into trouble. There, I gave birth to John."

Beth shifted in her seat. Olivia paused and looked down at her hands, which were creased with wrinkles.

Glancing from Beth to Melinda and back to Beth, Olivia paused. The two women remained silent. Olivia wrung her hands and continued, "He was the sweetest little angel, but they did not allow me to hold him." Olivia gazed again at her hands and turned them over as if searching for something. She twisted the gold band on her ring finger.

"They told me he was being adopted. And the parents were ready to take him.

"Late that night, I crept into the nursery and picked up my baby for the first and only time. I cradled him in my arms for hours, then a baby nearby whimpered and woke the attending nun. She and another nun approached me. They insisted I hand the baby over for his feeding. 'Go to your room,' they said. I didn't want to disturb my son or the other infants, so I held back my tears.

"One nun took a moment to remind me of the Depression we were in at the time. 'There are long bread lines just outside our door. At least there is a couple who wants to take him,' she proclaimed. I had no means, not even a place to go. Homeless. I didn't know how I might take care of myself, let alone a baby. Many girls had left their babies on the doorstep, hoping the nuns would find a good family to raise them." Olivia hung her head and said, "I handed over my baby."

The conversation halted when the waitress returned with the tea. She lingered, wiping up crumbs that weren't there. Beth suspected she was well seasoned and knew when something interesting was in the air.

When the waitress moved away from the table, Olivia continued. "Days later, I watched from the window as a couple walked away with my baby." Tears filled Olivia's eyes and rolled down her cheeks. She wiped them away and apologized. "I was distraught for a long time, but never did a day go by when I didn't think of him."

Beth squirmed. Not knowing what to say, she tapped Melinda under the table.

Melinda swallowed hard. "Why now? And where's his father?"

"His father didn't know at the time."

Beth's eyes widened. "Why didn't you tell him?"

"His father, my boyfriend, had disappeared. I didn't know what happened to him until only weeks ago. Thirty-two years ago, we were dating steadily and very much in love. He was busy working long hours. During this time, we exchanged love letters, which I kept, but then his letters stopped coming. I continued writing, but the postman returned my letters. They were stamped RETURN TO SENDER. I tried to phone him. His telephone was disconnected. I went to his apartment. It was empty. I knocked on doors. Some of them opened, but no one knew at the time where the family had gone. Something was terribly wrong, but I didn't know what. Finally, disowned by my parents, I was sent off to give birth. John did not abandon the baby because he never knew he had a son until recently." Olivia paused and took a deep breath. She took a sip from her tea.

"It all sounds so desperately sad and lonely," Melinda said.

Olivia nodded. "As it turned out, my boyfriend—well, my boyfriend at the time—had suffered a horrible accident and became handicapped. Crippled. John didn't want me to know. He said he became half a man and could never give me a child. He kept himself from me, hoping I would have a better life without him."

"And did you?" Beth said.

"I never married any man," Olivia said.

Beth leaned forward. "What do you mean? I see a ring on your finger!" Beth rose to her feet and said, "Come on, Melinda. I've heard enough. The ring on her finger makes no sense."

Melinda shifted but stayed seated.

"Wait, please let me explain," Olivia said. "There's a good explanation. I promise… I married God instead. I became a nun."

"You what?" Beth smirked. "You don't look like a nun. This story sounds far-fetched."

"I had no place to go. The convent of Sisters became my family."

"Then why don't you dress like a nun?" Beth asked.

"How can a sinner, one who gave birth out of wedlock, be allowed to join the convent?" Melinda asked.

"I confessed my sin, and God forgives all."

"I'm confused," Melinda said. "How did you get to this place? It's apparent you left the convent since you're not wearing a nun's habit."

Olivia folded her hands on the table. "It's a long story, but I will try to tell you as simply as possible. Please stay for a little while longer so I can explain."

Beth released a breath she didn't realize she was holding. She sat back and glared.

"While teaching my fifth-grade class, I gave detention to one of my

STRANGERS SAINTS AND SINNERS

students for an act she shouldn't have committed. Her name is Kaylee. I made her sit in the convent across the street from the school until her mother picked her up. While there, she stole love letters—the ones that were exchanged between John and me."

"How did she find these letters? Didn't you hide them away?" Beth asked.

"Yes. I locked away the letters in a drawer, but she found the key. She is a very bold and curious young one. Amazingly, along with her older sister, she tracked down John and visited him, something I tried to do many years ago. Finally, after much ado, she confessed this to me. She met John, but she didn't tell me everything about her visit with him."

"What do you want from us?" Beth asked.

Olivia managed a smile. "I would love to meet my son. My grandson too."

Beth squeezed her hands together as the words conjured up an image of her new baby. Beth couldn't imagine having to say goodbye to a newborn. "Well, I'm sorry for your troubles, but my husband isn't interested in meeting you, and he would be angry if he knew I was here talking to you. It's getting late, and I need to get back to my baby. His grandmother is watching him. She does not know about any of this. She's a good woman. Stubborn but good. She and her husband raised my Harry as if he had been born to them."

"Harry… Harry. That's a nice name," Olivia said.

"If Harry's mother knew we were here talking with you, it would break her heart. She and my father-in-law gave Harry the home and the love he needed when no one else did. No one." Beth squinted as her eyes locked with Olivia's. "Now you come along and want to change all that."

"I would never want to change the relationship Harry has with his mother and father. I just ask that he meet me."

Beth shifted and turned her gaze toward the door.

"If he won't meet me, would he at least consider meeting his father? I mean, his biological father. He's innocent. Innocent. It's true he did not know he was a father until recently." Olivia hesitated.

"Only… well, he had a feeling that came to him in a dream. He dreamt he had a son with the hand of God pressed upon him. He did not know about the baby or the birthmark. I was the only one who knew Harry had a birthmark. I saw it. I can't replace all the lost years or change the past, but if Harry will allow me to meet him or if he would at least meet John, we would be forever grateful."

Beth rose. "I need to go now. I don't think I can do anything for you." Beth turned away.

Melinda rose. "Is there anything Beth and… well, Beth should know about a medical history for the… the one you gave birth to?"

Beth turned back.

"Nothing at all I can think of," Olivia said. "No concerns that I am aware of."

The women turned to leave.

Olivia stood with slumped shoulders. "Please, wait. Take this with you, Beth." She held out a small parcel.

"What is it?" Beth asked.

"It will explain itself. Please take it." Beth took the package, and she and Melinda made their way to the door.

Olivia waved a hand in goodbye, but they were already gone.

CHAPTER 32

A LULLABY

Beth set baby John down for a diaper change. Twisting the cap of the talcum powder, she inhaled its familiar soothing scent before sprinkling baby John's bottom. Beth snuggled him into a fresh diaper and finished nursing him. Then she cradled the infant in her arms and softly sang.

"Lullaby and goodnight.
Sleepyhead, close your eyes.
Mother's right here beside you.
I'll protect you from harm.
You will wake in my arms."

Beth gently kissed his smooth velvety cheek and laid him in his bedroom cradle for his nap. She moved to the kitchen, checked the oven's temperature, and returned to the living room. Taking a seat on the sofa next to her husband, she nervously patted her thighs. The aroma of a baking roast wafted from the kitchen.

"Harry," she began, "there is something I want to tell you. But don't be upset with me."

Harry kissed Beth on the cheek. "How could I possibly be upset with you? You're a lovely, darling wife and mother."

Clasping her hands together, Beth stood and walked to the window.

"Something's bothering you." Harry rose. "Talk to me, Beth. What is it?"

Beth turned to face him, her hands falling to her sides. She scratched the top of her head, a sure sign she was nervous. "Harry, sometimes things take a direction beyond one's control."

"Is there something you did beyond your control? I wish you would just get to the point."

Beth moved closer. "Sit down, Harry. Please try not to interrupt for a bit."

Harry sat and looked up into Beth's eyes.

"I met your mother—your biological mother. Her name is Olivia."

Harry's eyes narrowed, and his voice rose. "You did what?"

Beth's mouth turned down.

"It's hard to believe that you, my wife, would go behind my back." A scowl crossed Harry's face. He rose again and headed to the bedroom, slamming the door shut behind him.

Baby John erupted into an explosive cry. Beth remained where she was, afraid to follow Harry, hoping to give him time to calm himself as well as the baby. Time stood still.

A short while passed before Beth knocked on the bedroom door, entered, picked up the baby, and rocked him to sleep. After laying the baby down, Beth said, "Please, Harry, let me explain."

She sat on the bed beside him. Harry held his head in his hands.

"I'm sorry. It's just that it felt important to take the chance to meet this woman. After all, like it or not, she is our son's biological grand-mother. Let me tell you about her—Olivia, that is. I can explain a little why she did what she did, well… put you up for adoption. I had time to think. The circumstance that led up to…" Beth exhaled sharply and continued, "To a time in a foundling hospital when you were born." Beth carefully selected her words. "I went with Melinda and met her. We went to a diner."

"Oh, Melinda put you up to this, didn't she? It's none of her business. I wish she'd never found out I'm adopted."

"It's not her fault. I could've said no, but I was curious. Besides, there might be some medical history we should know. Anyway, Harry, I spotted her right away when we entered the diner. I knew she was your mother the moment I set my eyes on her—"

"She's not my mother," interrupted Harry.

"Well, biological mother," Beth said. "Harry, you look like her. You have her almond-shaped eyes and the oval of her face. You even have her dimples. She's pretty in an understated way, maybe because her dress was plain and she wore no makeup. We ordered tea, then she told us about the day her parents sent her to a place for unwed mothers, where she eventually gave birth to you."

"What about my biological father? Where was he in all of this?"

Beth, grateful for his interest, said, "His name is John... John Sullivan, but I'll get to that—"

"John?" Harry interrupted. "What? You named our son after him? You've got to be kidding."

Beth crossed her arms. "I didn't know when I chose the name. I tried to tell you later, but the timing was never quite right. Then the next thing you know, the name was on his birth certificate."

Harry narrowed his eyes and locked them with Beth's. "Is there anything else you haven't told me... something else I should know?"

Beth's voice quivered. "Let me start with what I found out at the diner, and when I get to the John part, it will begin to make some sense."

Harry's face wrinkled into a frown, and Beth told Harry the story Olivia had recounted in the diner, starting with how her parents had disowned her and sent her away. She got to the part about Olivia staying on at the foundling hospital after giving birth to care for the young mothers-to-be and the orphans who weren't chosen for new homes.

"Think about it," Beth said. "She stayed for quite some time, and then another surprising change came about for her. Olivia said that she never lost her faith throughout all the hard times. She couldn't imagine ever being with another man and became a nun. The story would have seemed to be very far-fetched had I not met her and heard it with my own ears."

"Why now?" Harry asked. "Why did she wait so long to search for me?"

"I'm not sure, but it has something to do with a schoolgirl by the name of Kaylee who found old love letters or stole them or something. Somehow, she stirred things up. And it was only recently that your father—I mean, your biological father—became aware of you. He had no idea you existed. And he wants to meet you. Surely you can see his innocence in this."

"He can't be too innocent if he became a father out of wedlock," Harry said.

"Well, he couldn't have given you up for adoption if he didn't know he was a father," Beth said. "Besides, we had a scare ourselves. Remember? Before we decided to start a family? How worried we were when I was late? This could have happened to us before we married. It happens more than we know. And why? Because it's a secret. Think of all those children born out of wedlock. Think of all the abortions. And what if Olivia had an abortion?"

"I don't think there were too many abortions going on back then, at least not out in the open," Harry said.

"If Olivia had an abortion, where would you be then? Where would we be? Nowhere," she said before he could answer.

"I can't see it," Harry said. "How do you know for sure these are my birth parents?"

"Olivia described your birthmark. I don't know how she could possibly have known about it."

Harry stood. A shiver moved through him. He rolled his shirt-sleeves down and covered a mark on his arm. A small birthmark in the shape of a hand lay beneath his left sleeve.

"You look like her, and you can't hide that. Will you meet them?" Beth asked.

Harry slowly shook his head. "How could I? How would my parents, the ones who lovingly cared for me, the ones who raised me… How do you think they would feel about this? I can't betray them."

Harry took Beth's hand and held it close to him then dropped it at the sound of the apartment's buzzer. Harry's parents were arriving for their usual Sunday dinner.

Before Beth rushed to the kitchen to finish dinner preparations, she went to the door with Harry to say hello.

Beth looked at Harry's parents with fresh eyes. They wanted to spend time with family, and she wondered about those parents who didn't or couldn't. How lucky Dan and Lois must have felt thirty-two years ago when they adopted Harry. God blessed them with an infant boy who brought so much joy into their lives.

Beth missed her own parents, who lived far upstate. She envied Harry's parents for living nearby, which made visiting easy for them.

When Harry's parents entered the apartment, Dan hung up his fedora and set down an umbrella, even though there was barely a sprinkle in the air. He removed his galoshes and handed flowers to Beth and a bottle of champagne to Harry. Lois set down a package, checked her pearl earrings in the mirror, and removed her pillbox hat. Then she pulled off her kid gloves.

Lois's efforts to maintain the fashion of donning hats had not waned, even though hats were fading as fast as blue jeans were taking over. And the dawn of hippies coincided with the further demise of millinery fashion. She hung her coat on the rack.

A quiet awkwardness hung in the air.

"Is everything all right?"

Harry glanced from Beth to his mother. "Yes, of course."

"Something feels different," Lois said in a low voice.

Dan put on a smile, opened a bottle of champagne, and raised his flute. "Let's toast to a family dynasty. Here's to new birth." Glasses clinked as the smiling couples toasted. "Here's to Abbott's millinery business my father inherited and to Harry when he takes it over, and if we're lucky, eventually to baby John's takeover."

Harry was not the first child to be abandoned in the family. Dan's grandparents died in the flu epidemic of 1918, leaving Dan's father an orphan. Dan's father had still been in high school when his uncle, a New York milliner, took him into his home. It wasn't long before he learned the business of ladies' hat making, which Dan eventually took over. Harry had yet to share his ideas with his father of expanding the business into the rag trade, especially women's dresses, including bridal gowns.

Halfway through dinner, the buzzer sounded. Beth rose and pressed the intercom button.

"Hi, it's me. Melinda." Her voice crackled through the speaker, louder than necessary.

"We're having dinner. I'm sorry," Beth said.

Dan and Lois exchanged glances, and Lois set down her eating utensils.

"Oh, I forgot. It's your Sunday night dinner. Don't worry. I won't stay. I'll just drop off the matching pillow cover I knitted for baby John. You know, it matches the blanket I made," Melinda said.

Beth buzzed Melinda into the building and opened the door. Beth had barely greeted her when Melinda entered the small foyer and followed the short hallway to the dining room. She greeted John and his parents and turned to hand her gift to Beth.

"Thank you. It'll be lovely in John's crib," Beth said, putting emphasis on John's name. "I'm trying not to call him baby or at least to break the habit before he's twelve." Beth giggled.

"By then, we can call him Junior," Melinda said.

"But my name isn't John, so he can't be a junior," Harry said.

"That's right. I forgot. Even though your father is John, he can't be a junior. He could be John the third if you were named John," Melinda said. She swung her long pearl necklace like a lasso and wrapped it around the fingers.

Silence. It was like the music stopped, but there wasn't any music. There wasn't any sound, not even the clinking of silverware against china.

"Well, I guess I best be going so you can finish your dinner. Sorry for the intrusion," Melinda said and scurried out.

"Can someone tell me what in God's name is going on?" Lois asked. She bent her head sideways as though recalling something. "John was Harry's given birth name." The room fell silent.

Beth finally spoke. "I'll try to explain. Melinda answered an ad in the classifieds posted by a woman looking for her son. A son she gave up for adoption. She described Harry's birthmark, so we felt she was legitimate, and Melinda and I met her."

Lois's eyes widened. "Is that where you and Melinda went while I babysat?"

Beth lowered her head and nodded.

"Do you mean to tell me while I was here babysitting for baby John, you and your heartless friend Melinda were off meeting Harry's biological mother? How could you? How could you be so insensitive? To do such a thing? And behind my back? We're the ones who raised Harry. We're the ones who did all the caring. And the loving."

Beth stammered, "I-I thought we should at least like to know our child's medical history."

Lois rubbed her forehead and turned her gaze to Harry. "I was afraid this might happen someday. Harry, did you know about this?"

"No, not at the time."

"If you ever see this woman who thinks she's your mother, then don't see me—your real mother. Come on." She turned to Dan. "Let's go."

"Of course you're my actual mother"—Harry turned to Dan—"and my real father."

"But wait. There's dessert, and you haven't finished your dinner. Please stay," Beth said.

Dan looked at Harry. "You do like running the family business, the business that someday will be yours, don't you... Harry?"

Dan rose and put on his galoshes. Beth walked to the door.

"Don't. We will let ourselves out," Lois said.

"That stupid girl, Melinda!" Harry said after they left.

"At least we know how they feel about this," Beth said.

"Of course that's how they feel, and I don't want to hurt them. After all they did for me and still do, and with the business and all."

Quiet followed until the sound of a baby's cry filled the space. Beth hummed a lullaby.

CHAPTER 33

HARRY AND BETH

When Harry entered the bedroom, a sudden movement caught his eye. He turned in time to see Beth slip something beneath the throw on her chair. "What's that?" he asked.

"Oh, nothing."

"Well, it must be something you're hiding."

"If I tell you, you might get upset, and I don't want you to feel bad."

"You know I'm going to find out anyway. What is it? Does it have something to do with Melinda?" Harry asked.

"It has more to do with Olivia."

"Spill it."

"Okay, but will you let me read something to you?"

"Go on then."

"I have some of the love letters written between your biological parents. Olivia gave me a package before I left the diner. When I opened it, I found these. I'll read a couple to you." Beth looked into Harry's eyes. "There's no harm in listening. She's giving us a peek at her early life with John."

Harry hesitated. After more of Beth's convincing, Harry agreed and listened to Beth's readings.

"Sounds like a true love story," Harry said.

Beth held up a couple of letters. "These were at the bottom of the stack and stamped RETURN TO SENDER. You see, it's all there, the truth... he disappeared without a word, Olivia tried to tell him she was pregnant. It must have been a terrible time for both of them. I know some of the story seems far-fetched, but all the pieces of the puzzle are coming together and making sense. Olivia didn't seem to have any choice in the matter."

"Tragic," Harry said.

"She didn't turn to drugs or alcohol like some have. She didn't have an abortion. She turned to her faith. She became a nun."

Harry cast his eyes downward and rubbed his chin. "I guess Olivia was dealt a bad hand."

Perhaps it's making more sense to Harry, Beth thought. She picked up baby John and sat beside Harry.

Harry leaned into Beth and put his arm around her. "I don't want to meet a nun."

"A nun or not, if I were in her shoes, Harry, I don't know what I would've done. And as for her boyfriend, John... Could you imagine him leaving her because he was a cripple, even though they were in love?"

Harry whispered in Beth's ear, "I would not have left you. I love you too much."

"I know. I love you, too, but we didn't walk the same path." Beth looked away. "It was different for them. Won't you please meet your biological father? You don't have to form a relationship with him."

"No."

Beth moved to the crib, kissed the sleeping baby on the forehead, and turned to Harry. "Let's just take a chance and meet our son's biological grandparents. You wouldn't want to wonder about them for the rest of your life. You must be curious. What if you never get this chance again? What if they die? Knowing them or just meeting them will not hurt your relationship with your mother and father. Let's find a way to convince them. And perhaps someday they'll come around."

"I'm really not interested."

Beth stood and walked into the kitchen. She put the phone number Olivia had passed to her at the diner into her address book.

* * *

It was a week later on a warm spring day when Harry told Beth he had been thinking about meeting his biological mother. Beth called Olivia, who encouraged them to meet her in Central Park.

On the day of the meeting, Harry and Beth left the baby with Lois with the excuse they were taking time for themselves. Hand in hand, the couple walked to Central Park and waited at an east entrance for Olivia to appear.

Beth stood at the corner of 66th Street and looked up and down Fifth Avenue before spotting Olivia. "Too bad your biological father is not with her."

"Just meeting Olivia is more than enough."

Olivia reached the couple and offered an outstretched, trembling hand to Harry. "I'm Olivia."

"I'm Harry," he said, his voice uneasy. He shook her hand.

"I'll meet you later by the boat pond," Beth said, referring to the ornamental pond where enthusiasts remotely maneuvered miniature sailboats or rented life-size rowboats. She looked over her shoulder at Harry and Olivia as she walked away.

"Fine," said Harry.

He and Olivia strolled along the path in silence. Olivia cleared her throat and made small talk about how the weather was warming and how summer would be here before long. Harry remained silent.

They paused in front of the statue of Shakespeare. "I don't know where to begin," Olivia said. "Perhaps Beth has relayed my situation to you. I don't want to upset you or your family and your relationship with your parents. I imagine you feel I don't deserve to know you, and perhaps I don't. But I do want to say I'm grateful for your parents adopting you. I'm sorry that I didn't feel capable of taking care of you. I hardly knew how to take care of myself. There were several things that made it a difficult time. I'd rather not get into them now unless you want to know more."

"Can you tell me about my biological father?"

"He was... no, he *is* a very loving and caring man. A man who wanted the best for me. If he had known of you, I believe matters would have been different somehow."

"Why didn't he know?"

"John had a terrible accident, an accident so bad it separated us. It was during the Depression. The accident on the job did more than put him out of work. He's a good man, and until then he took good care of his parents. He paid the rent and cared for relatives. His relatives were less fortunate than he was. At least, less fortunate at the time. After the accident John was in a coma, and his family had to move to something more affordable. That is when my letters were returned."

Olivia said more, some of which Harry had learned from the letters. They continued to stroll, and the conversation halted.

After a time, Olivia asked, "Would you like to see an old photo of John and myself?"

Harry affirmed with a nod.

Olivia produced the photo, and Harry gazed at the picture. He could not help but see the resemblance between the man in the photo and himself. There was no denying it. Even though he resembled Olivia, it was as though he was looking at himself in a mirror, transported to another era, sometime in the past. He saw himself dressed in clothes he didn't recognize, standing beside a woman, their pinky fingers locked together.

He felt himself soften. "Sometimes I hold Beth's pinky finger in mine. It was a habit that began early in our relationship. May I keep the photo?"

"Oh, please do. You have his hair and a cowlick, too, except John's was above his left temple. I used to tease him about it, and he would say jokingly, 'A cow licked my hair, and so it got stuck in a swirl.'" She smiled at Harry.

Harry smiled at Olivia for the first time. "Sounds like he has a sense of humor."

"Yes, he does. And he's also smart, kind, and handsome. Besides taking care of family, he was known to make sandwiches for the homeless."

"What's he like now? Can he get around?"

"He's the same lovely man he's always been except not as mobile and naturally has put on some weight. But that seems to be changing, improving. He gets about with crutches."

"What kind of relationship do you have with him now?" Harry asked.

Olivia looked away as though she hadn't expected the question. "We're certainly friends, but frankly, beyond that… well, honestly, I'm not sure. I realize this is odd, but I'm still a nun, even though I'm not wearing a nun's habit. I'm praying and taking some time to decide how to go forward. The Sister who is principal of the school where I teach has been exceptionally patient as she waits to hear from me."

"I hope you find your answer." He paused. "No, I'm sure you will."

Olivia glanced at Harry. "I hope one day you and John meet."

Harry didn't answer.

"John had a dream about a child who had a birthmark in the shape of a tiny hand. Perhaps God had a way of telling him he had become a father." Olivia hesitated then asked, "Would you be so kind as to let me see the birthmark on your arm? May I see it, please?"

Harry rolled up his right sleeve. "What birthmark?" he asked and laughed.

Olivia smiled. "You have your father's sense of humor."

Harry rolled up the left sleeve for Olivia to see a birthmark she hadn't seen for over thirty-two years. Her mouth gaped open. She caught her breath.

"Thank you," she said in a low voice then looked away to contain the tears welling in her eyes. After Olivia composed herself, she said, "Thank God for that birthmark. It's largely responsible for us meeting here today."

They walked along a path until they reached the boat pond where

Beth waited. Olivia reached out to take Harry's arm but then withdrew her hand.

Sensing the motherly instinct, Beth reached out and took Olivia's hand. Olivia placed her free hand over Beth's. Each held onto a peaceful grace.

"This has been a blessing, thank you." Olivia turned to Harry. "Will you meet your biological father?"

"We have your telephone number," Harry said before Beth could answer.

They said their goodbyes, and Olivia walked away with a slight lilt in her step.

CHAPTER 34

MAY PROCESSION

KAYLEE

Once Kaylee had finished washing the supper dishes, she polished her saddle shoes and handwashed her school uniform to ensure it would not disappear in a heap of laundry.

"Squeeze out the moisture by rolling it between two towels. Like this," Mary said. Then, using an iron, she showed how to press out the creases and put the pleats back in the uniform skirt. Kaylee took over the tricky process. Steam sizzled, rising from the hot iron as she glided the iron back and forth. Determined, she pressed in pride and pressed out teasing. Finally, she hung up the uniform, and by morning, it was completely dry.

Kaylee slipped the jumper over her white blouse with the Peter Pan collar. After snapping on a bow tie and putting on polished saddle shoes, she inspected herself in the long mirror at the end of the hallway.

"Neato," Mary said. "You'll have to fix up the blouse and knee socks next time since they look even worse than before against your crisp jumper. Just do it the same way, and you'll look brand new."

I am new, Kaylee thought as she rode the school bus. She smiled the entire ride. No one picked on her.

Spring was in the air. Mrs. Baxter opened the windows in the classroom, welcoming in a fresh breeze. Classmates took turns reading aloud. A bluebird flew in and lit on Angela Marie's head then hopped off, leaving a piece of her hair sticking straight up in the air.

"So your halo fell off," Louella said, making the girls giggle.

The bluebird alighted on Kaylee's pen before flying out the open window.

"Neato," Kaylee said. She hooked her thumbs together and wiggled her fingers like bird wings.

Mrs. Baxter stood in front of the class. "The bluebird is a symbol of joy, of happiness, of good things to come. It will help set you free. It brings to mind Ecclesiastes 3:1-8. *To everything there is a season, a time for every activity under heaven. A time to be born and a time to die. A time to plant and a time to harvest. A time to kill and a time to heal.*"

Mrs. Baxter looked over at her flock. "And heal, we will."

She gave Louella the job of handing each girl a piece of paper and a blue satin ribbon. "Now girls, this is the season for dreaming. You will each write your dreams, hopes, and prayers on the paper, roll it into a scroll, then tie it with the blue ribbon. This afternoon we will, along with all our schoolmates, join in the May procession. You will place your scrolls in the bin at the foot of the Blessed Mother Mary in the convent's garden. Mother Mary will send your wishes to heaven."

Kaylee thought for a long time about her dreams. She wrote:

> *Dear Mary, mother of God,*
> *Please bless Mother, especially because she's pregnant.*
> *Please help me get good grades so we can go to the*
> *   World's Fair or somewhere just as good. Then I*
> *   won't have to play hooky next year.*
> *Please help Mary become a concert pianist. Mrs. Clef*
> *   says she's real good.*
> *Please help Joey and make him a priest. Mother would*
> *   like that, even though that probably won't happen.*

Please bless Sister Killian and make her a happy
*   person. I think she once was.*
Please find a wonderful home for Patches.
Please bless the whole family. Dad too.
Oh, and my classmates, too, I guess.
Amen

Kaylee rolled up her paper and tied it with a blue ribbon.

After lunch, the entire student body formed a line that stretched around the playground and far down the street. The Brothers shepherded their flock in a straight line to the convent's garden. Each schoolmate dropped their scroll into a barrel set before the statue of the Blessed Virgin Mary. Kaylee stole a glance at what had once been Sister Killian's bedroom window. Repairs had been made since the day Kaylee and Joey conspired in the garden to return the letters. A shiver ran through Kaylee. She dropped her scroll into the barrel and looked up into the statue's eyes. Kaylee felt as though the Blessed Mother smiled down upon her.

Sister Agatha led with a prayer. "Hail Mary, full of grace. The Lord is with you. Blessed are thou among women, and blessed is the fruit of thy womb, Jesus. Holy Mary, Mother of God, pray for us sinners, now and at the hour of our death. Amen."

Father Halligan lit the papers in the barrel. Flames burst and danced as smoke rose to heaven, carrying prayers, hopes, and dreams with it. Blessed Mother Mary's song rang out.

Immaculate Mary,
Your praises we sing.
You reign now in splendor
With Jesus Our King.
Ave, Ave, Ave Maria.
Ave, Ave Maria.

In heaven, the blessed your glory proclaim.
On earth, your children invoke your sweet name.

Ave, Ave, Ave Maria.
Ave, Ave Maria.

Kaylee glanced again at Sister Killian's bedroom window. She suspected that something she had done—something to do with the letters—was partly responsible for Sister's disappearance. Though what exactly, she didn't know. Kaylee prayed to the Blessed Mother to send extra blessings to Sister Killian.

When Kaylee arrived home from school, her mother handed her a letter that had come in the mail. Kaylee had never received a letter before. She had written thank-you notes to aunts at Christmas at the request of her mother, but outgoing mail was the only mail experience Kaylee had. So excitedly she tore open her first incoming letter.

Dear Kaylee Reagan,

In an answer to prayers, I have a new beginning in my life. If you are wondering about the letters and how they might be related to my new life, I can only say it has made an impact.

You were wrong to go into my private belongings and take what you did. I'm sure you have confessed your sins, asked for forgiveness, and did your penance as I have. I forgive you. I am also sorry we did not see eye to eye.

I am told you are doing well in class, as I have inquired about you. May you shine in your journey forward. Build on all your good qualities of inquisitiveness, intelligence, and even rambunctiousness but only when warranted.

Go forth, and may God be with you,

Sincerely,
Sister Killian, Olivia Hunter
P.S. There is a bluebird singing in my garden.

Kaylee noted the return address on the envelope and knew she would exchange letters. She held the letter close to her chest.

CHAPTER 35

REPORT CARD

KAYLEE

When Kaylee finished her after-dinner chores, Dad summoned her to the living room. Kaylee stood before him and fidgeted with her sleeve. Dad set the last report card of the school year down on the newspaper. Kaylee looked him in the eye and smiled, hoping her improvements would be good enough that she could go on vacation, as he had promised.

"Sit down, Kaylee. We have something to discuss."

Kaylee sat on the couch, knees together, just as Mother had taught her. She sat still and waited.

Dad drummed his fingers on the table. "You've done a fine job, and your teacher promoted you to the sixth grade. Applied yourself, you did. Paid off, it did. I'm proud of you, and so is Mother, and the good news is the whole family will go to the World's Fair."

Kaylee jumped from the couch and threw her arms around Dad. "What will it be like? How much will it cost? Is it like going to the circus?"

"It's that and much more. It costs two dollars for adults and one dollar for kids under twelve. But there are other expenses, so save your nickels. First, we'll go to the UNICEF building. It's like going to Disneyland, thanks to good old Walt. All you kids will love it. Then we'll go to the Vatican Pavilion for Mother and the Music Hall for Mary."

Kaylee jumped up and down and clapped her hands.

Dad continued, "The company I work for constructed the Westinghouse building. We'll see groundbreaking science."

"How will we get there?"

"We could take the train to Queens. The World's Fair is in an enormous park called Corona, right by Shea Stadium. But I think we should take the old woody station wagon just in case we come back after dark. It will be easier to manage the whole family, and that way we can see the light show. People will come from all over the world, and we'll learn something about their customs and understand more about their way of life. In fact, the theme of the fair is Peace Through Understanding."

"I understand. Well, I think I understand," Kaylee said.

"Understand, you will. You'll see. And so will I."

Dad pinched Kaylee on the nose then made a fist, letting the tip of his thumb peek out. "Got your nose," he said as he wiggled his thumb.

Kaylee giggled and said, "I'm too big for that."

"Never." Dad grinned.

After the last day of the school year, the old woody pulled out of the driveway and headed to Queens. Mother gave a lecture about how all the kids would have to stick together. She suggested each child have a partner and always keep track of that person. Everyone paired up, and naturally, Mary and Kaylee became partners. The littlest ones held hands with the biggest ones and stayed close to Mother and Dad while they pushed a baby carriage carrying Orla, Emma, and a new baby girl through the crowd. Three-year-old Orla sat cross-legged in the pram, holding the infant and practicing the baby's name—Fi-ona, Fiona. One-year-old Emma smothered Fiona with kisses, and Dad warned Joey not to run off by himself.

"If you get lost, go to the RCA pavilion near the UNICEF building. They will put you on television and broadcast it on all the televisions throughout the park," Mother said.

Before they entered the gate, Dad handed each child an admission ticket. Kaylee proudly handed hers over to the attendant. She stepped through the gate. Her mouth gaped open, so wide she could have caught a fly, as she scanned the sights.

She and Mary led the way, swinging their linked hands, and Kaylee let go long enough to do a cartwheel. Little Liz bounced on the balls of her feet. Near the entrance stood a huge steel Unisphere that looked like planet Earth. The family posed in front of it, and a stranger adjusted his stance to fit everyone in the frame.

"The next stop will be the UNICEF building," Dad said. But before they got there, they looked up to the Tower of the Four Winds. It stood twelve stories high and full of mobiles driven by the wind. Wheels of all shapes and sizes and colors spun round. Crowds of people from all over the globe looked up at the sky and pointed.

Disney characters emerged from every direction, greeting people. Kaylee pivoted, not knowing where to turn first. Snow White led the seven dwarfs in a procession, followed by Mickey Mouse and Donald Duck.

Joey reached out to Snow White. "Hey, toots," he said.

Sneezy turned to Joey and put his hands on his hips.

"Aren't you Dopey?" Joey said. Sneezy sneezed in his direction, and Grumpy raised a fist. Bashful marched right on by.

"It's A Small World," written by Richard and Robert Sherman, sang out from every speaker. The family boarded a train of little open cars that moved along rails to view the spectacle of a hundred lands. All around, automatons moved like robots, singing in their native languages and laughing. The Dutch ones clicked their wooden shoes. The French cancan dancers did not disappoint, and neither did the leprechauns, Scottish bagpipers, and Asian snake charmers. The Reagans rode past the rainforests of Brazil, gondolas of Venice, African giraffes, and flying carpets soaring above the Taj Mahal.

When the little train stopped, Dad's face was lit up like a kid in a candy store. "What do all these children who speak different languages have in common?"

"They all laugh the same," Kaylee said.

"Right, you are!"

Mother held her hands in prayer pose. "I'll bet they all pray too."

"Pray they do, I'll bet, just not all to the same God," Dad said.

"God is everywhere," said Kaylee.

"Yes, he just looks different to different people."

"Differences, yet we are all the same. If only we could all understand that," Mother said.

The Reagans went off to have a family picture taken at the Kodak building. After that, Dad treated the kids to Eskimo Pies for fifteen cents apiece, much more than what the Good Humor man charged from his truck. Then, at the Mobile building, Mother tested her driving skills as Joey ducked and crossed his arms in front of his face. It was obvious why Dad didn't let her drive to the city.

The next stop was the Vatican Pavilion, where Mother stood in quiet reverence before Michelangelo's Pieta. She made the sign of the cross and held her hands in prayer. She seemed to be in a trance. The children looked to Dad for an explanation, but he wasn't looking much different from Mother. Yet somehow the children knew to give them this special moment.

While making their way to the Westinghouse building, Mary's eyes popped as she pointed to one of the many television cameras. "Holy guacamole," she exclaimed, using one of Grandma's expressions.

Everyone turned to see Joey on the television screen. He was eating another ice cream with a cigarette tucked into the flap of his right ear. He paused long enough to smile for the camera.

* * *

Mother turned red with embarrassment. "I didn't miss Joey. RCA building!" was all Mother said.

She looked up to the Tower of the Four Winds to orient herself, remembering it stood near the UNICEF and RCA buildings. Mother dodged her way through parading Disney characters and understood why the Tower of the Four Winds represented the boundless energy of children. She greeted the greeters, trying to convince them she was Joey's mother, but Joey was too busy watching himself on television to pay much attention to Mother. After much ado, when Dad and the rest of the clan arrived, Joey finally stated she was his actual mother. Mother was so mad she didn't want to hold Joey's hand, so she made Dad do it. It was a trade-off, and she had to push the baby carriage herself. Kaylee and Mary held on to each side to help push it along, making their way to the place Dad had so patiently waited for—the Westinghouse building.

Science exhibits full of new technologies lit up the building. Kaylee played with the hands-on exhibits. Dad chatted with the attendant of the time capsule about its contents, which included a report of civilization. It contained millions of words on microfilm, information on space and science, and everyday items such as an electric toothbrush, credit cards, the Westinghouse guest book, and many other objects.

Dad signed the guest book and received a pin for his lapel. The pin read, *My name is in the Westinghouse Time Capsule for the next five thousand years.* Joey signed it too. Kaylee hesitated then forged her mother's name so she could go down in history with Dad. Then she attached the pin to her shirt. The capsule was to be opened in the year 6939.

The family ate Japanese food for the first time, but Dad was still hungry and ate a bagel. They watched the dancing waters and the light show marked by spectacular fireworks set to music.

It was dark when the family exited the park and headed to the station wagon. When Joey thought no one was looking, he kissed Mother, whispered, "I'm sorry," and fixed his pin to her blouse. She smiled and hugged him. Kaylee kept secret about the forgery at the time capsule, but she thought Dad might have noticed.

They piled into the old woody. And for once, the only noise heard was the rumble from under the woody's hood.

CHAPTER 36

IN SEARCH OF SELF

OLIVIA ~ A TIME TO HEAL

O nce again, Olivia Hunter found herself pausing on a doorstep and inhaling deeply. She raised her hand to knock, but it fell back to her side before making contact with the door. Olivia shifted her weight and raised her arm again. She knocked at a door she had passed through a thousand times, a door which she had never stopped to knock on until now.

The sounds of beeping horns and people shouting spilled out around her, but nothing stirred from behind the curtains of the house, and the place appeared eerily empty. It was hard to tell if anyone lived there anymore. Olivia waited. Soon her head drooped, and she turned to leave.

Just then, the door slowly opened, and a gray-haired lady appeared. Olivia's mother, Gloria Hunter, had a thin, fragile frame and a face marked with deeply etched lines. She blinked, as though trying to register who the person was standing before her. Her puzzled look disappeared as she cupped one hand to her mouth.

"Mother," Olivia said, hardly recognizing the woman who stood before her.

Olivia's mother took a step backward, blinked, then moved toward Olivia with outstretched arms. They held each other, feeling their tensions lessen. Olivia's watery eyes gazed over her mother's shoulder, searching for her father, but he did not appear. Words didn't come from either of them, and Olivia held back her tears.

When they finally released their embrace, Olivia followed her mother inside. Her mother had always taken pride in her household, but a hint of Italian seasoning seemed to mask a dank smell. Long gone was the sweet scent of freshly baked butter cookies bringing joy.

Mother sat in Father's old easy chair, a place that used to be reserved only for him.

A cool shiver ran through Olivia as she sat on the hard sofa, which was once her mother's spot. She suddenly wondered if Mother had always wanted an easier chair, an easier marriage, an easier life—or at least a more interesting one.

Olivia glanced around the room at objects that held memories of a time long ago. Her eyes fell on an old photograph of her parents. She swallowed hard and asked a question, even though her instincts knew the answer.

"Where's Dad?"

Mother looked down. "He's no longer with us... passed on."

"I had a feeling. I'm sorry." Olivia brushed away a tear and didn't know what more to say. The two sat still and quiet.

Olivia surveyed the old living room. Some memories flooded back, yet some stayed beneath the surface. Dusty photos covered her mother's organ with its closed-up keyboard. The furniture and the deep-blue sofa sat in the same place they always had. A song by the Shirelles, "Will You Still Love Me Tomorrow," could barely be heard through the neighboring walls of the brownstone. A light layer of dust covered the entire room. Photographs on the bookshelves were arranged differently from what Olivia remembered. Some held fingerprints, yet a few of Olivia looked as though someone had recently taken them out of hiding for her.

Olivia moved to the bookcase and picked up a photograph of her parents. They were young, full of joy, and dressed in their Sunday clothes. It was likely taken before they got married. Olivia had her mother's eyes and the pretty shape of her face, but the resemblance had grown less pronounced over the years.

Olivia picked up a framed photograph of a little girl, an only child, sitting on a pony, wearing a beaming smile. "I don't remember this."

"You were four or five years old when your father took it. We were at a park where a man offered pony rides for a small fee. Your father was so excited, he picked you up and placed you in the saddle. Then he took your picture. The man held the reins and began pulling the horse along to give you a ride. Father was so nervous he walked alongside and wouldn't let you out of his sight or his reach, for that matter."

Olivia set the photo down and sat back on the sofa, and a hint of a smile crossed her face.

"You're probably wondering what happened to Dad," Mother said.

"Can you talk about it?"

Mother folded her hands in her lap and pursed her lips. "I'll have to sooner or later." Mother sank deeper into her chair, looking like a lost sheep. "He had a heart attack. It's been almost a year now. He died of a broken heart and without ever apologizing to you. I'll have to do that for both your father and myself." Mother closed her eyes for a moment. Then she leaned forward, opened her eyes, and looked squarely at Olivia. "I'm sorry for how we treated you, how wrong we were. Dad was determined, of course, to protect the family name, but he paid for it. As did I. But you paid dearly."

"I'm curious about one thing," Olivia said. "What did you tell people… where I went?"

"Off to college. What else could we say?"

"And after that?"

"You went off and got a teaching job."

"How did you explain my lack of visits? Or any visit?"

"I said you were busy and that we went to see you. Once we even faked a trip to Ohio or someplace like that. There were so many lies I can't remember them all. But, after a while, people stopped asking. They must have realized something was out of place." Mother took a deep breath.

"Forgive me, Olivia. I've been sorry since the day you left here.

Unfortunately, I was not strong enough to stand up to your father, and he was not strong enough to let go of his stubbornness."

Olivia wanted to offer forgiveness, but she was still comprehending all the events that led to this day. She thought about seeing John after thirty-two years and now her mother—all of it— and learning of her father's passing. Besides, the reality of finding her son was weighing on her. And to think of how the actions of a fifth-grade student had affected her life. She waited for her mother to ask her where she had been, but she did not. Perhaps Mother wondered if she had lost all her motherly rights.

The smell of Italian meat sauce hinted at a prepared meal.

"Will you stay for dinner?" Mother asked.

Olivia's appetite was lacking, but with nothing urgent on her schedule, she agreed.

After dinner, Olivia offered to do the dishes, and Mother conceded. Dishes done, they sat for tea, and Olivia started to talk. "It was a boy. I spent very little time with him before a couple adopted him. Took him away."

"Somehow, I knew it. I knew he was a boy."

Olivia told her mother about the birth and the recent visit with her son and her old boyfriend. Then, in a shaking voice, she explained the part about becoming a nun. Even to Olivia, the story seemed unreal. Mother reached out, and they held hands the way they had a long time ago.

Mother squeezed Olivia's hand, and both women released tears, tears that waited a long time to flow. Then finally, as a wave of relief left Olivia's body, she said, "I've been angry for too long. I forgive you. I'll work on doing that for Dad too."

Mother smiled. "I suppose he spent quite a bit of time in purgatory before reaching heaven. He may have grabbed the devil's pitchfork and poked a few demons on his way."

Olivia grinned, remembering her mother's light side.

"When will you go back to the convent?" Mother asked.

"I'm not sure. I have more than a little searching to do. We'll see."

"Your bedroom is still here. The door is open and will stay open for you as long as you like."

Olivia rose and walked to her old bedroom. She glanced in before entering. Things appeared the same as they had years ago. A bed with a dust ruffle and a pink canopy sat near the middle of the room next to a dresser. Rosary beads lay coiled on the bed pillow. At the foot of the bed sat a hope chest. Olivia stood before the hope chest and closed her eyes. Then she ran her fingers along the top, inhaled, and opened the chest.

A wave of memories rolled out and hit Olivia like an ocean wave crashing on the shore. She took a step back and steadied herself. Then she moved closer, reached in, picked up a seashell she had collected with John, and held it to her ear. The shell whispered its lost song. She turned the seashell over in her hands before setting it down and picked up the wedding dress her mother had once worn. Olivia knew Mother had intended her daughter, her only child, to someday walk down the aisle, wearing the same white lace gown. Olivia held the lacy gown against herself and swayed gently as though in a slow dance until a movement appeared in the doorway.

Gloria Hunter smiled. "You don't have to go back."

Olivia cradled the dress over one arm and picked up the rosary beads. She looked from one to another. "I don't know what I should do. The nuns took me in after I abandoned a child. I don't want to betray them... or God. My life in the convent is a simple one, which I'm accustomed to."

"Is it a betrayal if your life changes course? God will still love you. If I could turn back the hands of the clock, I would." Olivia's mother took a step closer. "I made a wrong decision before. Circumstances have changed. We changed. And we can change more. We are not yet done. But either way, we are back in one another's lives. I won't lose you again."

CHAPTER 37

KAYLEE

Dear Sister Killian,

It's the end of the school year, and lo and behold, I'm promoted to sixth grade. Louella is too. It was hard work but not as hard as I thought. And I got eyeglasses. My dad and my mother took us to the World's Fair. Dad said it was a reward for doing good in school, but I think he would have taken us anyway. It was so much fun. I want to move there.

I'm trying to make friends with Brenda Mullarkey, but that's hard. It's not working out so well. Mother says keep trying. Dad says cheeks you have, turn the other one. Joey says use your middle finger. And Louella says so what.

I got to go watch my sister Mary at her recital. She's a wonderful piano player, and she doesn't crack her knuckles as much anymore. Her teacher, Mrs. Clef, is looking after a dog named Patches. We rescued him. I hope she can keep him. Mother is afraid of animals of any size, even small worms.

My mother brushed out Mary's pigtails for the recital and put her hair up in a beautiful French twist. I hardly recognized her. My mother said she looked like Audrey Hepburn.

I'm sorry about stealing your letters, but only if, in the end, it made things worse. Otherwise, I'm not sorry or sad.

I'm glad you had a bluebird in your garden. Mrs. Baxter says the bluebird is a sign of joy and happiness to come. You must be joyful and happyful. I saw one outside your old window at the convent during May procession. One time, one even flew into the classroom and landed on my pen. My pen has been happy ever since, and my penmanship has improved, especially now that it is writing to you.

We saw a film on menstruation. Louella got hers. I hope I never get mine.

Oh, my father signs my homework notebook for now because my mother had another baby. That makes nine of us kids. She doesn't seem to be sad that it's another girl. Neither is my brother Joey. Dad is so happy he's giving away cigars.

Many more bluebirds to you!

Sincerely, and oh, have a splendid opportunity,
Kaylee Reagan
P.S. Do you want a dog named Patches if Mrs. Clef won't keep him?

CHAPTER 38

TO EVERYTHING THERE IS A SEASON

ECCLESIASTES

Olivia removed a piece of Juicy Fruit gum Kaylee had sent with her latest letter and popped it into her mouth. The little girl had been writing to Olivia regularly since she'd sent her first letter about being promoted to sixth grade. Olivia placed the letter in her bureau along with the others. Then she put on a pale-green dress and combed her hair in front of the mirror. By now, it reached her shoulders, and she styled it into a flip with one large, long sweeping curl.

Summer followed spring and spring drifted into fall. A brilliant canopy of autumn gold colored the Central Park sky and leaves floated in the wind like elegant ballerinas. Children kicked balls and lovers rowed boats.

A year had passed since Olivia walked the paths of Central Park with her son Harry. There—in the middle of the park, the Angel of the Waters stood gracefully atop the fountain at Bethesda Terrace. The angel seemed to bless the birds landing on her wings. Water trickled down beneath her feet and sprayed against a blue sky. A bluebird alighted on her wing and harmonized with the cascading waters. Folks ambled along paths dusted with leaves, and the world slowed to match their pace.

A horse and buggy halted near the fountain. Olivia stepped down. With the help of crutches, John made his way down and over to a bench. Olivia took her place beside him as children ran through the grass and mothers pushing strollers called to them. Off in the distance, Olivia recognized a young family as they made their way to the fountain. A toddler broke free of his mother's hand and waddled into the arms of Olivia before crawling onto his Grandpa John's lap. Olivia looked about to see if Harry's parents were with him. Perhaps they were just late.

Something sparkled on Olivia's ring finger, caught by the light of the sun. There was a lot of love to go around.

Amen

ACKNOWLEDGMENTS

Much gratitude to Liz Curtis, Ellen Morse, Mary Botnovcan, Peggy Best, Millard Johnson's writing group, Paper Pens and Pals, the Wannabees writers of the Villages, and the librarians of Lady Lake. Grateful also to the Leo House of NYC.

"When a mischievous Catholic schoolgirl finds something unexpected, the discovery sets off a far-reaching chain of events with unexpected consequences. By turns heartwarming and heartbreaking, this riveting tale of love lost and found will delight readers. "

— IRENE S., RED ADEPT EDITING

ABOUT THE AUTHOR

As a youngster, Susan told stories while sitting around the Girl Scout campfires, causing the campers to scream or laugh. As a middle child in a large, grand Catholic family, she enjoyed the attention storytelling afforded her. Finally, as a young adult, she began to write the stories. Her Catholic school upbringing inspired the novel.

Susan Dwyer graduated from North Rockland H.S., Rockland Community College, SUNY Geneseo, and later earned her Master's Degree from Nazareth College of Rochester, NY.

Teaching experiences include a private college prep school, private practice in Early Intervention, and as an adjunct college professor - SUNY Geneseo.

Born in NYC, Susan spends her time between Cape Cod and Florida. She has a son, a daughter, and two grandchildren.

Author contact:
Oysterb@yahoo.com
Ask about availability for book clubs and signings.

Thank you and with hopes you enjoyed the read, please leave a review. I read every review and they help readers discover the book.

Made in the USA
Columbia, SC
18 January 2023

75513776R00138